A MOST REVEALING CLUE

Chan stood there holding the letter in his hand. Could it be true? Was the answer to this puzzle so soon within his grasp?

The floor lamp furnished the only illumination in the room. Chan took a step nearer it; he had the envelope open now, and was about to remove the contents. Suddenly the lamp went out. There followed the sound of a blow, then another, a cry and the fall of a rather solid body.

The place was in an uproar. As the lamps in the wall brackets flashed on, Charlie was slowly rising from the floor. He rubbed his right cheek, which was bleeding slightly.

"Overwhelmed with regret," he said. "Famous god Jove, I hear, nodded on occasion. For myself, I fear I have just taken most unfortunate nap." He held out his left hand in which there was a tiny fragment of envelope. "Vital portion of letter," he added, "seems to have traveled elsewhere."

The Black Camel

EARL DERR BIGGERS

THE BLACK CAMEL

A Bantam Book / January 1975

Published simultaneously in the United States and Canada

Bantam Books are published by Bantam Books, Inc. Its trademark, consisting of the words "Bantam Books" and the portrayal of a bantam, is registered in the United States Patent Office and in other countries. Marca Registrada. Bantam Books, Inc., 666 Fifth Avenue, New York, New York 10019.

PRINTED IN THE UNITED STATES OF AMERICA

CONTENTS

Chapter I

MORNING AT THE CROSSROADS

The Pacific is the loneliest of oceans, and travelers across that rolling desert begin to feel that their ship is lost in an eternity of sky and water. But if they are journeying from the atolls of the South Seas to the California coast, they come quite suddenly upon a half-way house. So those aboard the *Oceanic* had come upon it shortly after dawn this silent July morning. Brown misty peaks rose from the ocean floor, incredible, unreal. But they grew more probable with each moment of approach, until finally the watchers at the rail were thrilled to distinguish the bright green island of Oahu, streaked with darker folds where lurk the valley rains.

The *Oceanic* swung about to the channel entrance. There stood Diamond Head, like a great lion—if you want the time-worn simile—crouched to spring. A crouching lion, yes; the figure is plausible up to that point; but as for springing—well, there has never been the slightest chance of that. Diamond Head is a *kamaaina* of the islands, and has long ago sensed the futility of acting on impulse—of acting, as a matter of fact, at all.

A woman traveler stood by the starboard rail on the boat deck, gazing at the curved beach of Waikiki and, up ahead, the white walls of Honolulu half hidden in the foliage behind the Aloha Tower. A handsome woman in her early thirties, she had been a source of unending interest to her fellow passengers throughout that hot monotonous voyage from Tahiti. No matter in what remote corner of the world you have been hiding, you would have recognized her at once, for she was Shelah Fane of the pictures, and hers was a fame equal to that of any president or king.

"A great piece of property" film salesmen had called her

for eight years or more, but now they had begun to shake their heads. "Not so good. She's slipping." Golden lads and lasses must, like chimney-sweepers, come to dust, which is something the film stars think about when they can not sleep of nights. Shelah had not been sleeping well of late, and her eyes, as they rested on peaceful Tantalus with its halo of fleecy cloud, were sad and a little wistful.

She heard a familiar step on the deck behind her and turned. A broad, powerful, keen-looking man was smiling down at her.

"Oh—Alan," she said. "How are you this morning?"

"A bit anxious," he replied. He joined her at the rail. His was a face that had never known Klieg lights and make-up; it was deeply lined and bronzed by tropic suns. "Journey's end, Shelah—for you at least," he added, laying his hand over hers. "Are you sorry?"

She hesitated a moment. "Rather sorry—yes. I shouldn't have cared if we had just sailed on and on."

"Nor I." He stared at Honolulu with the bright look of interest that comes naturally to British eyes at sight of a new port, a new anchorage. The ship had come to a stop at the channel entrance, and a launch bearing the customs men and the doctor was speeding toward it.

"You haven't forgotten?" The Britisher turned back to Shelah Fane. "This isn't journey's end for me. You know I'm leaving you behind here to-night. Sailing out at midnight on this same ship—and I must have your answer before I go."

She nodded. "You shall have it before you go. I promise."

For a brief moment he studied her face. A marked change had crept over her at the sight of land. She had come back from the little world of the ship to the great world whose adoration she expected and thrived on. No longer calm, languorous, at peace, her eyes were alight with a restless flame, her small foot tapped nervously on the deck. A sudden fear overwhelmed him, a fear that the woman he had known and worshiped these past few weeks was slipping from him for ever.

"Why must you wait?" he cried. "Give me your answer now."

"No, no," she protested. "Not now. Later to-day." She glanced over her shoulder. "Were there reporters on the launch, I wonder?"

A tall, handsome, hatless youth with a mop of blond hair waving in the breeze rushed up to her. His energy was a challenge to the climate.

"Hello, Miss Fane. Remember me? Met you when you went through here on your way south. Jim Bradshaw, of the Tourist Bureau, press-agent of beauty, contact man for Paradise. Our best aloha—and here's a lei to prove it." He hung a fragrant garland about her neck, while the man she had called Alan moved quietly away.

"You're awfully kind," Shelah Fane told him. "Of course I remember you. You seemed so glad to see me. You do now."

He grinned. "I am—and besides, that's my job. I'm the door-mat on the threshold of Hawaii, with 'welcome' written all over me. Island hospitality—I have to make sure that my advertisements all come true. But in your case, I—well, believe me, it isn't any strain." He saw that she looked expectantly beyond him. "Say, I'm sorry, but all the newspaper men seem to be lingering in the arms of Morpheus. However, you can't blame them. Lulled as they are by the whisper of the soft invigorating trade-winds in the coco-palms—I'll finish that later. Just tell me what's doing, and I'll see that it gets into the papers. Did you complete the big South Sea picture down in Tahiti?"

"Not quite," she answered. "We left a few sequences to be shot in Honolulu. We can live here so much more comfortably, and the backgrounds, you know, are every bit as beautiful——"

"Do I know it?" the boy cried. "Ask me. Exotic flowers, blossoming trees, verdant green hills, blue sunny skies with billowy white clouds—the whole a dream of the unchanging tropics with the feel of spring. How's that? I wrote it yesterday."

"Sounds pretty good to me," Shelah laughed.

"You'll be some time in Honolulu, Miss Fane?"

She nodded. "I've sent for my servants," she told him. "They've taken a house for me on the beach. I stifle in hotels—and then, too, people are always staring at me. I hope it's a large house——"

"It is," Bradshaw cut in. "I was out there yesterday. They're all set and waiting for you. I saw your butler—and your secretary, Julie O'Neill. Speaking of that, some day I'd like to ask you where you find secretaries like her."

Shelah smiled. "Oh, Julie's much more than a secretary. Sort of a daughter—almost. Though of course that's absurd to say, for we're nearly the same age."

"Is that so?" said the boy—to himself.

"Julie's mother was a dear friend of mine, and when she died four years ago, I took the child in. One must do a good deed occasionally," she added, modestly looking down at the deck.

"Sure," agreed Bradshaw. "If we don't we'll never be tapped for the Boy Scouts. Julie was telling me how kind you've been——"

"I've been amply repaid," the star assured him. "Julie is a darling."

"Isn't she?" replied the boy heartily. "If I had my rhyming dictionary along, I'd give you a good description of the girl right here and now."

Shelah Fane looked at him suddenly. "But Julie got in only two days ago——"

"Yes—and so did I. Made a flying trip to Los Angeles, and came back on the same boat with her. The best crossing I ever had. You know—moonlight, silver seas, a pretty girl——"

"I must look into this," said Shelah Fane.

Two of the passengers joined them: a weary, disillusioned-looking man whose costume suggested Hollywood Boulevard, and a dashing girl of twenty. Shelah yielded to the inevitable. "Mr. Bradshaw, of the Tourist Bureau," she explained. "This is Miss Diana Dixon, who is in my new picture, and Huntley Van Horn, my leading man."

Miss Dixon lost no time. She sparkled instantly. "Honolulu is an adorable place. I'm always so thrilled to come here—such beauty——"

"Never mind," cut in the star. "Mr. Bradshaw knows all that. None better."

"Always happy to have my ideas confirmed," bowed the boy. "Especially from such a charming source." He turned to the man. "Mr. Van Horn—I've seen you in the films."

Van Horn smiled cynically. "So, I believe, have the natives of Borneo. Has Shelah told you anything about our latest epic?"

"Very little," Bradshaw replied. "Got a good part?"

"It always has been a good part," Van Horn said. "I trust my rendering of the rôle will not impair its future usefulness. If it does, many of our leading studios will have to close. I'm a beach-comber, you see, and I've sunk lower and lower——"

"You would," nodded the star.

"I'm wallowing in the depths, and quite comfortable, thank you," went on Van Horn, "when—if you can believe it—I'm saved. Absolutely rehabilitated, you know, through the love of this primitive, brown-skinned child."

"Which child?" asked Bradshaw blankly. "Oh, you mean Miss Fane. Well, it sounds like a great plot—but don't tell me, don't tell me." He turned to the star. "I'm glad you're going to take a few shots in Honolulu. That sort of thing makes us very happy at the Tourist Bureau. I must run along—one or two other celebrities on the ship. Fellow named Alan Jaynes—very wealthy——"

"I was talking with him when you came up," Shelah said.

"Thanks. I'll go after him. Diamond mines—South Africa—he sounds good. We're strong for the arts in Hawaii, you know, but as for money—well, when that appears in the harbor, then we really get out the flags. See you all later."

He disappeared down the deck, and the three picture people moved over to the rail.

"Here comes Val," said Huntley Van Horn, "looking like the man who wrote the tropics."

He referred to Val Martino, director of Shelah's latest picture, who was rapidly approaching along the deck. He was a short, stocky, gray-haired man, dressed in a suit of immaculate white silk. Above a flaming red tie loomed his broad heavy face. It was almost the same shade as the tie, suggesting that Mr. Martino had never concerned himself with such trivial matters as blood pressure and diet.

"Hello," he said. "Well, here we are. Thank heaven, Tahiti has been attended to. From this on, I'll take my tropics after they've been ruined by American plumbing. Was that a newspaper man you were talking with, Shelah?"

"Not precisely. A boy from the Tourist Bureau."

"I hope you laid it on thick about the new picture," he continued. "You know, we'll need all the publicity we can get."

"Oh, let's forget the picture," returned the star a bit wearily.

The *Oceanic* was drawing slowly up to the pier, on which a surprisingly meager crowd was waiting. Shelah Fane gazed at the group with interest and some disappointment.

She had rather hoped for a vast throng of schoolgirls in white, bearing triumphal leis. But this had happened when she went through before; she could not expect history to repeat itself—and it was, too, only seven in the morning.

"There's Julie," she cried suddenly. "There—near the end of the pier. See—she's waving." She returned Julie's signal.

"Who's that beside her?" Van Horn inquired. "Good lord—it looks like Tarneverro."

"It is Tarneverro," Miss Dixon said.

"What's he doing here?" the leading man wondered.

"Perhaps he's here because I sent for him," said Shelah Fane.

A quiet black-garbed maid stood at her side. "What is it, Anna?"

"The customs men, madam. They're going through everything. You'd better come. They want talking to, it seems."

"I'll talk to them," said the star firmly, and followed the maid into her suite.

"Well, what do you know about that?" Van Horn remarked. "She's sent for that phony fortune-teller to come all the way from Hollywood——"

"What do you mean, phony?" cut in Miss Dixon. "Tarneverro is simply wonderful. He's told me the most amazing things about my past—and about my future, too. I never take a step without consulting him—and neither does Shelah."

Martino shook his great head impatiently. "It's a rotten scandal," he cried, "the way most of you Hollywood women have gone mad over voodoo men. Telling them all your secrets—some day one of them will publish his memoirs, and then where will you be? A few of us try to lift the industry to a dignified plane—but, oh, lord—what's the use?"

"No use, my dear fellow," said Van Horn. He looked across the intervening stretch of water at the tall lean figure of the fortune-teller. "Poor Shelah—there's something rather touching in such faith as this. I presume she wants to ask Tarneverro whether or not she shall marry Alan Jaynes."

"Of course she does," Miss Dixon nodded. "She wants to know if she'll be happy with him. She cabled Tarneverro the day after Jaynes proposed. Why not? Marriage is a serious step."

Martino shrugged. "If she'd only ask me, I'd read her future quick enough. She's nearly through in pictures, and she ought to know it. Her contract expires in six months, and I happen to know—in strict confidence, you understand—it won't be renewed. I can see her taking a long journey by water then—going abroad to make a picture—the beginning of the end. She'd better grab this diamond king quick before he changes his mind. But no—she's fooling round with a back-parlor crystal-gazer. However, that's like you people. You won't grow up." He walked away.

The formalities of the port were quickly ended, and the *Oceanic* docked. Shelah Fane was the first down the plank, to be received by the eager arms of her secretary. Julie was young, impetuous, unspoiled; her joy was genuine.

"The house is all ready, Shelah. It's a knockout. Jessop is there, and we've found a Chinese cook who's a magician. The car's waiting."

"Really, dear?"

The star looked up into the dark deep-set eyes of the man at Julie's side. "Tarneverro—what a relief to see you here. But I knew I could depend on you."

"Always," said the fortune-teller gravely.

What the crowd lacked in numbers, it made up in noise and confusion. Anna, the maid, was overwhelmed with boxes and bags, and seeing this, Tarneverro went to help her. There was no condescension in his manner; he treated her with the same courtly grace he would have shown the star.

Alan Jaynes and Bradshaw appeared on the scene. The latter went over to greet Julie with as much warmth as though he had just arrived after a long hard voyage from some distant port. Jaynes stepped quickly to Shelah's side.

"I shall be damnably anxious," he said. "This afternoon—may I come then?"

"Of course," she nodded. "Oh—this is Julie—you've heard about her. Julie, please tell him the number of our house. We're just beyond the Grand Hotel, on Kalakaua Avenue."

Julie told him, and he turned back to Shelah. "I shan't keep you——" he began.

"Just a moment," said the star. "I want to introduce an old friend from Hollywood. Tarneverro—will you come here, please?"

The fortune-teller handed a couple of bags to Shelah's chauffeur, and came at once. Jaynes looked at him with some surprise.

"Tarneverro—I want you to meet Alan Jaynes," the star said.

They shook hands. "Glad to know you," remarked the Britisher. As he gazed into the other man's face, he experienced a sudden sensation of deep dislike. Here was power; not the power of muscle, which he had himself and could understand; but something more subtle, something uncanny, inexplicable and oddly disturbing. "Sorry, but I must dash along now," he added.

He disappeared into the crowd, and Julie led them to the waiting car. Tarneverro, it appeared, was stopping at the Grand, and Shelah offered to drop him there.

Presently they were bowling along through Honolulu's streets, under a flaming blue sky. The town was waking to another leisurely day. Men of many races languidly bestirred themselves; at the corner of King Street a boy offered the morning paper, and a fat brown-skinned policeman lazily turned a stop-go sign to let them pass. Shelah Fane, like all passengers newly descended from a ship at this port, felt rather dazzled by the brightness and the color.

"Oh, I shall enjoy this," she cried. "I've never stayed here longer than one day before. What a relief to be out of the South Seas."

"But they're romantic, aren't they?" Julie asked.

"The illusions of youth," the star shrugged. "I shan't destroy them. Only don't mention Tahiti to me again as long as I live."

"Not quite like the books," Tarneverro nodded. He sat, mysterious even in that bright world, at Shelah's side. "I discovered that for myself, long ago. You're staying here for some time, I take it?"

"A month, I hope," the star answered. "A couple of weeks still to go on the picture, and then, I trust, a fortnight's rest. I want it badly, Tarneverro. I'm tired—tired."

"You need not tell me that," he said. "I have eyes."

He had, indeed, eyes; eyes that were cold and piercing and rather disquieting. The car sped on past the old royal palace and the judiciary building, and turned off into Kalakaua Avenue.

"It was so good of you to come over here," Shelah told him.

"Not at all," he replied evenly. "I started the day after I got your cable. I was due for a vacation—my work, you know, is not precisely restful. Then, too, you said you needed me. That was enough. That will always be—enough."

Julie began to chatter about the islands: she mentioned

the warm caressing waters of Waikiki, the thrill of haunting native music in the purple night, the foreign pageant of the streets.

"All of which," smiled Shelah, "sounds very much to me like James Bradshaw in one of his more lyric moods."

Julie laughed. "Yes, I guess I was quoting Jimmy. Did you meet him, Shelah?"

"I met him," the star nodded.

"He's really very nice," Julie assured her. "Especially when he isn't talking shop."

The pink walls of the Grand Hotel appeared at that moment through a network of majestic palms, and Shelah directed the chauffeur to turn in at the gates.

"I must talk with you very soon," she said to Tarneverro. "I have so much to ask you. You see——"

He raised a slim white hand. "Don't tell me, please," he smiled. "Let me tell you."

She glanced at him, a little startled. "Oh—of course. I need your advice, Tarneverro. You must help me again, as you have helped me so often in the past."

He nodded gravely. "I shall try. With what success—who knows? Come to my apartment at eleven o'clock—it is number nineteen, on the first floor. There is a short flight of stairs leading to my corridor just at the left of the hotel desk as you enter. I shall expect you."

"Yes, yes." Her voice was trembling. "I must settle this thing to-day. I'll be there."

Tarneverro bowed from the hotel steps, and as the car drove off Shelah was conscious of Julie's frank young eyes fixed on her with a disapproval that was almost contempt.

The head bell-man touched Tarneverro's sleeve. "Excuse. There is a man who waits to see you. This one."

The fortune-teller turned to perceive a bulky Chinese who approached him with an amazingly light step. The ivory face was wearing a somewhat stupid expression; the black eyes were veiled and sleepy-looking. Not a very intelligent Chinese, Tarneverro thought, wondering vaguely what this visit presaged.

The Oriental placed one hand on his broad chest, and achieved a grand bow despite his waist-line.

"A thousand pardons," he remarked. "Have I the undisputable honor to address Tarneverro the Great?"

"I am Tarneverro," answered the other bruskly. "What can I do for you?"

"Permit that I introduce myself," continued the Chinese, "unworthy of your notice though I am. The name is Harry Wing, and I am humble business man of this island. Do I extend my remarks too far when I say I wish to see you alone?"

Tarneverro shrugged. "What for?"

"The matter is of pressing urgency. If I might suggest—your room——"

The fortune-teller gazed for a moment into that placid mask of a face, behind which life seemed nonexistent. He capitulated. "Come along," he said. Obtaining his key at the desk, he led the way.

Once inside the door of number nineteen, he turned to confront his odd visitor, who had followed on noiseless feet. The curtains of the sitting-room were drawn back as far as they would go, and the place was flooded with light. With his customary forethought, Tarneverro had selected an apartment on the mountain side of the hotel, and a restless cool wind from the Koolau Range swept in at the window and stirred the papers lying on a desk.

The countenance of the Chinese was still without expression, even under the piercing scrutiny the fortune-teller now gave it.

"Well?" said Tarneverro.

"You are the famous Tarneverro," began Harry Wing in a respectful singsong. "Among Hollywood people you have vast reputation as one who lifts dark veils and peers into uncertain future. Black as lacquer that future may be to ordinary eyes, but to yours, they say, it is clear as glass. Permit me to add this reputation pursues you even to Hawaii, dogging like shadow at your heels. The rumor of your mystic skill floods the street."

"Yes?" put in Tarneverro shortly. "What of it?"

"I am, as I say, business man of small importance to everybody but myself. Now I begin to speak to you frankly that opportunity arouses itself in my path. I can amalgamate my business up together with that of my cousin from a north province. Future looks bright, but qualms assail me. Will the merge have success? Is my cousin honorable as cousin of mine should naturally be? Can I trust him? In fewer words, I desire dark veil lifted, and you are man to do the business. I stand ready to make generous payment for this lifting."

Tarneverro's eyes narrowed, and for a long time he stood staring at this unexpected customer for his wares. The Chinese waited motionless as a Buddha, with his hands in his trousers pockets, his coat thrown back. The fortune-teller's glance rested for a moment at a point just below the fountain-pen pocket on his visitor's waistcoat.

"Impossible," he said, with sudden decision. "I am here on a vacation, not to practise my profession."

"But rumor remarks," objected the other, "that you have already done work with crystal——"

"For one or two of the hotel managers—as a friendly gesture," Tarneverro cut in. "I received no fee of any sort. I will not do this kind of thing for the general public."

Harry Wing shrugged. "The matter then becomes sad disappointment for me," he answered.

A grim smile spread over the seer's dark face. "Sit down," he said. "I have spent some time in China, and I understand how great is the interest of your people in fortune-tellers. So for a moment, while you were telling me why you came, I thought you were speaking the truth."

The visitor frowned. "I am now rapidly failing to understand you."

Still smiling, Tarneverro dropped into a chair facing the Oriental. "Yes, Mr.—ah—er—Wing, I believe you said—momentarily I was deceived. And then a certain little gift of mine came to my aid. You have been kind enough to speak of my success. I have succeeded—why? Because I happen to be psychic, Mr. Wing——"

"Chinese people are psychic, too."

"Just a moment. As I stood there listening to you, a psychic wave swept over me. I had a feeling—a feeling of—what? Of stern men who sit in police stations and are sworn to enforce the laws. Of detectives pursuing evil-doers, landing them at last—and then, a court of justice, so-called, a learned judge. That, my friend, is the feeling I had. Rather amazing, don't you think?"

His visitor's expression had lost suddenly all its stupidity. The little black eyes snapped with admiration.

"Amazing smart act on your part, yes. But as for me, I do not think it was psychic feeling. A moment ago I beheld your eyes resting with fierce understanding on locality of my own waistcoat from which detective badge was recently removed. The pin has left indelible marks. You are number one detective yourself, and I congratulate you."

Tarneverro threw back his head and laughed. *"Touché!"* he cried. "So you are a detective, Mr.—er——"

"The name is Chan," said the bulky Chinese, grinning broadly. "Inspector Chan, of the Honolulu police—former times Sergeant, but there has been upheaval in local police department, and I am rewarded far beyond my humble merits. Trap which has just failed so flatly, I add in justice to me personally, was not my idea. I informed Chief it would not work unless you happened to be extreme dull-wit. Since you turn out clever beyond expectation, it did not. No bitter feelings. I pause only to call attention to local ordinance which says men like you must not practise dark arts in this town without obtaining permission. A word being spoken to the wise, I rise to accomplish my exit."

Tarneverro also stood up. "I am not going to practise among your townspeople," he announced. He had dropped the tense air of mystery which he evoked for the benefit of film stars, and seemed quite human and not unlikable. "It has been a pleasure to meet you, Inspector. As for my own detective prowess, I may say in confidence that it is rather useful in my work."

"Must be so," returned Chan. "But such skill as yours should be at service of public. Frequently in Los Angeles murder mystery leaps into print and never gets solved. I study them all with fiery interest. The Taylor case—what an amazing happening was there—*haie,* it is still mystery. And case of Denny Mayo, famous actor of handsome countenance, dead in his home at night. How many years—three and more—and Denny Mayo is still unavenged by Los Angeles police."

"And never will be," added the fortune-teller. "No, Inspector, that is not in my line. I find it safer to dwell on the future and soft-pedal Hollywood's past."

"In such course, wisdom may abide," agreed Chan. "None the less, how happily I would welcome your aid if some such worrisome puzzle stared into my face. I will say good-by, Mr. Tarneverro. Memory of your cleverness will linger in my poor mind for long time to come."

He slipped quietly out, and Tarneverro glanced at his watch. With a leisurely air, he placed a small table in the middle of the room, and taking from a bureau drawer a gleaming crystal, stood it thereon. Then he stepped to the window and drew the curtains part way across, shutting out a goodly portion of the bright light outside. Glancing about the darkened room, he shrugged his shoulders. Not such an impressive stage-setting as his studio in Los Angeles, but it would have to serve. Sitting down by the window, he took out of his pocket a bulky letter and, slitting the flap of the envelope, began to read. The curtains, caught in the fierce grip of the trade-wind, swirled about his head.

At eleven o'clock Shelah Fane knocked on the door, and he ushered her into his sitting-room. She was gowned in white and appeared younger than she had at the dock, but her eyes were clouded with worry. Tarneverro's manner was professional now; he was cold, remote, unsympathetic. He seated her at the table behind the crystal; then, drawing the curtains all the way, plunged the room into almost complete darkness.

"Tarneverro—you must tell me what to do," she began. He sat down opposite her.

"Wait," he commanded. He looked fixedly into the crystal. "I see you standing at the rail on the boat deck of a steamer, under a brilliant moon. You are wearing a dinner gown—it is gold and matches your hair. There is a scarf of the same color about your shoulders. A man is standing at your side; he points, and offers you a pair of glasses. You raise them to your eyes—you catch the last faint glimmer of the lights along the front at Papeete, the port from which you sailed a few brief hours ago."

"Yes, yes," murmured Shelah Fane. "Oh, Tarneverro—how do you know——"

"The man turns. I can see him only dimly, but I recognize him. To-day, on the pier—Alan Jaynes—was that his name? He has asked you a question—marriage, perhaps—but you shake your head. Reluctantly. You want to say yes—yet you don't. You put him off. Why? I feel you love this man."

"I do," the star cried. "Oh, Tarneverro—I really do. I knew him first at Papeete—only a week—but in a place like that—— The first night out—it was just as you say—he proposed to me. I haven't given him my answer yet. I want to say yes—to have a little happiness now—I've earned it, I think. But I—I'm afraid——"

He lifted his piercing eyes from the crystal. "You're afraid. Something in your past—you fear it will return to haunt you——"

"No, no," the woman cried.

"Something that happened long ago."

"No, no—it isn't true."

"You can not deceive me. How long ago? I can not quite determine, and it is necessary that I know."

The trade-wind mumbled at the curtains. Shelah Fane's eyes wandered helplessly about the darkened room, then came back to Tarneverro's.

"How long ago?" the man demanded again.

She sighed. "Three years ago last month," she said in a voice so low he had to strain to hear.

He was silent for a moment, his mind racing like an engine. June—three years ago. He gazed fixedly into the crystal; his lips moved. "Denny Mayo," he said softly. "Something about Denny Mayo. Ah, yes—I see it now."

The wind tore the curtains apart, and a wide strip of dazzling light fell across Shelah Fane's face. Her eyes were staring, frightened.

"I shouldn't have come," she moaned.

"What about Denny Mayo?" Tarneverro went on relentlessly. "Shall I tell you—or will you tell me?"

She pointed to the window. "A balcony. There's a balcony out there."

As one who humors a child, he rose and looked outside. He came back to the table. "Yes, there's a balcony—but no one is on it."

He sat down again, and his bold commanding eyes sought hers. She was trapped, and helpless.

"Now!" said Tarneverro the Great.

Chapter II

THE HOUSE ON THE BEACH

After a brief twilight, the dark sweeps over Waikiki Beach like Old Man Mystery himself. In the hours before the moon, like a climbing torch, ascends the purple sky, the sense of hearing comes into its own. Blackness covers the coco-palms, yet they may be heard rustling at the trade-wind's touch; the white line of the breakers is blotted out, yet they continue to crash on that unseen shore with what seems an added vigor. This is night in the real sense of the word, intriguing, awe-inspiring, but all too short, for the moon is waiting an early cue.

A solitary floor lamp was burning in the huge living-room of the house Shelah Fane had rented at Waikiki. The paneled walls, the furniture and the floor, all fashioned of rare native woods, gleamed faintly in the half-light; the green of exotic plants was everywhere. The French windows that faced the street were closed, but those on the ocean side, leading on to a great screened lanai, stood wide, and through them at regular intervals came the roar of the surf, which was running high.

Shelah Fane came into the room. She walked with a quick nervous step, and in her eyes was a look of apprehension—almost of terror. It was a look that had been there ever since her return from that interview with Tarneverro in his apartment at the Grand Hotel. What had she done? She asked this of herself over and over. What had she done? What was the secret of this dark man's power that he had so easily dragged from the inner recesses of her mind a story she had thought safely buried for ever? Once away from the strange influence of his presence she had been appalled at her own indiscretion. But it was too late then for anything save regret.

With her unerring instinct for the spotlight, she sat down under the single lamp. Many cameras had clicked in Hollywood since that distant time when, like a rocket, she had flashed into the picture sky, and nowadays the spotlight was none too kind to her. Kind to her hair, yes, which seemed to spring into flame, but not so considerate of the lines of worry about her eyes, about her small tense mouth. Did she know? Longer than most rockets she had hung blazing in the sky; now she must endure the swift lonely drop in the dark.

Her butler, Jessop, came in, a spare elderly Englishman who had also found in Hollywood the promised land. He carried a florist's box. Shelah looked up.

"Oh, Jessop," she said. "Did Miss Julie tell you? The dinner hour is eight-thirty."

"I understand, madam," he answered gravely.

"A few of the young people are going for a dip before we dine. Mr. Bradshaw for one. You might show him to the blue bedroom to dress. The bath-houses are dark and need cleaning. Miss Julie and Miss Diana will dress in their rooms."

Jessop nodded, as Julie came in. The girl wore an afternoon gown, and her face was innocent of make-up. She was enthusiastic, happy, young—a touch of envy darkened the star's fine eyes.

"Don't you worry, Shelah," Julie said. "Jessop and I have planned everything. It will be like all your parties—a knockout. What's that, Jessop? Flowers?"

"For Miss Fane," explained the butler, and handing the box to the girl, left the room.

Shelah Fane was looking about her, a frown on her face. "I've been wondering, Julie. How in the world can I arrange a good entrance on the party, in a place like this? If only there were a balcony, or at least a broad flight of stairs."

Julie laughed. "You might come suddenly through the lanai, strumming a ukulele and singing a Hawaiian song."

The star took her seriously. "No good, my dear. I'd be entering on the same level with the guests, and that is never effective. To make the proper impression, one must appear suddenly from above—always remember that, darling. Now, in Hollywood——"

The girl shrugged. "Oh, just come in naturally for once, Shelah. There's a lot in novelty, you know." She had torn the cord from the box of flowers, and now she lifted the lid. "Lovely," she cried. "Orchids, Shelah."

The star turned, without interest. Orchids were nothing new in her life. "Nice of Alan," she said languidly.

But Julie shook her head. "No," she announced, "they're not from Mr. Jaynes, evidently." She read the card aloud. " 'With love from one you have forgotten.' Who could that be, Shelah?"

"Who couldn't it be?" smiled the star a bit wistfully. She rose with sudden interest. "I wonder—let me see the card." She glanced at it. " 'With love from one——' " Her eyes lighted with quick understanding. "Why, it's Bob's writing. Dear old Bob! Just fancy—with love—after all these years."

"Bob?" inquired the girl.

Shelah nodded. "Bob Fyfe—my first and only husband, dear. You never knew him—it was long ago. I was just a kid, in the chorus of a musical show in New York, and Bob was an actor, a legitimate actor—such a good one, too. I adored him then, but along came Hollywood, and our divorce. And now—with love—I wonder? Can it be true?"

"What's he doing in Honolulu?" Julie asked.

"Playing in stock," Shelah replied. "Leading man at some theater here. Rita Ballou told me all about him, this morning when I called her up." She took the orchids. "I shall wear these to-night," she announced. "I never dreamed he would even speak to me. I—I'm touched. I'd like to see Bob again." A thoughtful look crossed her face. "I'd like to see him at once. He was always so kind, so clever. What time is it—oh, yes——" She glanced at a watch on her wrist. "Seven-twenty. What was the name of that theater? Rita told me. The Royal, I think she said——"

The door-bell rang briskly, there ensued a snappy bit of dialogue in the hall and Jimmy Bradshaw burst through the curtains. He was, it seemed, in a light-hearted mood.

"Here we all are," he cried. "Everybody who really matters. Well, Miss Fane, how does it feel to be foot-loose and care-free on a palm-fringed shore—way down in the warm southern seas?"

"It's really very restful," Shelah smiled. She nodded at Julie. "I'll be back in a moment. I want a pin for these flowers."

She disappeared into the hall, and Bradshaw turned quickly to the girl.

"You're looking great," he cried. "It's the climate. Not that you didn't look fairly good at the start——"

"Tell me," she cut in. "What do you think of Shelah?"

"Shelah?" He paused. "Oh, she's all right. Nice and friendly but—a bit artificial—a good actress, on and off. In the past two years I've met enough screen stars to start a Hollywood of my own, and what I always say is—doffing my hat to southern California—you can have 'em."

"You don't really know Shelah," protested the girl.

"No, I guess not. She's been kind to you, and that makes her aces up with me. But my own preference in women—and I've looked very carefully over the field——"

"Oh, you have, have you?"

"My ideal—since you've asked me, and I'm glad you have—is a rather different sort. Lovely, of course, young, innocent, ingenuous—and pretty crazy about yours truly. That—and you may quote me freely—is the girl for me."

Diana came suddenly through the curtains. She, too, still wore an afternoon gown.

"Hello, big boy," she said. "You ready for that swim with me?"

"Sure," replied Bradshaw. "With you—and anybody else who wants to come along." He looked at Julie. "Let's go. Before the moon rises is my idea. It's the best time. Any one else going—or is it just—the three of us?"

Julie shook her head. "No one else, I guess. The others are afraid of spoiling their make-up."

"Which is one advantage of youth over doddering age," the boy returned. "Well, come along——"

Shelah appeared, wearing the orchids on her shoulder.

"Just about to dip into the world-famed waters of Waikiki," Jimmy informed her. "Won't you join us?"

"Some other evening," she told him. "You know, I'm hostess to-night."

"You are missing," said Bradshaw impressively, "one of the thrills of a lifetime. The silken surf beating on coral sand, the dark, star-strewn sky above, perhaps the pastel loveliness of a lunar rainbow—boats run from Los Angeles and San Francisco once a week, and the fare is within the reach of all——"

The door-bell rang again. Accompanied by Shelah, the young people went out into the hall.

"Get your suit," Julie said to the boy. "I'll show you

where to change. Let's make it a race. The first one into the water gets a prize."

"I'll win it," answered Bradshaw. "I'll name it too." They clattered up the polished stairs.

Again the bell sounded. Shelah was just beside the door, but she did not open it; she considered such an act beneath the dignity of a star. Instead she returned to the living-room and waited for Jessop to do his duty. After a brief delay, he did it, and two new guests appeared in the living-room. Shelah advanced to meet them—a dark, rather faded woman of thirty, followed by a big blond man who had an air of nonchalant authority.

"Rita Ballou," the star cried. "Why—it's ages! And Wilkie—I'm so glad."

"Hello, darling," said the woman she called Rita.

The man came forward. "Look here, Shelah. What time did you say dinner was to be?"

"Eight-thirty—but it doesn't matter——"

Ballou turned to his wife. "Good lord—can't you ever get anything straight?"

"What's the difference?" the woman replied. "We can have a chat with Shelah before the others come." She turned to the star. "So sorry we missed you when you went through before. We were on the mainland."

"Haven't missed you this time, thank heaven," added Wilkie Ballou. "By gad, you're as blooming as ever."

"How *do* you do it?" inquired Rita sweetly. Her cold eyes flashed green with envy as she looked at Shelah.

"She's found the fountain of youth," suggested Wilkie admiringly.

"I've always heard that was in Hawaii," smiled the star. She looked hard at Rita. "But it isn't," the look added.

Rita understood. "Not at all," she said grimly. "It's in the beauty shops of Hollywood, and you know it. Over here, women fade quickly——"

"Nonsense," protested Shelah.

"Yes, they do. Oh—I've learned my lesson—too late. I should have stayed in Hollywood and gone on with my career."

"But, my dear,—surely you're happy with Wilkie?"

"Of course. The way I would be with the toothache."

Wilkie shrugged. "Overlook it, Shelah," he said. "We've been rowing all the way out here. Rita's nerves, you know."

"Is that so?" remarked his wife. "I guess any one would have nerves with a husband like you. Honestly, Shelah, he's got a better imagination than what's his name—Shakespeare. If he'd only drop sugar planting and go in for writing scenarios—but never mind us. Tell me all about Hollywood. I'd love to be back."

"I'm making a long stop here—we'll have lots of time to chat later," Shelah explained. "Some of the crowd are going for a swim before dinner. Care to go along?"

Rita put one hand to her perfect coiffure, and shrugged "Not for me," she cried. "I'm so sick of swimming I gag at the sight of my tub. You've no idea, my dear—three years married and living in Honolulu—these people over here are like fish. They suffocate when you bring 'em ashore."

They heard the noise of a new arrival in the hall, and Alan Jaynes came into the room, handsome and upstanding in his dinner clothes. Shelah's heart sank suddenly at sight of him. While she was introducing him to the Ballous, Julie and Jimmy Bradshaw rushed in, wearing gay beach robes over their bathing-suits. They paused, with obvious reluctance, for further introductions.

"Where's Miss Dixon?" Bradshaw inquired. "She hasn't gone out, has she?"

"Nonsense," cried Julie. "Diana will take ages. She always does."

"Then the race is between us two," said the boy, and dashed through the open window on to the lanai, with Julie at his heels.

"What a good-looking boy," Rita remarked. "Who is he?"

Shelah explained Mr. Bradshaw's place in the world's work. Rita stood up.

"Let's all go down to the beach," she said.

"The beach—in high-heeled slippers?" protested Wilkie.

"I can take them off, can't I?" Rita demanded. She was moving toward the window.

"Go along," the star said. "We'll follow later."

Rita went out.

Without enthusiasm, Wilkie lifted his great bulk from the chair. "That means I go, too," he explained, and did so.

Shelah turned to Alan Jaynes with a nervous little laugh. "Poor Wilkie—he's so jealous. And with reason, I'm afraid—at least, he had reason in the old days."

Jaynes came quickly to her side. "So sorry I couldn't

see you this afternoon. Your headache—it's better, I trust?"

She nodded. "Much better."

"I've brought you a bit of an offering. It's hardly worthy of you, of course." He handed her a corsage bouquet wrapped in tissue-paper.

She unwrapped it. "Lovely," she said.

"But too late," remarked Jaynes. "I see you're wearing some one's orchids."

Shelah laid his gift on a table. "Yes, Alan."

"I hope that doesn't mean——" he began, frowning. "Shelah—it can't mean that. I—I couldn't go on without you."

She faced him. "You'll have to, Alan. I'm so sorry. But I—I can't marry you."

His expression clouded. "It's true, then," he said.

"What's true?"

"The thing Van Horn told me this afternoon. I refused to believe it of you—it's too childish—too ignorant. You sent for that damned fortune-telling charlatan, and he decided it for you. He advised you not to take me." She turned away, without speaking. The man's face flushed with anger. "If you had any sane reason," he continued, controlling himself with an effort, "I'd take my medicine quietly. But this—this is too much. To let a fakir—a crystal-gazer—a cheap fraud, come between us—by the lord, I won't stand for it. I thought on the boat you loved me——"

"Maybe I did," she answered sadly.

"Then nothing in this world shall stop me——"

"Wait, Alan, wait, please," she cried. "It's for you—I'm doing this for you. You must believe that. There could be no happiness for us——"

"So that's what he told you, eh?"

"That's what he told me, but he was only repeating what was in my heart. The past, Alan—the past won't die——"

"I've told you I don't give a hang about what's past."

"Oh, but you don't know, Alan—and I can't tell you. I'm trying to do the decent thing—you're so fine and straight—I couldn't bear it if I ended by dragging you through the dust. Please, Alan, please——"

"I don't want to understand," Jaynes cried. "I only want you—to love and take care of—see here, my time is brief, so pitifully brief. I must leave at midnight—you know that. Forget this fool of a fortune-teller. I can't understand your faith in him, I can't approve it, but I'm willing to overlook it. You aren't to blame, I fancy. Your temperament, your way of life. Forget him, my dear, and give me your word before I go——"

She shook her head. "I can't," she said brokenly. "I can't."

For a long moment Jaynes looked at her. Then, with great dignity, he turned on his heel.

"Where are you going?" Shelah cried.

"I don't know," he answered. "I must think this thing out."

"But you're dining here——"

"I don't know," the man repeated. "I couldn't talk to your friends just now. I want to be alone for a few minutes. I may return later." He seemed dazed, uncertain of himself.

Shelah was at his side, her hand on his sleeve. "Alan, I'm so sorry—so unhappy."

He turned, and took her in his arms. "By heaven—you loved me on the ship. I won't give you up. I can't." His glance fell on the orchids, fastened to the shoulder-strap of her gown by a small diamond pin. "No one shall take you from me," he cried and, releasing her, went quickly out.

Shelah Fane walked slowly to a chair, and dropped into it. Pain and a desperate unhappiness were in her face, and she was not acting now. For a few moments she sat there, then gradually came back to her surroundings. She glanced at her watch—a quarter of eight. Quickly she rose and went to the French windows at the rear.

The moon was still in hiding, and the broad lawn that lay between the house and the pounding surf was shrouded in darkness. She heard, far away, the exultant cry of Julie battling with a breaker, and then the answering call of Jimmy Bradshaw. There was an odd air of expectancy about her as she stepped out on the lanai. She crossed it to the screen door that opened on to the lawn and stood there, peering out. Under a near-by hau tree she thought she saw, in the blackness, an even blacker shadow. Suddenly it moved. With a little cry of recognition, she flung open the door and ran swiftly across the grass.

Meanwhile, Alan Jaynes was striding grimly along Kalakaua Avenue in the direction of the Grand Hotel. Five minutes brought him to the cool lofty lobby of that famous hostelry. He passed the head bell-man, whose smile of welcome froze suddenly on his face as he caught the look in the Britisher's eyes.

Jaynes turned to the left, moving past shop windows filled with jade and Oriental silks, then past the flower booth where, earlier in the evening, he had purchased the bouquet which now lay unappreciated on Shelah Fane's table. In another moment he reached the entrance to the big lounge of the hotel, and stood there at the top of a short flight of steps.

It was a beautiful room, with those three great arches opposite the entrance like triple paintings of the tropic sky. But Jaynes had no eye for beauty to-night. Most of the guests were at dinner, and the lounge had a deserted air. Seated not far away, however, talking pleasantly with an elderly couple who had the look of tourists, the Britisher saw the man he wanted.

He descended the steps, and crossed to this man's chair. "Stand up," he ordered in a husky voice.

Tarneverro the Great looked at him with an expressionless face. "I should have expected a bit more courtesy," he said evenly. "But then—I scarcely know you."

"Stand up," Jaynes repeated, "and come with me. I want a talk with you."

For a moment the fortune-teller sat, quietly measuring the man who towered above him. Then he rose, and making his apologies to the two old people, he walked at Jaynes' side down the long room.

"What is all this——" he began.

They stopped at an archway near the far end. Outside a series of brilliant lights bathed the hotel lawn in white, making an ideal stage-setting for some drama of the tropics. But the stage was empty; the drama was all inside the lounge.

"I want an explanation," said Jaynes roughly.

"An explanation of what?"

"I have done myself the honor of asking Miss Shelah Fane to marry me. I had every reason to believe she intended to do so—but to-day she consulted you about the matter—a matter that concerns you not at all. You advised her against a marriage with me."

Tarneverro shrugged. "I do not discuss with outsiders what goes on at my readings."

"You're going to discuss it with me. Make up your mind to that!"

"Suppose I did—what could I say? I tell my clients only what I see in the crystal——"

"Rot!" cried Jaynes. "You tell them whatever happens to suit your fancy. What was your reason for this advice to Shelah?" He came closer and stared into the seer's face. "Are you, by any chance, in love with her yourself?"

The fortune-teller smiled. "Miss Fane is most charming——"

"We don't need your evidence on that point——"

"Most charming, but I do not permit myself the unwise luxury of a sentimental attachment for my clients. I advised her as I did because I saw no happiness possible in this proposed marriage." His tone grew serious. "Incidentally, whether you appreciate it or not, I did you a favor to-day."

"Really?" said Jaynes. "But I'm not asking favors of a mountebank like you."

A dark flush spread over Tarneverro's face. "There can be no point in prolonging this interview," he remarked, and turned away.

Jaynes seized him quickly by the arm. "We'll prolong it this far. You are going to Miss Fane at once and tell her you're a fraud, a fake, and that you wish to retract all you said to her to-day."

Tarneverro shook off the other's grasp. "And if I refuse?" he said.

"If you refuse," Jaynes answered, "I propose to give you a thrashing you won't forget for many a day."

"I do refuse," said Tarneverro quietly.

Jaynes' arm shot back, only to find itself in a surprisingly firm grip. He turned. Val Martino, the director, was at his side; his was the grip on the Britisher's arm. Beyond Martino, Huntley Van Horn, resplendent in Hollywood evening garb, looked on with an air of amused interest.

"Now, now," bellowed Martino, his face even redder than usual. "Cut this out, please. Too much of it in the pictures already. We can't have it, Jaynes, we can't have it."

For a moment the four stood motionless. A new figure strolled upon the scene, a broad bulky Chinese in a dinner coat. Tarneverro hailed him. "Ah, Inspector Chan. Just a moment, please."

Charlie came closer. "It is Mr. Tarneverro," he remarked. "The lifter of the veil."

"Inspector," the fortune-teller said, "may I present Mr.

Van Horn, and Mr. Martino? And this is Mr. Alan Jaynes. Inspector Chan, of the Honolulu police."

Chan bowed gracefully. "The honor is immense. Distinguished company, as a blind man could see."

Jaynes glared at Tarneverro. "Very good," he sneered. "Hide behind the skirts of the police. It's what I would expect of you."

"Now, now," Martino interposed. "A slight misunderstanding, Inspector. There will be no trouble—I am sure the good name of the industry is too precious to all of us. It is certainly very precious to me."

Van Horn looked at his watch. "Eight o'clock," he announced. "I believe I'll roll along down to Shelah's. Anybody coming?"

The director shook his head. "Not yet. I'll be down presently." The actor walked slowly away. Martino, his grip still firm on the Britisher's arm, sought to lead him off. "Come out on the terrace," he pleaded. "We'll talk this matter over."

Jaynes turned to the fortune-teller. "I'm not sailing until twelve," he said. "In the meantime, we may meet again." He permitted Martino to lead him down the room.

"I trust that last prediction falls short of truth," Chan said to Tarneverro. "I do not have much liking for light I observe in gentleman's eye."

Tarneverro laughed. "Oh, he'll come around. I have offended him, quite unintentionally." He looked thoughtfully at Charlie. "By the way, Inspector, this is a happy meeting. I was thinking of calling you up. Just how do you plan to spend the evening?"

"I attend Rotary Club banquet in this hotel," Chan explained.

"Good. You'll be here some time?"

Chan nodded. "I fear so. It happens very few after-dinner speeches are equipped with self-stopper."

"Until eleven, perhaps?"

"It seems terribly possible."

"I am dining at a friend's house down the beach," Tarneverro said. "At the house of Miss Shelah Fane, in fact. Some time between now and eleven o'clock I may have a very important message for you, Inspector."

Chan's eyes opened slowly. "A message? Of what nature?"

Tarneverro hesitated. "This morning you happened to

speak of certain murder cases in Los Angeles that remain unsolved. I told you then that I preferred to keep out of that sort of thing. We are not always able to follow our preferences, Inspector." He moved away.

"One moment," said Chan. "You have sought to quench the fire of my curiosity by tossing upon it a handful of straw. May I repeat my question—what sort of message?"

The fortune-teller gave him a long look. "A message calling upon you to arrest the murderer of—but there, I mustn't say too much. There's many a slip, as you have no doubt learned from your own experience. I shall be happy to have you so near—until eleven, at least. After that I presume I can reach you at your home?"

"With ease," Charlie told him.

"Let us hope for success," smiled Tarneverro cryptically, and went to rejoin his elderly acquaintances in the center of the lounge. For a second Chan looked after him. Then, shrugging his broad shoulders, he turned to find the banquet room.

Chapter III

FLOWERS FOR SHELAH FANE

Huntley Van Horn strolled down Kalakaua Avenue in the direction of Shelah Fane's house. On this tiny island in the midst of the rolling Pacific, few outward signs of a romantic past survived. He might have been on Hollywood Boulevard: the parade of automobiles along that stretch of American asphalt was constant, a trolley clattered by, he walked on a concrete sidewalk under the soft yellow glow of modern street-lamps. Yet, beyond the range of those lamps, he was conscious of the black velvet of a tropic night. He caught the odor of ginger blossoms and plumeria, a croton hedge gave way to one of hibiscus, topped with pale pink flowers that were doomed to die at midnight.

He came to the number Shelah had impressed on his memory and turned in through the gates on to a broad drive that curved before a wide front door. Passing beneath a prolific banyan tree, two centuries older than the motion pictures, he rang the bell. Jessop admitted him.

"Oh, Mr. Van Horn," the butler said. "I'm happy to see you again."

"How have you been?" the actor inquired.

"In splendid health, sir. I trust you enjoyed your little jaunt to Tahiti?"

Van Horn tossed down the straw hat he had substituted for the silk topper in which he had won the approval of several million women. "A primitive country, Tahiti," he smiled. "It would have reminded you of Hollywood, Jessop."

The butler permitted himself a discreet smile. Van Horn pushed on into the living-room, and Jessop followed.

"No one here?" the actor cried. "Lord—am I as early as all that?"

"Oh, no, Mr. Van Horn. Some of the guests are enjoying the bathing, which I understand is rather famous in certain quarters. A few, I believe, are on the beach. Would you care to join the—er—the other young people in the water, sir?"

Van Horn grinned. "The diplomatic service lost a good man in you. No—much as I am tempted to classify myself with youth, the matter involves too damn' much dressing and undressing. I shall remain, high and dry, on the shore."

"Just as well, sir," nodded Jessop. "It is already eight-fifteen, and the dinner hour is rapidly approaching. I shall be forced to summon them in shortly."

Van Horn stared about the room. "What—no cocktails?"

"There has been a slight delay, sir. The gentleman who was to supply us with the raw material—the very raw material, between you and me, sir—has only just come. I was busy with the shaker when you rang." He went over and stood by the French window opening on to the lanai. "You will find the ocean just out here, sir," he explained.

Van Horn laughed, and stepped on to the lanai. The butler followed him to the screen door, and held it open.

"Ah, yes," said the actor. "I hear the roar of surf. No doubt I shall find the sea in that same general neighborhood." He paused in the doorway, and indicated a light gleaming through the trees some distance to the right. "What's over there?"

"It's a sort of summer-house, or pavilion, sir," Jessop explained. "At least, it would be a summer-house in England, where we have summers. It may be a few of the guests are in there."

Van Horn went out on the lawn, and started across it in the direction of the light. Suddenly he heard, above the pounding of the breakers, voices on the beach. He stood for a moment, undecided which way to go.

Jessop, meanwhile, returned to the living-room. An old bent Chinese came shuffling in.

"My dear Wu Kno-ching," the butler protested, "in a well-run house, the cook's place is in the kitchen."

The old man blandly ignored the rebuke. "What time dinnah?" he asked.

"As I have told you, the dinner is set for eight-thirty," replied Jessop. "It may, however, be somewhat delayed."

Wu Kno-ching shrugged. "Wha' kin' house this is? Dinnah mebbe sometime plitty soon aftah while. I get dinnah leady boss say wait dinnah goes to hell." He departed, murmuring further reproof.

The screen door slammed behind Wilkie Ballou; he crossed the lanai aimlessly and entered the living-room.

"I fear this idea of a swim is going to delay dinner, sir," Jessop said to him.

"What? Oh, yes—I suppose so. Have you any cigarettes here? My case is empty."

Jessop proffered a box containing cigarettes, and taking one, Ballou dropped into a chair. The butler officiated with a match, then retired to the kitchen.

Returning fifteen minutes later, he found the Honolulu man sitting just as he had left him.

"Things are getting rather serious, sir," Jessop remarked. He carried a large dinner gong. "I had always supposed, from my reading, that the Chinese are a notably patient race."

"They have that reputation, yes," nodded Ballou.

"Their representative in our kitchen, sir, is doing nothing to sustain it," Jessop sighed. "He informs me with great passion that dinner is waiting. I'll just go down to the shore and see what this will do." He nodded toward the gong and disappeared. Presently he could be heard in the distance, beating a not unmusical tattoo.

Ballou lighted a fresh cigarette. Jessop returned, and at his heels came Rita Ballou and Van Horn.

"You should have stayed, Wilkie," Rita said. "I've just been getting all the latest Hollywood gossip."

"I'm not interested," Ballou growled.

"Poor Wilkie," his wife smiled. "It's close to his bedtime, and he hasn't even had his dinner. Cheer up. It won't be long now."

Diana Dixon arrived, quite out of breath. "I suppose we're late," she cried. "You should have been in with us. It was glorious—but not half long enough. I could have stayed for hours. Cocktails—that's an idea."

She took one from the tray which Jessop held before her. The other guests likewise needed no urging. Huntley Van Horn lifted his glass.

"To our hostess, if any," he remarked.

"That's right—what's become of Shelah?" Rita Ballou said. "We saw her for a moment when we came——"

"Shelah," said Van Horn, with a cynical smile, "is no

doubt lurking in the background waiting to make a grand and impressive entrance. She will ride in on a white charger, or descend on us from a balloon. You know, she goes in for that sort of thing——"

Julie and Jimmy Bradshaw rushed in, glowing and in high spirits. "Hello, Mr. Van Horn," the girl cried. "Are you all that's come?"

"To think," he groaned, "that you could be so rude to me."

"Oh, you know what I mean," she laughed. "Where are all our other guests? Val Martino, Mr. Jaynes, Tarneverro——"

"Tarneverro coming?" Van Horn lifted his eyebrows. "In that case, I will have a second cocktail. Thanks so much."

Quite unexpectedly there was the sound of steel guitars at the front door, and of many fresh young voices singing a Hawaiian song. Julie cried out with delight.

"A serenade from Shelah's admirers," she said. "Isn't that sweet? She will be pleased." Her beach robe streaming behind her, she ran to the door and threw it open. She stood gazing out at a vast throng of high-school girls, laden with flowers. They stopped their song, and a young Japanese girl stepped forward. "We would like to see Shelah Fane, please."

"Of course," said Julie. "Just wait, and I'll get her. While you're waiting, if you don't mind—will you sing *The Song of the Islands?* It's Miss Fane's favorite, you know."

She left the door open and returned to the living-room. "Come on, Jimmy—we'll find Shelah. I think she's in the pavilion."

"Sure," said Jimmy. They went out on the lawn.

"Couldn't be better," Julie cried. "For Shelah's entrance on the party, I mean. That crowd outside serenading her as she comes in—she'll love it."

"Good lord," said Bradshaw, disapproval in his voice.

"Oh, I know," the girl answered. "It's silly, but poor Shelah's what she is. Her life has made her so, and she can't change." They went on across the soft lawn under the hau trees and the algarobas. The sweet haunting strains of *The Song of the Islands* came to them on the evening breeze. "Hurry," Julie said, "Shelah must get in there before that song ends."

She ran up the steps of the pavilion, with Bradshaw

close behind. He pushed open the door of the single room. For a second he stood there, then he turned swiftly and caught the girl in his arms.

"No, no," he cried. "Don't go any farther."

His tone frightened her. "What do you mean?"

"Turn around and go back," he pleaded, but she tore away from him and ran inside.

"You'll be sorry," he warned.

And she was sorry, it seemed, for above the voices of the serenaders and the distant whine of steel guitars, her own voice rose in a sharp cry of fright and terror.

Shelah Fane lay on the floor beside a small straight-backed chair. She had been stabbed through the heart; her priceless ivory gown was stained with crimson. Outside, that little group of her admirers continued to sing fervently their serenade.

Julie knelt by the star's side, and Bradshaw looked away. In a moment he went over and lifted the girl to her feet. "We'd better go," he said gently. "There's nothing we can do."

He led her to the door. She looked up at him through her tears. "But who—who——" she murmured.

"Ah, yes——" he answered. "That, I'm afraid, is the big question now."

He found, on the inside of the pavilion door, an unexpected key. They went outside, and the boy locked the door, putting the key in his pocket. Slowly they walked back to the house. Huntley Van Horn greeted them.

"Did you tell Shelah?" he said. "The stage is all set. Her guests are gathered in the living-room, her great public is singing lustily at the door—it's a grand entrance——" He stopped at sight of Julie's face.

"What's happened?" cried Rita Ballou shrilly.

Bradshaw stood looking about the little group. Jessop came in and, picking up the silver tray on which he had served the cocktails, prepared to collect the empty glasses. Outside the door, *The Song of the Islands* trailed off into silence.

"Shelah Fane has been murdered in the pavilion," said the boy in a low voice.

There was a sudden crash. Jessop had been guilty of his first error in forty years of service. He had dropped the silver tray.

"I beg pardon," he said to no one in particular.

Outside, Shelah Fane's admirers began another song. Bradshaw dashed through the curtains to the front door.

"Please," he cried. "Please—no more to-night. You must go away now. Miss Fane can't see you. She is—she is ill."

"We are so sorry," said the girl who seemed to be the leader. "Will you give her the flowers, please?"

They began to load him down with fragrant blossoms. Presently he staggered back into the hallway, his arms filled with a riot of color. Julie was standing there, her eyes wide, her face deathly pale.

"Flowers," said Bradshaw. "Flowers for Shelah Fane."

With a choking cry, Julie fell in a heap at his feet.

Chapter IV

THE CAMEL AT THE GATE

Down at the Grand Hotel, Charlie Chan was well started on what he perceived was going to be an excellent dinner. The hour of Rotarian oratory was not near enough to worry him, the food was good and he felt at peace with the world. He did not know the name of the small fish that lay on the plate before him, but one taste had led him to approve most heartily of its quality. He was leaning forward to apply himself with increased diligence to the task at hand, when a bell-boy touched him on the shoulder.

"You are wanted on telephone very quick," said the boy.

A sense of vague unrest troubled him as he walked down the long lobby to the telephone booth. He would have preferred a life of quiet meditation, but a ruthless fate was always breaking in upon him with some new problem that must be solved. What now, he wondered, as he entered the booth and pulled the door to behind him.

He was greeted by an excited young voice. "Say, Charlie,—this is Jim Bradshaw of the Tourist Bureau. Huntley Van Horn told me I could find you at the hotel."

"Yes—and now you have found me. What is it that has brought you to this state of high disturbance?"

In jumbled phrases Bradshaw poured out his story. Charlie listened calmly.

"Shelah Fane," the boy was saying. "You know what that means, Charlie. This news of mine will be cabled all over the world to-night. You're going to be in the limelight as you never were before. Better get down here as fast as you can."

"I will arrive at once," Charlie answered. Was that a sigh, Bradshaw wondered, that came over the wire? "Let nothing be touched until I touch it," the detective added.

He hung up, then called the police station and gave certain directions. At last he came from the booth, mopping his perspiring brow with his handkerchief. For a moment he stood motionless, as though gathering his strength for the task that lay before him. Another case, another murder, and he knew that what the boy had said was true: this time he would work in a bright spotlight indeed. Shelah Fane! Not for nothing did he have numerous children who, as he often said, were movie crazed. He knew only too well the interest that had always centered about the woman who now lay dead a short distance down the beach.

"A thousand-mile journey begins with one step," he sighed, and took it—in the direction of his hat.

When he returned to the door of the hotel, he encountered Tarneverro. The fortune-teller also carried a hat, and seemed on the point of going out. "Hello, Inspector," he said. "You haven't finished your dinner already?"

"I have not," Charlie answered. "I am rudely wrenched away by important business. The most important I have encountered for some time."

"Yes?" returned Tarneverro lightly.

Charlie's small eyes were fixed upon the other's face with a fierce intensity. Not too soon to collect impressions, to weigh, to measure, to study.

"Miss Shelah Fane," he said slowly, "is just now found murdered at her home."

For hours afterward he was to speculate upon the look that crossed that dark mysterious face.

"Shelah!" Tarneverro cried. "Good God!"

"You were on your way there, perhaps?" Charlie continued.

"I—I—yes—of course——"

"Do me the honor to ride with me. I desire to ask questions."

Val Martino hurried up. "I say, Tarneverro—are you going down the beach?"

Tarneverro told him the news. The director heard it with surprising calmness.

"Too bad," he said evenly. He was thoughtful. "Well, there goes six months' hard work. That picture's ruined. I'll never find anybody to double for her—I've tried it——"

"Good lord, man!" cried Tarneverro angrily. "Shelah is dead, and you babble about your picture."

"Sorry," said Martino. "Sorry for poor Shelah. But even in the movies, the show must go on."

"What became of that fellow Jaynes?" Tarneverro asked suddenly.

"Right after we left you, he shook me off and strolled down the beach. He was in a state of mind—well, you saw that. Wasn't coming to the dinner—but I fancy I'd better find him and bring him down, eh?"

"Yes, yes," Chan said hurriedly. "I must see him. Come, Mr. Tarneverro. Speed is necessary." He led the fortune-teller out to the drive, where his battered flivver was waiting. "The vehicle is none too grand," he apologized, "but it moves. Will you kindly leap inside?"

Silently Tarneverro climbed into the little two-seater. Charlie started the car.

"This is a terrible thing," the fortune-teller said. "Poor Shelah—I can scarcely realize it."

Charlie shrugged. "Time to be philosophical," he suggested. "You have perhaps heard old Eastern saying. 'Death is the black camel that kneels unbid at every gate.' Sooner or later—does it matter which?"

"I know, I know," Tarneverro continued. "But, in a way, I'm afraid I'm responsible for this. Oh, lord, the more I think about it, the clearer it becomes. Poor Shelah's blood is on my head."

"Your remarks have interesting sound," Charlie remarked, as the car moved through the hotel gates on to the avenue. "Explain, if you will be so kind."

"This evening," the fortune-teller went on, "I told you I might call on you to make an arrest in a very important murder case. I fully expected to do so. I'll tell you what I meant by that, as briefly as possible.

"Shelah Fane had cabled me from the ship, asking me to meet her here. It seems that this fellow Jaynes had proposed to her, and she wanted my advice. For some time past she had been in the habit of coming to me with all her problems. She loved Jaynes, she wanted to marry him—but she was afraid of what the future might hold in store. She feared that at any moment the world might discover that for three years or more she had gone about burdened with a terrible secret."

"What secret?" Charlie inquired.

"This morning," Tarneverro continued, "you spoke of

Denny Mayo, who was found dead in his home in Los Angeles some three years ago. The police have been at sea on the case from the start. But Shelah Fane—she knew who murdered Denny Maro. She was in Mayo's house, paying a harmless call, on the night of the murder. The door-bell rang, and she foolishly hid in another room. She saw the thing done. All this she confessed to me this morning. What is more, she told me that Denny Mayo's murderer is at this moment in Honolulu."

Charlie's eyes gleamed in the dark. "She told you the name?"

Tarneverro shook his head. "I'm sorry. She didn't want to, and I made no effort to press her. Her reason, of course, for not revealing her connection with this affair at the time, was that to do so would ruin her career. She has kept silent all these years, but she hesitated to marry a man of whom she was really fond and perhaps drag him through some very unpleasant publicity later on."

"A natural hesitation," Chan approved. "You encouraged it?" He had stopped the car in the drive of Shelah's house, but he made no move to alight.

"I did, of course," Tarneverro said. "More than that, I strongly advised her to lift this burden from her mind and find peace at last. I assured her that if she revealed the name of the guilty person of her own accord, no police in the world would be inclined to punish her for her long silence. I trust I was right in that?"

"Speaking for myself only, yes," nodded Charlie.

"I suggested she refuse Jaynes for the present, and go through with this unpleasant duty which I felt she owed to society. I said I thought it would be extremely foolish for her to marry any man with such a threat hanging over her happiness. If he really cared for her, I pointed out, Jaynes would marry her in the end. If he didn't care that much, then it was better to discover it now."

They alighted and stood under the banyan tree. Charlie peered into the fortune-teller's face. "And if Jaynes did not marry her——" he suggested.

Tarneverro shrugged. "You are on the wrong track there," he said. "I had no sentimental interest in Shelah Fane. But I didn't fancy my rôle—the secret she confided in me was a bit more than I'd bargained for. I felt, too, that for the sake of her own happiness she ought to get rid of this burden at last. So I pleaded with her to make public the name of the guilty person in the Mayo case."

"And she agreed?" Charlie asked.

"Not precisely. The idea rather frightened her. She said she would think it over, and give me her decision to-night. 'Write me a brief statement, with that name included,' I told her, 'give it to me at dinner this evening, and I will make everything as easy for you as possible.' I was confident of gaining my point, or I would never have spoken to you about it. Yes, I would have gained it—but now—now——"

"Now," Chan said, "the killer of Denny Mayo has silenced this woman for ever."

"Precisely."

"But in what manner did this person discover she was hovering on a point of revealment?"

"I can't tell you," Tarneverro replied. "There is a balcony outside my room. That's a possibility, but not a likely one, I fear. Or it may be that Shelah consulted the killer, told him—or her—that she could no longer remain silent. It would have been like her. She was indiscreet, impulsive." They moved toward the steps. "I hope that what I have told you will prove helpful, Inspector. It gives you the motive, at least, and it narrows your search. Believe me, I shall be at your side through this investigation. You are going to have all the help I can possibly give you. I want, even more than you, the name of Shelah's murderer."

"Your help will be valuable indeed," Chan told him. "What did I say to you this morning—you are number one detective yourself. I did not dream that so soon we would be working side by side."

Jessop admitted them, and they went into the living-room where the two Ballous and Van Horn sat in gloomy silence. Charlie stood gazing at this small group with thoughtful deliberation. Jimmy Bradshaw entered behind him, his bathing-suit abandoned for dinner clothes.

"Hello, Charlie," he said in a low voice. "You're needed here, all right. In the pavilion—clear over to the right on the lawn. I locked the door as soon as we found what had happened. Here's the key."

"You are bright boy," said Charlie, pleased. "That fact has long been apparent as the morning sun." He turned to the others. "It will naturally be understood that no one leaves this house until I grant permission. Mr. Tarneverro, will you kindly accompany me?"

He walked with the fortune-teller in silence across the lawn, white now under the rising moon. Chan went up the steps first, and unlocked the door. With marked reluctance, Tarneverro followed.

Charlie went over and dropped down on one knee beside Shelah Fane. Slowly he looked from her to the fortune-teller. "Long time I have been in present business," he said softly, "but rough blunt feelings do not come natural to me yet. I am sorry for this lady. Never before this moment have I seen her—yet I am so very sorry." He stood up. "The black camel has knelt at plenty famous gate to-night," he added.

Tarneverro remained some distance from the body. He seemed to control himself with an effort. "Poor Shelah!" he muttered. "Life was very sweet to her."

"It is sweet to all of us," Charlie nodded. "Even the beggar hesitates to cross a rotting bridge."

"I can never forgive myself," the other continued. "What you see here began this morning in my apartment."

"What is to be, will be," Chan comforted. "We will not move unfortunate one until arrival of coroner. I have already telephoned the station. But we will look about, Mr. Tarneverro. Do not forget—you are to help." He knelt again, and lifted Shelah Fane's left arm. "Here is already some evidence. There has been a struggle, and wrist-watch was smashed in process. Crystal is broken, and"—he placed the watch to his ear—"the working of the timepiece immediately ceased to function. The hands remain stationary at two minutes past eight. So soon, without an effort, we know exact moment of tragedy. That is indeed something."

"Two minutes after eight," Tarneverro said. "At that moment, Jaynes, Martino, Van Horn, you and I were in the lounge of the hotel. Remember—Van Horn looked at his watch, remarked it was eight o'clock, and said he was starting down here."

"Of course," Chan nodded. "The alibis arrive in one huge flock." He pointed to the orchids, crushed on the floor. "Further evidence of the struggle. Bouquet was torn off, trampled under foot."

"All of which looks a bit like jealousy," responded Tarneverro, frowning. "Can we be wrong about the motive, after all? No—it might be anger, too."

Charlie was crawling about the rug. "Peculiar thing," he remarked. "Flowers were fastened by pin—you may note the shoulder-strap is torn—but no pin is here now." He examined the orchids, and made a thorough search of the floor, while Tarneverro watched him. "It is true," he added, standing up, "the pin which fastened flowers is strangely missing."

He stepped to an old mahogany dressing-table, a handsome piece in its day, but now banished to the beach house. The table had a glass top, and leaning over, he studied this with a microscope he had taken from his pocket. "One more point," he said. "This corner here has lately received fierce nick. What can that mean?"

Tarneverro had picked up an expensive gold mesh bag that was lying on the table, and was studying the contents. "No use," he said. "The usual compact, and a few dollars. For a moment I had a crazy thought that perhaps Shelah had already written down for me that name we want. It would have been a very happy chance. The case would have been over before it started."

"Cases do not permit themselves the luxury of such easy solution," sighed Chan. "If letter such as you warmly desire had been in this room, murderer would have it now. No—fate is never so kind. We must take long way round. Come—we have finished here for the present. Much more to be done later."

They went out, and Charlie locked the door. As they moved across the lawn, he enumerated the clues. "A watch stopped at two minutes past eight in fierce struggle. A bouquet of orchids crushed in same, the pin that held them in place oddly lost. A fresh nick on glass corner of dressing-table. Enough for the moment, maybe."

As they entered the living-room, Jessop was ushering in Martino and Alan Jaynes. The latter's face was pale beneath its bronze, and he was obviously much upset.

"We will all acquire chairs," Chan suggested. "Many questions must now be asked."

Jessop came forward and faced Tarneverro. "I'm sorry, sir," he said. "With all the excitement, I quite forgot it."

"Forgot what?" asked Tarneverro, surprised.

"This letter, sir." He took a large elaborate envelope from his pocket. "Miss Fane requested me to give it to you the moment you arrived."

Tarneverro stretched forth his hand, but Charlie stepped quickly between them. He took the envelope. "So sorry. But the police are in charge here now."

"Naturally, sir," Jessop bowed, and backed away.

Chan stood there, a rather helpless-looking figure, holding the letter in his hand. Could it be true? Was the answer to this puzzle so soon within his grasp? A long understanding look passed between him and Tarneverro. The room seemed filled with people, milling about, seeking chairs. Charlie lifted his right hand to slit the envelope.

The floor lamp furnished the only illumination in the room. Chan took a step nearer it; he had the envelope open now, and was about to remove the contents. Suddenly the lamp went out, and the room was plunged into darkness. There followed the sound of a blow, then another, a cry and the fall of a rather solid body.

The place was in an uproar. Out of the blackness came an insistent demand for lights. The lamps in the wall brackets flashed on, revealing Jessop at the switch.

Charlie was slowly rising from the floor. He rubbed his right cheek, which was bleeding slightly.

"Overwhelmed with regret," he said, glancing at Tarneverro. "Famous god Jove, I hear, nodded on occasion. For myself, I fear I have just taken most unfortunate nap." He held out his left hand, in which was a tiny fragment of envelope. "Vital portion of letter," he added, "seems to have traveled elsewhere."

Chapter V

THE MAN IN THE OVERCOAT

For a long moment Chan stood with that fragment of letter in his hand. His expression was calm and unruffled, a very inaccurate indication of what was going on in his heart. Before a room filled with people some person had tricked and therefore disgraced the famous detective of the Honolulu police.

Charlie Chan had lost face in the presence of seven witnesses. Though he had lived many years in Hawaii, he was still Oriental enough to feel a hot bitter anger that startled even himself.

He sought to conquer that feeling immediately. Anger, he had been taught, is a poison that destroys the mind, and he would have need of all his faculties in the ordeal that impended. In this affair he was face to face with an adversary who was not only in a desperate mood, but who was also clever and quick to act. Well, so much the better, Charlie told himself; he would find all the more satisfaction in defeating such an opponent in the end. For he would win out; on that he was fiercely determined. The unknown person who had killed, first Denny Mayo, and then, to protect that secret, Shelah Fane, would be brought to justice at last, or Inspector Chan could never find peace again.

Tarneverro was glaring at him with ill-concealed indignation. "So sorry," he remarked coldly, "but the police are in charge here now."

Chan nodded. "You are eminently correct in that sneer. Never before in my life has such a happening aroused itself in my path. But I give you my word"—he looked slowly around the little group—"the person who struck that blow will pay. I am in no mood that turns the other cheek to-night."

He took out his handkerchief and applied it to the cheek that had, unfortunately, been already turned. It did not need the trace of red on the white linen to tell him that the hand that had hit him wore a ring. His right cheek—then the blow had probably come from some one's left hand. On the left hand of Van Horn, he noted a large seal ring; he turned to Wilkie Ballou, and on that gentleman's left hand he caught the glint of a diamond. Covertly he pursued his study; Bradshaw, Martino, Tarneverro and Jaynes were all innocent of jewelry.

Tarneverro held his arms aloft. "You may start with me," he said. "You are, of course, going to search every one in this room."

Charlie smiled. "I am not quite such fool as that. Person who favored me with vigorous blow is not likely to hold incriminating letter in guilty possession. Besides," he added casually, as he walked away, "the matter is of small importance anyhow."

Tarneverro lowered his arms. It was quite evident from his expression that he heartily disapproved Charlie's omission of what he considered an essential move. But Chan ignored him. The detective was making a swift examination of the cord which stretched from the lamp to an electrical socket a few inches above the floor. The plug, wrenched from its place, lay before him, its two protruding prongs mute evidence that its removal had been a simple matter. It had only been necessary to step on the cord anywhere along its length, move the foot a short distance away from the wall, and the thing was done. Simple, yes, but a bit of quick thinking on some one's part. Charlie restored the plug, and the lamp flashed on again.

He came back to the center of the room. "We waste no time in fruitless search for letter now," he remarked. "I propose instead to fix in my mind our little group of characters, and perhaps learn from their lips just what they were engaged in doing at two minutes past eight to-night." He stood gazing at them thoughtfully. "I have some hesitation where to begin. Mr. Ballou, yours is familiar face, so I will start in your vicinity. Will you kindly state position in this house of yourself and Mrs. Ballou?"

The millionaire looked at him with all the arrogance of the white man who has lived for a long time among what he considers inferior races. "Why should I do that?" he inquired carelessly.

"Murder has been committed," replied Charlie sternly. "I recognize your high position on this island, but you are not above question. Will you deign to reply, please?"

"We came here as dinner guests," Ballou said. "We are —we were—old friends of Miss Fane."

"You knew her in Hollywood?"

"Yes."

"Mrs. Ballou was, before her marriage to you, herself actress on famous silver screen?"

"What if she was?" flared Ballou.

"Why not be polite, Wilkie?" rebuked his wife. "Yes, Inspector, I was in the pictures, under the name of Rita Montaine. And if I do say it, I was rather well known."

Chan bowed. "Could one of your charm be otherwise? May I inquire, please, how long you have been married?"

"Three years this month," she told him amiably.

"You resided, perhaps, in Hollywood up to moment of your marriage?"

"Oh, yes."

"Do you recall—was Mr. Ballou in Hollywood for some time previous to that marriage?"

"Yes—he hung around for several months, pleading with me to give up my career and take him." Her husband snorted. "You may not recall it now, Wilkie, but you did."

"What the devil," cried Ballou irritably, "has all that got to do with the murder of Shelah Fane? I believe, Inspector, that you are exceeding your authority. You'd better be careful—I'm not without influence——"

"So sorry," said Chan soothingly. "I will come at once to the present. You arrived here to-night at what hour?"

"At seven-thirty," he answered. "The dinner was not until eight-thirty, but Mrs. Ballou got the invitation over the telephone, and as usual"—he glared at his wife—"she balled things up."

"At seven-thirty," put in Chan hastily, cutting off Rita's reply. "Describe actions down to present moment, please."

"What are you getting at?" objected Ballou roughly. You don't think I killed Shelah Fane, do you? By gad, I'll speak to some one down at the station about this. Do you know who I am——"

"Oh, who are you, anyhow, Wilkie?" his wife put in wearily. "Why not tell the Inspector what he wants to know and have done with it?" She turned to Chan. "We arrived about seven-thirty, and after a little chat with Miss Fane, stepped out on the beach to watch the bathers. It was about a quarter to eight when we went out there, I imagine."

"You were engaged in this manner how long?"

"Answering for myself, I was on the beach until Jessop came out at eight-thirty. About ten minutes before that, Mr. Van Horn joined us and my husband got up and strolled toward the house."

"At two minutes past eight, then, yourself and husband were seated side by side on sand. You heard no cry or other indication of disturbance?"

"None at all. The two girls in the water were doing more or less screaming—you know how people will. But that's not the sort of thing you mean?"

"Not precisely," replied Chan. "Thank you so much. We drop you for the present."

Julie O'Neill came slowly into the room. The new pink evening gown she had looked forward to wearing at the party was back on its hangar, and she had donned a simple little dress of gray chiffon. Her face was still decidedly pale, but she seemad calm and collected now. Chan turned to her.

"Good evening. I am so sorry to be here. Not until this moment have I encountered the pleasant thrill of seeing you. Would you mind informing me just who you are?"

Bradshaw camd forward. He introduced Julie to Chan, and went on to explain the girl's place in the household.

"My heart's deepest sympathy," Charlie remarked. "As mere matter of form, I must ask about your actions during this most tragic evening."

"I can tell you all about that," Bradshaw informed him, "and kill two birds—oh, sorry—I mean to say, give you my own story at the same time. I arrived at the house early for a swim with Miss O'Neill. The last time we saw Miss Fane was in this room when we came down dressed for the water—that was about seventy-forty. She was here with Mr. and Mrs. Ballou, and Mr. Jaynes."

"You went immediately to the beach?"

"We did—and on into the water. It was marvelous—pardon me if I put in a small advertisement for the local bathing beach. What I mean to say is, Miss O'Neill and I were together from the time we saw Miss Fane until about eight-thirty, when Jessop rang the gong calling us in. It was soon after that we made our unhappy discovery."

"You remained in water at all times?"

"Oh, no—we came back to the beach now and then. Mrs. Ballou was there from the start, as she says. Mr. Ballow disappeared toward the last and Mr. Van Horn showed up."

"At two minutes past eight, then, you and Miss Julie were either in water or making brief excursion to shore?"

"One or the other—we had no means of knowing the time, of course. It went very quickly. We were surprised when Jessop called us in."

Chan turned to the girl. "Miss Fane was wearing tonight pretty nice bouquet of orchids on shoulder?"

Julie nodded. "Yes."

"Fastened with pin, no doubt?"

"Of course."

"Did you by any chance note the pin?"

"No, I didn't. But I remember her saying she was going to her room to get one. Perhaps her maid can tell you about that."

"Are you in position to know who it was sent those orchids?"

"I am," Julie replied. "There was no name, but Miss Fane recognized the writing on the card. She said they came from her ex-husband, Bob somebody—he's an actor playing with a stock company in Honolulu."

"Bob Fyfe," explained Rita Ballou. "He's in the company down at the Royal. They were married when Shelah was quite young, and I believe she was always very fond of him, even after their divorce."

Alan Jaynes rose and, taking a small cigar from a case, lighted it, then walked nervously about the room, seeking a place to throw the match.

"A discarded husband," mused Charlie. "Ah, yes, I would expect at least one of those. This man should be notified at once, and arrive here with all speed possible."

"I'll attend to it, Charlie," offered Jimmy Bradshaw.

"Warmest thanks," Chan remarked. As the boy left the room, he turned to the others. "We now resume somewhat rude questioning. Mr. Van Horn, you are actor, perhaps?"

"Perhaps?" laughed Van Horn. "Well, that's flattering. The reward of ten years' hard work."

"You have, then, been in Hollywood for the past ten years?"

"Ten years and a half—lost in what the amiable Mr. Mencken calls the sewers of Hollywood."

"And before that?"

"Oh, before that I led a most romantic life—ask my press-agent."

"I seek to determine facts," Charlie said.

"In that case I shall have to tell you that I came there, wide-eyed and innocent, from an engineering school. I planned to build bridges, but my fatal beauty intervened."

"You have appeared with Miss Shelah Fane in other pictures before this one?"

"No." Van Horn grew more serious. "I scarcely knew her until I was engaged for this part."

"I do not need to ask where you were at two minutes past eight to-night?" Chan continued.

"No, you don't," the actor agreed. "I was in the same room with you. You'll remember I looked at my watch and remarked that it was eight o'clock, and that I was toddling along down here. At two minutes past the hour I was still where you could see me—if you cared to avail yourself of the privilege."

"You came to this house immediately?"

"Yes—I walked. Exercise—that's how I keep in trim. I got here about eight-fifteen—I didn't hurry. Jessop let me in, we had a little chat, and at about eight-twenty I joined Mrs. Ballou on the beach, as you've already heard."

Jimmy Bradshaw returned. "I got that man Fyfe at the theater," he announced. "My news just about bowled the poor fellow over. He said he would be through after the second act, and would come right along."

"Thank you most warmly," Chan nodded. "You have most helpful nature." He turned to Martino. "You are what they call a director, I think."

"Yes, they call me that," replied Martino grimly. "Among other things."

"You have been engaged in this work a long time?"

"Not very long. I was formerly an actor, on the English stage. Got interested in the pictures, you know, and eventually went to Hollywood."

"Could you mention date of arrival?"

"Surely. I landed there two years ago last March."

"At that date, you saw the place for the first time?"

"Yes—of course."

Charlie nodded. "With regard to this evening, I can

also omit to ask from you your exact location at two minutes past eight."

"Naturally. I was with you and these other chaps at the hotel. As I believe I told you, when I left you just after eight o'clock, I went with Mr. Jaynes on to the terrace. I tried to calm him a bit, but he broke away and wandered down the beach. I sat there on the beach walk for some twenty-five minutes, admiring the set. When I saw you again, I had just been upstairs to get my hat, intending to come down here."

Charlie looked over at Alan Jaynes, nervously smoking his small cigar in a distant corner. "Mr. Jaynes," he said.

The Britisher rose and approached him, consulting his watch as he did so. "Yes?" he remarked.

Charlie regarded him gravely. "You are, I believe, one of the people who suffer most from this death to-night?"

"What do you mean by that?"

"It is reported that you loved Shelah Fane."

"Reported—by whom?" The man looked angrily at Tarneverro.

"No matter," said Chan. "You had asked her to marry you?"

"I had."

"Then you loved her?"

"Look here—must you make a public inquisition of this?"

"So sorry. It is, I perceive, somewhat indiscreet on my part. Mr. Bradshaw has told me you were in this room at seven-forty to-night."

"I was. I had come to dinner."

"And to have, first of all, a private conversation with Miss Fane?"

"Yes. But the nature of that conversation is none of your business."

Charlie smiled. "Alas! I know so much that is none of my business. You ask for her final decision in the matter of marriage. She rejects you, and you suspect Mr. Tarneverro here is responsible for the action. You tramp angrily back to hotel, seeking to make quarrel with this same Tarneverro. So, at two minutes past eight, you stand in hotel lounge, glowering. Which, dear sir, is fortunate affair for you."

"I take it," Jaynes said, "that you have fixed the moment of this—this murder, at two minutes after eight?"

"I have," Chan replied.

Jaynes tossed his cigar into an ash-tray with a gesture of deep relief. "Thank God for that. Have you any more questions?"

"You saw Miss Fane for final time when you left this room at about fifteen minutes before eight?"

"That was the last time I saw her—yes."

"Then you did not return here between eight-five and eight-thirty-five?"

"I did not."

"Have you ever been in Hollywood, Mr. Jaynes?"

The Britisher laughed bitterly. "I have not—and I'm not likely to go there."

"That is all, sir," Chan nodded.

"Thank you. I'll say good-by. I happen to be sailing on the *Oceanic* at midnight."

Charlie looked at him in sudden surprise. "You are leaving Hawaii to-night?"

"I am."

The detective shrugged. "I am so sorry to disappoint you. The matter is impossible."

"Why should it be?" Jaynes demanded.

"You are somewhat deeply involved in this affair."

"But you say you've fixed the moment of the murder—and at that moment I was standing in your presence. It's a perfect alibi."

"Perfect alibis have way of turning imperfect without warning," Charlie informed him. "I regret that I can not allow you to sail. The *Oceanic* will be carefully watched, and no one connected with this affair will be permitted to leave the island aboard her. Or on any other ship, for the present."

An angry flush spread over the Britisher's face. "On what grounds do you keep me here?"

"As an important witness in present case," Chan replied. "I will go to extreme length of swearing out warrant, if necessary."

"I can at least go back to the hotel," Jaynes suggested.

"When I permit it," Charlie said gently. "Meanwhile, I hope you will find for yourself a comfortable chair."

"Jaynes glared at him, then receded into the background. The door-bell rang, and Jessop admitted two men. One was a tall angular American with a deputy sheriff's badge, the other a small anxious-looking Japanese.

"Ah, Mr. Coroner," Chan greeted the deputy, who doubled in that rôle. "And Kashimo. As usual, Kashimo, you are demon for speed to get on job. Is it too much to assume that you arrive here with horse and carriage?"

The deputy spoke. "They sent him to fetch me, and he finally managed it. Where did this thing happen, Charlie?"

"In a moment I lead you to the place," Charlie said.

"Maybe I search house," suggested Kashimo.

Chan regarded him sadly. "It would appear that there was great shortage of detectives at station house to-night," he said. "No, Mr. Kashimo, please do not search house—at least, not until somebody tells you what you are searching for." He turned to the deputy. "If you will follow me——"

Diana Dixon came into the room. She wore a white evening gown, and her elaborate make-up was sufficient explanation of the long delay in her appearance. Chan looked at her with interest.

"Here is some one about whom I have not heard before," he said.

"Who in the world——" began Diana, staring at him.

"Do not be alarmed," smiled Charlie. "I am Inspector Chan, of Honolulu police. You are in Hawaii now."

"Oh, I see," she answered.

"Your name, please?"

She gave it.

"You are guest in house, perhaps?"

"I am. Miss Fane was kind enough to take me in. You know, I've just come up from the South Seas with her—I acted in her last picture."

"An actress," nodded Chan. "I find myself dazzled by so much fame and beauty. All the same, I collect myself to inquire—what have you been engaged in doing this evening?"

"Why, I've been in swimming," she told him.

"When did you last see Miss Fane?"

"When I went up-stairs to put on my bathing-suit—I don't know what time that was. Mr. Bradshaw had just come, and Miss Julie and he and I went up to change. We left Miss Fane standing here in the hall. Some one was ringing the door-bell."

"You came down and entered the water with these young people?"

"Oh, no—it took me a lot longer to change. It was eight o'clock when I was finally ready—I noticed the clock on my dressing-table just before I left my room. I'd no idea it was so late—so I hurried down——"

"You did not see Miss Fane?"

"No, I didn't. This room was empty when I came through it. I crossed the lanai and stepped out on the lawn——"

"At a little time past eight?"

"Yes—it must have been three or four minutes past the hour. As I ran over the lawn, I saw a man come hurriedly away from the pavilion——"

"You saw a man leaving the pavilion? Who was he?"

"I don't know. I couldn't see his face. I thought he was one of the guests, and I shouted hello. But he didn't answer."

"You are able to describe him?" Chan asked.

"Not his face—that was in shadow, as I told you. But he was wearing a coat—an overcoat—I thought it odd on a night like this. The coat was open, and a streak of light from the kitchen window fell on his shirt-front. He was dressed in evening clothes, you see, and across his white shirt——" Suddenly she turned pale and sat down weakly in the nearest chair. "Oh, my God," she cried, "I never thought of it before."

"You never thought of what before?" Charlie prompted.

"That stain on his shirt—that long, narrow, bright red stain," she gasped. "It—it must have been blood."

Chapter VI

FIREWORKS IN THE RAIN

For a moment, stunned by the picture Miss Dixon's words presented, the assemblage was silent. Then a low murmur, a buzz of amazed comment, filled the room. Charlie Chan stood looking at his newest witness speculatively, as though he asked himself whether her statement could possibly be true.

"Most interesting," he said at last. "There has been, then, on these grounds to-night, a gentleman whose presence was up to this moment unsuspected by me. Whether or not he carried blood-soaked shirt bosom——"

"But I tell you I saw it," the girl protested.

Chan shrugged. "Perhaps. Oh, most humble pardon—I do not question your truth. I merely mention overwrought nerves, or maybe optic illusion. You must excuse if I say I might admit murderer would be so clumsy at his work as to inundate himself, but reason totters on pedestal to add that such a man would rush from scene of crime with coat flapping open on his error. Rather I would picture him with garment wrapped close to hide away this crimson evidence. But what does it matter? We must at any rate pursue thought of man with overcoat. The idea in itself presents portrait of queer human being. Overcoat in smiling tropics, even over evening dress, is unaccustomed garb." He turned to Julie. "And what, please, is name of man servant in this house?"

"You mean Jessop?" she inquired.

"I mean the butler. Will you summon him—if I am not getting too obnoxious?"

Julie went into the hall, and Charlie turned to the deputy sheriff. "I find it impossible to accompany you to scene of crime just yet. Same took place in small beach house at right of lawn—please accept this key. You may begin examination, and I will join you when I have interrogated servants here."

"Did you find the weapon, Charlie?" asked the coroner.

"I did not. That was, I think, carried off by the assailant. He was person, you will find, who had wits in good control." Charlie turned to the Japanese. "Kashimo, you may enjoy yourself by keen observation of the neighborhood. But if you repeat one former performance and spoil any footprints for me, I will at once arrange for you to return to former position as janitor of fish market."

The coroner and the little Japanese went out. At the same moment Jessop held open the curtains and followed Julie into the room. The butler was pale and agitated.

"The name is Jessop?" Charlie inquired.

"Yes—ah—sir."

"You understand who it is that I am?"

"I take it you represent the local constabulary, sir."

Chan grinned. "If it will help you to endure society of person like me, Jessop, I offer statement that my humble efforts on one occasion met with the complete approval of a gentleman from Scotland Yard."

"Really, sir?" answered Jessop. "The memory must be most gratifying to you."

"It is, indeed. How long is it now that you have been Miss Fane's butler?"

"Two years, sir."

"You were in Hollywood before that, maybe?"

"For about eighteen months, I was."

"A butler, always?"

"Always a butler, sir. I had a number of berths before I went with Miss Fane. I am bound to say that I was unhappy in all of them."

"The work was, perhaps, too difficult?"

"Not at all, sir. I objected to the familiarity of my employers. There is a certain reserve that should exist between servant and master. I found that lacking. The ladies I worked for would often weep in my presence and tell me stories of unrequited love. The gentlemen who engaged me were inclined to treat me like some long-lost brother. One in particular was accustomed to address me as 'old pal' and when a bit under the influence, would embrace me in the presence of guests. A man has his dignity, sir."

"It has been well said, without dignity there can be no

stature," Charlie assured him. "You found Miss Fane of a different type?"

"I did indeed, sir. A lady who knew her place as I knew mine. There was never any undue informality in her treatment of me."

"Relations were, then, of the happiest?"

"That they were. I should like to add that I am quite heart-broken by this evening's business, sir."

"Ah, yes—coming to this evening—did any of the gentlemen whom you admitted here to-night wear an overcoat, Jessop?"

"An overcoat, sir?" Jessop's white eyebrows went up.

"Yes. With dinner costume, you understand."

"No, sir," replied Jessop firmly. "No such gaucherie of dress was evident, Constable."

Chan smiled. "Kindly look about the room. Do you recall admitting any visitor with exception of those now visible to your view?"

"No, sir," returned Jessop, surveying the party.

"Thank you. When did you last see Miss Fane?"

"It was in this room, at about twenty minutes after seven, when I brought her a box of flowers. I heard her voice after that, but I did not see her."

"Please detail your activities from hour of twenty minutes past seven onward," Chan requested.

"I was engaged with my duties, sir, in the dining-room and the kitchen. I may add that it has been a rather trying evening, in my department. The Chinese cook has exhibited all the worst qualities of a heathen race—I'm sure I beg your pardon."

"A heathen race," repeated Charlie gravely, "that was busy inventing the art of printing at moment when gentlemen in Great Britain were still beating one another over head with spiked clubs. Pray excuse this brief reference to history. The cook has been in uproar?"

"Yes, Constable. He has proved himself sorely deficient in that patience for which his people have long been noted. Then, too, the—er—the bootlegger, to use one of your—or their—American phrases, has been unforgivably late."

"Ah—you already possess bootlegger?"

"Yes, sir. Miss Fane was a temperate woman herself, but she knew her duties as a hostess. So Wu Kno-ching, the cook, arranged with a friend to deliver a bit of liquor just out of the laboratory, and a wine of the most recent vintage."

"I am deeply shocked," Chan replied. "Wu's friend was late?"

"He was indeed, sir. As I say, I was busy with my duties from the moment I gave Miss Fane the flowers. At two minutes past eight——"

"Why do you make selection of two minutes past eight?"

"I could not help but overhear your questions to these others, sir. At that moment I was in the kitchen——"

"Alone?"

"No, sir. Wu was there, of course. And Anna, the maid, had dropped in for a cup of tea to sustain her until dinner. I called Wu's attention to the fact that it was already past eight o'clock, and we had a few words about the bootlegger's tardiness. The three of us remained there together until ten after eight, when Wu's friend made a rather sheepish appearance, and I immediately set about to do what I could with the ingredients he brought. At fifteen past eight, I came out to admit Mr. Van Horn. From that point on I was in and out of this room, sir, but I did not leave the house until I went to the beach and sounded the dinner gong."

"I am obliged to you for a most complete account," Charlie nodded. "That is all, Jessop."

The butler hesitated. "There is one other matter, Constable."

"Ah, yes. What is that?"

"I do not know whether or not it has any significance, sir, but it came back to me when I heard this terrible news. There is a small library up-stairs, and to-day, when I had cleared away the luncheon things, I went in there to secure a book, planning to take it to my room as a recreation during my siesta. I came suddenly upon Miss Fane. She was looking at a photograph and weeping most bitterly, sir."

"A photograph of whom?"

"That I couldn't say, sir, save that it was of some gentleman. She held it so I could not obtain a better view of the face, and hurriedly left the room. All I can tell you is that it was a rather large photograph, and was mounted on a mat that was Nile green in color."

Chan nodded. "Thank you so much. Will you be kind enough to dispatch heathen cook into my presence, Jessop?"

"I will indeed, sir," replied Jessop, and withdrew.

Charlie looked about the circle. "The matter lengthens itself out," he remarked kindly. "I observe beyond windows a cool lanai crowded with nice Hongkong chairs. Any who wish to do so may stroll to more airy perch. One thing only I ask—please do not leave these grounds."

There followed a general movement, and amid a low buzz of comment all save Bradshaw, Julie, Tarneverro and Chan went out on the dim lanai. The fortune-teller looked keenly at Charlie.

"What have you accomplished?" he wanted to know.

Charlie shrugged. "Up to the present moment, I seem to have been setting off fireworks in the rain."

"That's precisely what I thought," Tarneverro said impatiently.

"Do not lose heart," Chan advised. "Changing the figure, I might add that to dig up the tree, we must start with the root. All this digging is routine matter that does not fascinate, but at any moment we may strike a root of vital importance."

"I sincerely hope so," Tarneverro remarked.

"Oh, you trust Charlie," Bradshaw said. "One of Honolulu's first citizens, he is. He'll get his man."

Wu Kno-ching came in, mumbling to himself, and Charlie addressed him sharply in Cantonese. Looking at him with sleepy eyes, Wu replied at some length.

The high-pitched, singsong exchange of words between these two representatives of the oldest civilized nation in the world grew faster and louder, and on Wu's part, seemingly more impassioned. The three outsiders stood there deeply interested; it was like a play in some dead language; they could not understand the lines but they were conscious of a strong current of drama underneath. Once Chan, who had up to that point been seemingly uninterested, lifted his head like a bird-dog on the scent. He went closer to the old man, and seized his arm. One recognizable word in Wu's conversation occurred again and again. He mentioned the "bootleggah."

Finally, with a shrug, Chan turned away.

"What's he say, Charlie?" asked Bradshaw eagerly.

"He knows nothing," Chan answered.

"What was all that about the bootlegger?"

Charlie gave the boy a keen look. "The tongue of age speaks with accumulated wisdom, and is heard gladly, but the tongue of youth should save its strength," he remarked.

"Yours received and contents noted," smiled the boy.

Chan turned to Julie. "You have spoken of Miss Fane's maid. She alone remains to be interviewed. Will you be so good as to produce her?"

Julie nodded and went out. Wu Kno-ching still lingered at the door, and now he burst into a tirade, with appropriate gestures. Charlie listened for a moment, and then shooed the old man from the room.

"Wu complains that no one eats his dinner," he smiled. "He is great artist who lacks appreciation, and his ancient heart cracks with rage."

"Well," remarked Jimmy Bradshaw, "I suppose it's an unfeeling thing to say, but I could put away a little of his handiwork."

Chan nodded. "I have thought of that. Later, perhaps. Why not? Do the dead gain if the living starve?"

Julie returned, followed by Anna, the maid. The latter was a dark thin woman who moved gracefully.

"The name, please?" Chan inquired.

"Anna Rodderick," she answered. There was just a trace of defiance in her tone.

"You have been with Miss Shelah Fane how long?"

"Something like a year and a half, sir."

"I see. Before that you were perhaps employed elsewhere in Hollywood?"

"No, sir, I was not. I went with Miss Fane the day after my arrival there, and I have never been employed by any one else in the picture colony."

"How did you happen to go to California, please?"

"I was in service in England, and a friend wrote me of the higher wages that prevailed in the States."

"Your relations with Miss Fane—they were pleasant?"

"Naturally, sir, or I wouldn't have remained with her. There were many other positions available."

"Did she ever admit you into her confidence regarding personal affairs?"

"No, sir, she did not. It was one of the things I liked about her."

"When did you last see your mistress?"

"At a bit before seven-thirty. I was about to go down to the kitchen for a cup of tea, for I saw that my dinner was likely to be long delayed. Miss Fane came to her room—I was in the one adjoining. She called to me and said she wanted a pin for some orchids she had in her hand. I went and got it for her."

"Kindly describe the pin."

"It was a rather delicate affair, set with diamonds.

About two inches long, I should say. I fastened the flowers to the shoulder-strap of her gown."

"Did she remark about those flowers?" Charlie inquired.

"She said they were sent to her by some one of whom she was once very fond. She seemed a bit excited."

"What happened next?"

"She sat down at the telephone," Anna told him. "There is an extension in her room. She looked up a number in the telephone book and then busied herself with the dial, sir."

"Maybe you heard subsequent conversation?" Chan suggested.

"I am not accustomed to spying, sir. I left her at once and went down to the kitchen."

"You were in the kitchen at two minutes past eight?"

"Yes, sir. I recall the hour because there was a great deal of talk between Jessop and the cook about the bootlegger."

"You were still in the kitchen when this bootlegger came, at ten minutes past eight?"

"I was, sir. A little later I went back to my room."

"You did not see your mistress again?"

"No, sir, I did not."

"One other thing." Chan looked at her thoughtfully. "Kindly speak of her manner during the day. Was it same as always?"

"I noticed nothing unusual."

"You did not note that she was seen with a portrait—the portrait of a gentleman—during the afternoon?"

"I was not here this afternoon. It was our first day ashore, and Miss Fane kindly gave me a few hours off."

"Have you ever seen, among Miss Fane's possessions, portrait of gentleman mounted on Nile-green mat?"

"Miss Fane always carried with her a large portfolio, containing many pictures of her friends. It may be such a one is among them."

"But you never saw it?"

"I have never opened the portfolio. That would seem too much like prying—if I may say so, sir."

"Do you know where portfolio is now?" Charlie asked.

"I believe it is lying on a table in her room. Shall I fetch it for you?"

"A little later, perhaps. Just now I would inquire—you are familiar with jewelry usually worn by Miss Fane on occasion of evening party? Aside from diamond pin fastening orchids, I mean?"

"I think so, sir."

"Will you come with me, please?"

Leaving the others in the drawing-room, he led the maid across the moonlit lawn in the direction of the pavilion. They went in, and Anna lost her composure for a moment at sight of Shelah Fane. She gave a strangled little cry.

"Kindly conduct thorough search," Chan said to her, "and inform me if all jewelry is at present time in place."

Anna nodded without speaking. The coroner came over to greet Chan.

"I've made my examination," he said. "This is a pretty big thing, Charlie. I'd better send somebody to help you out."

Chan smiled. "I have Kashimo," he answered. "What more could any man ask? Tell Chief I will report entire matter to him at earliest convenience." They stepped out on the lanai of the pavilion, and at the same moment Kashimo crept like a correspondence-school sleuth from a cluster of bushes at the corner of the building.

"Charlie—come quick," he whispered hoarsely.

"Kashimo has discovered essential clue," Charlie said. "Please join us, Mr. Coroner."

They followed the Japanese through the bushes and out upon a public beach that bounded the property on the right. On that side of the pavilion, which stood flush with the dividing line, was a single window. Kashimo led them to this, and swept a flash-light over the sand.

"Footprints-s-s!" he hissed dramatically.

Charlie seized the light and knelt on the sand. "True enough, Kashimo," he remarked. "These are footprints, and peculiar ones, too. Shoes were old and battered, the heels are worn down unevenly, and in sole of one shoe was most unfashionable hole." He stood up. "I fear that fortune has not been smiling on owner of that footwear," he added.

"I am one to find things," remarked Kashimo proudly.

"You are," smiled Charlie, "and for once you do not destroy clue the moment you come upon it. You are learning, Kashimo. Warm congratulations."

They returned to the lawn of Shelah Fane's house. "Well, Charlie, this is up to you," the deputy said. "I'll see you early in the morning—unless you want me to stay."

"Your duty is accomplished," Chan answered, "or will

be when you have made proper arrangements in city. Body will of course be taken at once to mortuary."

"Certainly," the deputy replied. "Well, good-by—and good luck."

Chan turned to Kashimo. "Now great opportunity arises for you to perform your specialty," he said.

"Yes-s-s," Kashimo answered eagerly.

"Go to house, inquire for bedroom of Miss Shelah Fane, and search——"

"I go now," cried Kashimo, leaping away.

"Stop!" commanded Charlie. "You are one grand apprentice detective, Kashimo, but you never pause to inquire what it is you sleuth for. On table of that room you will find large portfolio of photograhs. I very much desire to see portrait of gentleman mounted on mat that is colored Nile green——"

"Nile is new word to me," the Japanese complained.

"Yes—and I have no time for geography lesson now," sighed Chan. "Bring me all photographs in room mounted on cardboard colored green. If none such is in portfolio, search elsewhere. Now be off. The portrait of a gentleman, remember. If you return with pretty picture of Fujiyama I will personally escort you back to private life."

Kashimo sped across the lawn, and Charlie again entered the pavilion. Anna was standing in the center of the room.

"You made investigation?" he inquired.

"I did," she said. "The pin that fastened the flowers is nowhere about."

"A matter already known to me," he nodded. "Otherwise the ornamental equipment is complete?"

"No," she replied. "It isn't."

He regarded her with sudden interest. "Something is missing?"

"Yes—an emerald ring—a large emerald that Miss Fane usually wore on her right hand. She told me once that it represented quite a bit of money. And—it has disappeared."

Chapter VII

THE ALIBI OF THE WATCH

Charlie sent the maid back to the house, and then sat down in the straight-backed chair before the dressing-table. The sole illumination in the little room came from two pink-shaded lamps, one on either side of the mirror. Thoughtfully he stared into the glass where, dimly reflected, he caught occasional glimpses of an ivory satin gown. Shelah Fane now lay on the couch where the coroner had placed her. All the loves and the hates, the jealousies, the glittering triumphs of this tempestuous career were ended to-night. A woman of flame, they had called her. The flame had flickered and died like a candle in the wind—in the restless trade-wind blowing from the Koolau Range.

Chan's small eyes narrowed in an intense effort at concentration. In one of her more indiscreet moments, Shelah Fane had seen Denny Mayo murdered. For three years she had carried the secret about with her until—and this moment was even more indiscreet—she poured it into the willing ears of Tarneverro the Great, a crystal-gazer—a charlatan, no doubt. That same night, the black camel had knelt before her gate.

Carefully in his mind, the detective began to go over the points his investigation had so far revealed. He was not one to carry a note-book, but he took an envelope from his pocket, and with a pencil began to write a list of names on the back. He was thus engaged when he heard a step behind him. Looking over his shoulder, he saw the lean mysterious figure of Tarneverro.

The fortune-teller came forward and dropped into a chair at Chan's side. He stared at the detective, and there was disapproval in that stare.

"Since you have asked me to work with you in this affair," he began, "you will perhaps pardon me if I say I think you have been extremely careless."

Charlie's eyes opened wide. "Yes?" he said.

"I refer to Miss Fane's letter," continued Tarneverro. "It may have been the answer to all our questions. In it the poor girl may have written the name we so eagerly seek. Yet you made no move to search the people in that room—you even pooh-poohed the idea when I offered it. Why?"

Chan shrugged. "You think, then, we have to deal with a fool? A miscreant who would take pretty complete pains to obtain the epistle, and then place it on his own person where a search would instantly reveal it? You are wrong, my friend. I had no taste for revealing how wrong you were, at the expense of further embarrassment for myself. No, the letter is hidden in that room, and sooner or later it will be found. If not—what of it? I have strong feeling that it contains nothing of the least importance."

"On what do you base that feeling?" Tarneverro inquired.

"I have plenty as a base. Would Shelah Fane have written big secret down and then given it to servant who must pass it along to you? No, she would have awaited her opportunity and then delivered it to you with her own hand. I do not reprove you, but I believe you attach undue importance to that probably innocent epistle."

"Well, the murderer certainly thought it important. You can't deny that."

"Murderer was in state of high excitement and took unnecessary risk. If he takes few more like that, we are at trail's end."

Tarneverro, with a gesture, dismissed the matter. "Well, and what have you discovered from all your questions?" He glanced at Chan's notes.

"Not much. You perceived that I was curious to learn who was in Hollywood three years ago last month. Assuming that the story is true—the story you say Shelah Fane told you this morning——"

"Why shouldn't it be true? Does a woman make a confession like that as a joke?"

"Never," answered Chan, somewhat sharply for him. "And for that reaon I am remarking I assume it to be true. It is, then, important to locate our many suspects in June three years ago. I have written here the names of all who were in Hollywood at that time, and consequently may have slain Denny Mayo. They are Wilkie Ballou, Rita his wife, Huntley Van Horn. And—ah, yes—Jessop, the butler. I regret that, overwhelmed by account of bloody shirt, I neglected to make inquiries of Miss Dixon."

"She has been in Hollywood six years," the fortune-teller informed him. "I know from what she has told me during the readings I have given her."

"One more." Charlie wrote down the name. "I may, I presume, add Miss Julie—though very young at the time. Of these, for the hour of two minutes past eight to-night, two have been accounted for. Jessop presents plenty good alibi and Huntley Van Horn has perfect one, to which I myself can swear. Other things I learned—not very important—but it struck my mind, as it must have struck yours, that Mr. Alan Jaynes was breathless with anxiety to leave Hawaii to-night. Do not forget—it is within grounds of possibility that Denny Mayo murder had nothing to do with death of Shelah Fane. This Jaynes was in overwrought state; his may be fiercely jealous nature; he may have looked at those orchids, the gift of another, on the lady's shoulder, and——"

"But he, too, has the alibi of the watch," Tarneverro suggested.

"Alas! yes," Chan nodded.

For a moment they sat in silence. Then Tarneverro rose, and walked slowly toward the couch. "By the way," he said casually, "have you made a thorough examination of this watch?"

"So sorry." Chan rose and followed him. "You now call my attention to fact that I have neglected most obvious duty." Tarneverro was bending over, but Chan stopped him. "I will remove it at once and have careful look at it—though I am so dense I do not quite grasp your meaning."

Taking a linen handkerchief from his pocket, he spread it over his left hand. With his other hand he unfastened the narrow black ribbon from Shelah Fane's wrist, and lifting the costly little watch, laid it on the handkerchief. He went back and stood directly under one of the lights, staring down at the timepiece.

"*Haie,* I seem in stupid mood to-night," he sighed. "I am still at sea. Crystal is broken, watch has ceased to function at precisely two minutes past eight——"

"Permit me," said Tarneverro. "I will be more explicit." He took both handkerchief and watch, and with the linen always between his fingers and the metal, turned the stem of the fragile timepiece. At his touch, the minute hand moved instantly.

A flash of triumph shone in the fortune-teller's eyes. "That," he cried, "is more than I dared to hope for. The murderer has been guilty of a small error—it was very kind of him. He adjusted the stem so that the time shown on the face of the watch could be altered at will—and in his haste he forgot to readjust it. Surely I needn't tell you what that means."

Charlie gave him a look of enthusiastic approval. "You are detective of the first class yourself—give me credit that I noted same this morning. I can never cease to be grateful to you. Of course I grasp meaning now."

Tarneverro laid the watch down on the glass top of the dressing-table. "I think we may be sure of one thing, Inspector," he remarked. "At whatever hour the murder took place, it was certainly not at two minutes past eight. We are dealing with a clever man. After he had killed Shelah Fane he removed her watch, set the time back—or perhaps forward—to two minutes past eight, and then smashed the thing as though to indicate a struggle." The fortune-teller's eyes lighted; he pointed to the corner of the dressing-table. "That's the explanation of the nick in the glass. He banged the watch against that corner until he had stopped its running."

Chan was instantly on the floor. "There is no glass beneath," he said.

"No, no," Tarneverro continued. "There wouldn't be. The broken glass was naturally found where Miss Fane fell. And why? Because this unknown person removed the watch with a handkerchief, as you have done; he swung it against the table in that handkerchief to catch the bits of crystal, and carried the wrecked remains intact to the spot where he wanted them. A bright boy, Inspector."

Charlie nodded. Obvious chagrin was in his manner. "But you are brighter boy. Almost I am on verge of resigning in disgust at my own stupidity. You should take my badge, Mr. Tarneverro, for you are the smart detective on this case."

Tarneverro gave him an odd look. "You think so, do you? I'm afraid you exaggerate—the matter was really simple enough. It came into my mind that too many of us had alibis in this affair. I thought how easy it would be to change the time on the face of a watch. That is what happened here.

The murderer set it at a moment then past, for which he had already established an alibi—or at a future time for which he proposed to get an alibi forthwith. However, when a man is excited he is likely to slip up somewhere—and this chap stumbled when he forgot to push down that little stem before he left."

Chan sighed. "I am, as I remarked, bubbling with gratitude toward you, and yet I am appalled. Whole flock of alibis is now quite ruined, and the field broadens like some boundless prairie. Van Horn's alibi is gone, the alibis of Martino and of Jaynes, they are gone too, and—begging humble pardon, Mr. Tarneverro—you have likewise destroyed the alibi you yourself possessed."

The fortune-teller threw back his head and laughed. "Do I need an alibi?" he cried.

"Perhaps not," Charlie grinned. "But when a tree falls, the shade is gone. Who knows? Even you might regret the loss of that shade in time."

"It may happen that I have another tree," suggested Tarneverro.

"If that is true, I congratulate you." Charlie glanced around the room. "I must have poor unfortunate lady removed now to house, then lock this place until finger-print expert can do work early in morning. You will observe we do not move with vast speed here in Hawaii. It is our lovely climate." He put the watch in the dressing-table drawer, and he and Tarneverro went out, Chan again locking the door. "We will now continue to living-room, which we will seek to obtain to ourselves. Perhaps there you will deign to keep on with remarkable research. I travel in luck to-night. What could I do without you?"

A little group of chairs on the lawn indicated the whereabouts of most of the guests. In the living-room they came upon Julie and Jimmy Bradshaw, seated close together. The girl had evidently been crying, and Mr. Bradshaw's manner suggested that he played the rôle of comforter. Chan gave Julie the key to the pavilion, and told her gently what must be done. She and the boy went out to seek the aid of the servants.

When they had gone, Charlie walked thoughtfully up and down the big room. He peered into receptacles that held flowers and plants, opened the few books he came upon and ruffled the pages.

"By the way," Tarneverro remarked, "have you made an inspection of Miss Fane's bedroom?"

"Not yet," Chan answered. "So much to do, and only you and I to do it. I have sent Kashimo, our Japanese sleuth hound, on an errand, from which he will doubtless return in course of week or two. As for myself——" He was walking across a rug, and paused. "As for myself——" he repeated. He rubbed his thin-soled shoe back and forth over a spot in the rug. "As for myself," he added a third time, "I have plenty good business here."

He stooped and threw back the rug. There on the polished floor lay the big envelope that had been snatched from his hand earlier in the evening. One corner was missing, but otherwise the letter was intact.

"Fortunate that Miss Fane preferred such thick note-paper," Charlie said. He picked up the envelope. "I fear I can not offer my unknown friend warm congratulations on his originality this time. But he was very hurried gentleman when this matter engaged his attention—I must remember that."

Tarneverro came close, his dark eyes gleaming. "By gad—Shelah's letter. And addressed to me, I believe?"

"I remind you again that the police are in charge," Chan said.

"They were in charge before," Tarneverro answered.

"Ah, yes. But history will not repeat just yet." Charlie removed the note from the envelope, and read. He shrugged his shoulders, and passed the missive to the fortune-teller. "Once I was right," he remarked.

Tarneverro looked down at the huge sprawling handwriting of one who was generous of note-paper as of all things. He frowned at what he saw.

"Dear Tarneverro:

"Please forget what I told you this morning. I must have been mad—mad. I intend to forget it—and so must you—oh, Tarneverro, promise me you will. Pretend that I never said it. I shall refuse poor Alan to-night—it will break my heart—but I'll do it. I am going on alone—perhaps in the end I may even find a little happiness. I want it so much.

"Yours ever

"Shelah Fane."

"Poor Shelah!" The fortune-teller stood for a moment, staring at the letter. "She hadn't the courage to go through with it—I might have known. A pitiful letter—I don't be-believe I would have insisted, after all." He crushed the paper in his hand fiercely. "The murderer of Denny Mayo was safe—she wasn't going to tell on him—he killed her for nothing. She's gone, and she might be here. By heaven—I'll get him if it's the last act of my life!"

Chan smiled. "I have a similar ambition, though I trust the accomplishment will not finish off my existence." His Japanese assistant came stealthily into the room. "Ah, Kashimo, have you enjoyed pleasant week-end up-stair?"

"Pretty hard job, but I got him," Kashimo announced proudly. "Found in jar under potted plant."

Chan reached out his hand. To his surprise Kashimo proffered, not the photograph Charlie expected, but a handful of torn bits of glazed paper and of heavy green cardboard. Some one had ripped the portrait on the green mat to bits, and then attempted to conceal the wreckage.

"What have we now?" Chan said. He stood looking in wonder at the handful of scraps that he held. His eyes sought Tarneverro's. "Here is a matter worthy of consideration. Person unknown does not wish me to look upon the photograph over which Shelah Fane wept this afternoon. Why? Is it then portrait of the man you had asked her to betray?"

"It may have been," Tarneverro agreed.

"Course now becomes clear," Charlie announced. "I must view this photograph, so with all patience at my command, I propose to fit these scraps together again." He pulled a small table up before the windows that faced the street.

"I investigate outside the house," Kashimo remarked.

"Much the safest place to have you," Chan returned. "By all means investigate very hard."

The Japanese went out.

Charlie removed the table cover, and sat down. On the smooth top he began carefully to lay together the pieces of the photograph. The task, he saw, was going to be long and arduous. "I never was bright man with jigsaw puzzle," he complained. "My daughter Rose was pride of family at that work. I would enjoy to have her at my side."

He had made scant progress when the door of the lanai opened, and a group of the guests entered the living-room.

Wilkie Ballou walked at the head, and after him came Van Horn, Martino, Jaynes and Rita Ballou. Diana Dixon followed; she seemed detached from the crowd, which had the air of a delegation.

A delegation it was, evidently. Ballou began to speak, in his most commanding tone.

"See here, Inspector—we've talked it over and there's no earthly reason why you should keep us here any longer. We've all been questioned, we've told you what we know, and now we propose to leave."

Charlie tossed down the as yet unplaced bits of the photograph and rose. He bowed politely.

"I recognize you are impatient with good reason," he said.

"Then you're willing for us to go along?" inquired Ballou.

"I am—and I say it with extreme pain—quite unwilling," Chan replied. "Unfortunately, new developments keep popping off like firecrackers on New Year holiday, and I have something still to talk about with you."

"An outrage!" Ballou cried. "I'll have your badge for this."

Charlie rewarded him with a maddening smile. "That may happen—to-morrow. But looking only at to-night, I am placed in charge of this case, and I say—you will remain here until I tell you to depart."

Jaynes pushed forward. "I have important business on the mainland, and I intend to sail at midnight. It is now long past ten. I warn you that you must call out your entire force if you propose to keep me here——"

"That also can be done," answered Charlie amiably.

"Good lord!" The Britisher looked helplessly at Wilkie Ballou. "What kind of place is this? Why don't they send a white man out here?"

A rare light flared suddenly in Charlie's eyes. "The man who is about to cross a stream should not revile the crocodile's mother," he said in icy tones.

"What do you mean by that?" Jaynes asked.

"I mean you are not yet safely on the farther bank."

"You know damn' well I've got an alibi," cried the Britisher angrily.

Chan's little eyes surveyed him from head to foot. "I am not so sure I do," he remarked calmly.

"You said yourself you had fixed the time of this affair——"

"How sad," cut in Charlie, "that we pass through this life, making so many errors as we go. Me, I am stupid blunderer. Your alibi, Mr. Jaynes, has been punctured like bubble with a pin."

"What!" cried Jaynes.

Van Horn and Martino stirred with sudden interest.

"Back off and cool down," Chan continued. "And accepting my advice, speak no more of alibis. You have already said too much."

Like a man dazed, Jaynes almost literally obeyed Chan's orders. Charlie turned to Rita Ballou.

"Madam, my humblest apologies and regrets. I hold you here with the utmost grief. It has occurred to me that there is a dinner long prepared—I fear the passage of time has wrecked most of it now. But if I might suggest——"

"Oh, I couldn't eat a thing," Rita told him.

"No, of course, the very thought is horrifying," Chan nodded. "Such heartlessness would be quite out of place." Julie and Bradshaw came in. "Nevertheless I urge that you all go out to your positions at the table and at least partake of one cup of coffee. The event will shatter strain, and make easier the period of waiting. Coffee, as you know, stimulates and fortifies the mind."

"Not a bad idea," said Huntley Van Horn.

"Miss Julie——" Chan suggested.

The girl smiled wanly. "Yes, of course. I'll tell Jessop to get things ready. You must forgive me. I'd quite forgotten we had guests to-night."

She turned and went out. Charlie walked back to the small table where his task lay uncompleted. At that instant a French window facing the street was thrust suddenly open, and the trade-wind swept into the room like a miniature hurricane. Instantly the air was filled with torn bits of photograph, swirling about like snow in a Minnesota blizzard.

Kashimo stuck his head into the room. "S-s-s," he hissed. "Charlie!"

"Splendid work, Kashimo," said Chan through his teeth. "What is it now?"

"I find window unlocked," announced the Japanese triumphantly, and withdrew, closing the aperture behind him.

Concealing his disgust, Charlie moved around the room, retrieving the bits of photograph from most unlikely places.

Tarneverro and some of the others came promptly to his aid. In a few moments, he again held a little packet of scraps in his hand. He walked about, still seeking, but no more were in sight.

He resumed his place at the table, and for a few moments he worked hard. Then he shrugged his shoulders, and stood up.

"What's the trouble?" Tarneverro asked.

Charlie looked at him. "No use. I have now little more than half the pieces I had before." For a moment he stood staring about that innocent-appearing little group. It was in his mind to search every one of them, but a glance at Ballou reminded him that such action would mean a hot battle, and he was ever a man of peace. No, he must reach his goal by some other path. He sighed, and placed what he had left of the photograph in his pocket, as Kashimo dashed in. More in sorrow than in anger Charlie regarded his ambitious confrère.

"Detectives were practically extinct at station house when they sent you out to-night," he said.

The door-bell rang, a loud, insistent peal. Jessop being in the distant kitchen, Jimmy Bradshaw went to the door. Those in the living-room heard a few sharp quick words in the hall, and a man strode into their midst. He was a handsome fellow of forty, gray at the temples, with great poise of manner and a keen eye. The grease-paint of the theater was still on his face. He stood, looking about him.

"Good evening," he said. "I am Robert Fyfe—at one time the husband of Miss Shelah Fane. This is terrible news some one telephoned me a short time ago. I came the instant my part in the piece was finished—without stopping to remove my make-up or change my costume. Most unprofessional—but I must ask you to overlook it."

"Shall I take your overcoat?" Jimmy Bradshaw asked.

"Thank you so much." He stepped to the curtains and handed Jimmy the coat. As he turned back toward the room, Diana Dixon's scream rang out, shrill and unexpected. She was pointing at Robert Fyfe's shirtfront.

Diagonally across that white expanse lay the bright red ribbon of the Legion of Honor. Startled, Fyfe looked down at it.

"Ah, yes," he said. "I came in my stage costume, as I told you. This week, you see, I happen to be playing the rôle of a French ambassador."

Chapter VIII

THE BEACH-COMBER'S SHOES

During the long silence that followed, Charlie stood gravely regarding this handsome actor who had, all unknowing, made the best entrance of his career. The actor looked back at him with a cool level stare. Still no one spoke, and Fyfe began to realize that the gaze of every one in the room was upon him. Accustomed though he was to the scrutiny of crowds, he found something a bit disconcerting in this situation. He stirred uneasily, and sought for words to break the spell.

"What is all this about Shelah? I came at the earliest possible moment, as I say. Though I had not seen her for many years——"

"How many years?" cried Chan quickly.

Fyfe looked him over casually. "You must pardon me," he said, "if I do not at once grasp your position here——"

Nonchalantly Charlie pushed back the left side of his coat, revealing his badge of office. It was a gesture of which an actor could approve—business, not words.

"I am in charge," Chan said. "You were, you say, at one time husband of Miss Shelah Fane. You have not seen her for many years. How many?"

Fyfe considered. "It was nine years ago, in April, when we parted. We were both playing in New York—Miss Fane in a Ziegfeld revue at the New Amsterdam, and I was doing a mystery play at the Astor. She came home one night and told me she had a splendid offer to go to Hollywood for a picture—she was so excited, so keen for the idea, that I hadn't the heart to oppose her. A week later, on an April evening, I said good-by to her at the Grand Central Station, wondering how long I could hold her love. Not very long, as it turned out. Within a year she went to Reno, and it was all quite painless—for her, I fancy. Not quite so painless for me—although I had felt it coming, that night at the station. Something had told me then that I was seeing her for the last time."

"You no doubt appeared in Los Angeles in later years," Chan suggested, "at moments when Miss Fane was in Hollywood?"

"Oh, yes—of course. But we never met."

"Do you happen to recall—were you playing in Los Angeles three years ago, in June?"

Charlie was struck by the look that came into the actor's eyes. Was it, perhaps, a look of understanding? "No," said Fyfe firmly. "I was not."

"You are plenty positive," Chan commented.

"I happen to be—yes," Fyfe replied. "Three years ago I was touring with a company that did not reach the coast."

"It is a matter that can easily be verified," the detective reminded him slowly.

"Certainly," agreed Fyfe. "Go ahead and verify it."

"Then you assert," Chan continued, "that you have not seen Shelah Fane since that moment in New York station, nine years ago?"

"I do."

"You did not see her in Honolulu to-day?"

"No."

"Or to-night?"

A pause. "No."

Julie entered. "The coffee is ready," she announced. "Please, all come into the dining-room."

"I make haste to endorse that suggestion," Chan put in.

Reluctantly they filed out, assuring one another that they could eat nothing, that the idea was unthinkable, but that perhaps a cup of coffee—— Their voices trailed away beyond the curtains. Of the dinner guests, only the fortune-teller lingered.

"Please go, Mr. Tarneverro," Chan said. "Small stimulant will increase action of that fine brain on which I lean so heavily."

Tarneverro bowed. "For a moment only," he replied, and left the room.

Charlie turned to Kashimo. "As for you, I suggest you travel out to lanai, sit upon a chair and think about your sins. When you appeared a moment ago like Jack of the box, you scattered precious evidence to the winds."

"So sorry," Kashimo hissed.

"Please be sorry on the lanai," Charlie advised, and hurrying him out, closed the windows after him. Turning, he came back to Robert Fyfe. "I am happy to be alone with you," he began. "Though you may not have guessed, you are most interesting figure who has yet popped into this affair."

"Really?" The actor dropped into a chair and sat there, a striking figure in his ambassadorial costume. His manner was calm, unperturbed, and seemingly he was in the frankest of moods.

"Very interesting indeed," Charlie continued. "I gaze at you, and I ask myself—why is he lying to me?"

Fyfe half rose from his chair. "Look here. What do you mean?"

Chan shrugged. "My dear sir—what is the use? When you visit lawn pavilions to call on ex-wives, how careless to flaunt distinctive red ribbon on chest. It might even be mistaken by excitable young women for—blood. Matter of fact—it was."

"Oh," said Fyfe grimly. "I see."

"The truth—for a change," went on Chan gently.

The actor sat for a moment with his head in his hands. Finally he looked up.

"Gladly," he answered. "Though the truth is a bit—unusual. I hadn't seen Shelah Fane since that night in the station—until to-night. This morning I heard she was in town. It was quite startling—what the news did to me. You did not know Miss Fane, Mr.—er—Mr.——"

"Inspector Chan," Charlie informed him. "No, I had not the pleasure."

"It was really that—a pleasure." Fyfe half smiled. "She was a remarkable girl, aflame with life. I'd once been very fond of her and—I never got over it. No other woman ever meant anything to me after Shelah left. I couldn't hold her—I don't blame her for that—no man could hold her long. She wanted romance, excitement. Well, as I say, I learned this morning she was in town, and the news thrilled me—it was as though I heard her voice again after nine years' silence. I sent her flowers, with a message—love from some one you have forgotten. Have I said she was impetuous? Wild, unreasoning, sudden—and irresistible. My flowers had barely reached this house when she called me on the telephone. She caught me at the theater, made up, ready to go on. 'Bob,' she said, 'you must come at once. You must. I want so much to see you. I am waiting.' "

He glanced at Chan, and shrugged. "Any other woman, and I would have answered: 'After the show.' Somehow, that was never the way one replied to Shelah. 'Coming'—that was always the answer when Shelah spoke.

"It was a rather mad idea, but possible. I had arrived at the theater early, I needn't go on for forty-five minutes. I had a car and could drive out here, if I rushed it a bit, in fifteen minutes each way. So, at seven-thirty, I went into my dressing-room on the ground floor of the building, locked the door on the inside, and stepped through a window into the alley that runs along beside the theater.

"Shelah had told me about the pavilion, she said she was giving a dinner party, but that I needn't meet any of the guests—my make-up, you know, and all that. She wanted to see me alone, anyhow. I reached here about seven-forty-five. Shelah met me on the lawn, and we went to the pavilion. She looked at me in a strange way—I wondered if she still cared for me. I was shocked at the change in her—when I knew her she was fresh and lovely and so very gay. Hollywood had altered her greatly. Oh, well—none of us grows younger, I suppose. We wasted precious time in reminiscences, living over the past—somehow, it seemed to make her happy, just to remember. I was nervous about the time—I kept looking at my watch. Finally I said that I must go."

He was silent. "And then——" Chan prompted.

"Well, it was odd," Fyfe continued. "I'd got the impression over the telephone, and even more so after I saw her, that she wanted my advice about some terribly pressing matter. But when I told her I was going, she only stared at me in a sort of pitiful way. 'Bob,' she said, 'you still care for me a little, don't you?' She was standing close to me, and I took her in my arms. 'I adore you,' I cried, and—but I needn't go into that. I had that moment—no one can take it from me. Thoughts of the happy past came back—I was torn between my love for Shelah and that damn' watch ticking in my very brain. I told her hurriedly that I would return after the play, that I would see her daily during her stay here, that we would swim together—I had a wild idea that perhaps I could win her all over again. And perhaps I could have done it—but now—now——" His voice broke. "Poor Shelah! Poor girl!"

Chan nodded gravely. "It has been well said, those who live too conspicuously tempt the notice of Fate."

"And I suppose no one ever lived more conspicuously than Shelah," Fyfe added. He gave Charlie a quick penetrating glance. "Look here, Inspector—you mustn't fail me. You must find out who has done this awful thing."

"Such is my aim," Chan assured him. "You departed at once?"

"Yes, I left her standing there—standing there smiling, alive and well. Smiling, and crying too. I dashed out of the pavilion——"

"It was now what time?"

"I know only too well—it was four minutes past eight. I rushed down the drive, found my car where I'd left it before the house, and motored back to town as quickly as I could. When I stepped through the window of my dressing-room, they were hammering like wild men on my door. I opened it, said I'd been having a nap, and went out with the stage manager to the wings. I was five minutes late—the stage manager showed me his watch—eight-twenty. But that wasn't serious—I went on and played my rôle—and I was just coming off after the first act when some young man telephoned me the terrible news."

He stood up. "That, Inspector Chan, is my story. My visit out here to-night may prove embarrassing for me, but I don't regret it. I saw Shelah again—I held her in my arms—and for that privilege I stand ready to pay any price you can name. Is there anything more I can tell you?"

Chan shook his head. "For the present, no. I ask that you remain on scene a brief time. Other matters may arise later."

"Of course," nodded Fyfe.

The bell rang, and Charlie himself went to the door. Peering into the night, he beheld a burly dark-skinned man in the khaki uniform of the Honolulu police.

"Ah, it is Spencer," he said. "I am very glad to have you here."

The officer came into the hall, dragging after him a figure that, anywhere save on a tropic beach, would have been quite unbelievable.

"I picked this up on Kalakaua Avenue," the policeman explained. "I thought you might like to see him. He's a little mixed on what he's been doing to-night."

The man to whom he referred shook off the officer's

grip and stepped toward Charlie. "I trust we're not too late for dinner," he remarked. He stood for a moment looking about the hall and then, as though prompted by old memories, removed from his head a limp and tattered hat of straw. "My chauffeur is really rather stupid. He lost his way."

His manner was jaunty and debonair, no mean triumph considering his costume. Aside from the hat, which he now clutched in a thin freckled hand, that costume consisted of a badly soiled pair of white duck trousers, a blue shirt open at the throat, a disreputable velvet coat that had once been the color of Burgundy and the remnants of a pair of shoes, through the holes of which peered the white of his naked feet.

The buzz of conversation from the dining-room had died, the group in there appeared to be listening, and Charlie hastily held open the curtains to the living-room. "Come in here, please," he said, and they entered to find Fyfe waiting there alone. For a moment the man in the velvet coat stared at the actor, and under the yellow ragged beard that had not known barber's scissors for a month, a slow smile appeared.

"Now," Chan said. "Who are you? Where do you live?"

The man shrugged. "The name," he replied, "might be Smith."

"It might also be Jones," Charlie suggested.

"A mere matter of taste. Personally, I prefer Smith."

"And you live——"

Mr. Smith hesitated. "To put it crudely, Officer, I'm afraid I'm on the beach."

Charlie smiled. "Ah, you uphold noble tradition. What would Waikiki be without beach-comber?" He went to the window that led to the lanai and summoned Kashimo. "Kindly search this gentleman," he directed.

"By all means," the beach-comber agreed. "And if you find anything that looks like money, in heaven's name let me know about it at once."

Kashimo's search revealed little—a piece of string, a comb, a rusty pocket-knife, and an object which at first glance looked like a coin, but which turned out to be a medal. Charlie took this and studied it.

"Temple bronze medal, Third Prize, Landscapes in Oils," he read. "The Pennsylvania Academy of Fine Arts." He looked inquiringly at Smith.

The beach-comber shrugged. "Yes," he said. "I see I shall have to confess it all now—I'm a painter. Not much of a one at that—the third prize only, you will observe. The first medal was of gold—it might have come in handy of late, if I'd won it. But I didn't." He came a bit nearer. "If it's not asking too much—just what is the reason for this unwarranted intrusion into my affairs? Can't a gentleman go about his business in this town without being pawed by a fat policeman, and searched by a thin one?"

"We are sorry to inconvenience you, Mr. Smith," Charlie replied politely. "But tell me—have you been on the beach to-night?"

"I have not. I've been in town. I walked out—for reasons which we needn't take up now. I was going along Kalakaua when this cop——"

"Where down-town have you been?"

"In Aala Park."

"You talked with some one there?"

"I did. The company was not select, but I made it do."

"Not on the beach to-night." Chan was staring at the man's feet. "Kashimo, you and Spencer will kindly escort this gentleman out to spot below window where you discovered footprints, and make careful comparison."

"I know," cried the Japanese eagerly. He went out with the other policeman and the beach-comber.

Chan turned to Fyfe. "Long arduous task," he commented. "But man, without work, becomes—what? A Mr. Smith. Will you be seated at your ease?"

The others entered from the dining-room, and to them also Charlie offered chairs, which most of them accepted with poor grace. Alan Jaynes was consulting his watch. Eleven o'clock—he sought Chan's eyes. But the detective looked innocently the other way.

Tarneverro came close to Charlie. "Anything new?" he inquired, under his breath.

"The inquiry widens," Chan answered.

"I'd rather it narrowed down," replied the fortune-teller.

The two policemen and the beach-comber returned through the lanai. Spencer again had the latter firmly in his grip.

"O. K., Charlie," said the uniformed man. "The footprints under the window could have been made by only one pair of shoes in Honolulu." He pointed at the beach-comber's battered footwear. "Those shoes," he added.

Smith looked down, smiling whimsically. "They are a shocking bad pair, aren't they?" he inquired. "But Hawaii, you know, seems to have no appreciation of art. If you've noticed the paintings they buy to hang in their parlors—the wooden waves put on canvas by the local Rembrandts—I may be a third-rater, but I couldn't bring myself to do stuff like that. Not even for a new pair of——"

"Come here!" cut in Charlie sharply. "You lied to me."

Smith shrugged. "You put things bluntly for one of your race, Officer. It may be that I distorted the situation slightly in the interests of——"

"The interests of what?"

"The interests of Smith. I observe that there is something wrong here, and I much prefer to keep out of it——"

"You are in it now. Tell me—did you enter that beach house to-night?"

"I did not—I'll swear to that. True, I stood beneath the window for a few minutes."

"What were you doing there?"

"I was planning to make the sand in the shelter of the pavilion my lodging for the night. It's a favorite place of mine——"

"Go back to beginning," cut in Chan. "The truth this time."

"I hadn't been out to the beach for three days and nights," the man told him. "I got a little money, and I've been stopping down-town. When I was out here last, this house was unoccupied. To-day my money was gone—I'm expecting a check—it hasn't come." He paused. "Rotten mail service out here. If I could only get back to the mainland——"

"Your money was gone," Charlie interrupted.

"Yes—so I was forced back to my old couch under the palm trees. I walked out from town, and got to the beach——"

"At what time?"

"My dear sir,—you embarrass me. If you will take a stroll along Hotel Street, you will see my watch hanging in a certain window. I often go and look at it myself."

"No matter. You got to the beach."

"I did. It's public, you know—this one out here. It belongs to everybody. I was surprised to see a light in the pavilion. Somebody's rented the house, I thought. The curtain of that window was down, but it was flapping in the wind. I heard voices inside—a man's and a woman's—I wondered whether it was such a good place to sleep, after all."

He paused. Charlie's eyes were on Robert Fyfe. The actor was leaning forward with a fierce intensity, staring at the beach-comber, his hands clenched until the knuckles showed white.

"I just stood there," Smith continued. "The curtain flopped about—and I got a good look at the man."

"Ah, yes," Charlie nodded. "What man?"

"Why, that fellow there," Smith said. He pointed at Fyfe. "The chap with the red ribbon across his shirt-front. I haven't seen one of those ribbons since the time when I was studying at Julien's, in Paris, and our ambassador invited me round for dinner. It's a fact. He came from my town—an old friend of my father——"

"No matter," Charlie cut in. "You stood there, peeping beneath the curtain——"

"What do you mean?" cried the beach-comber. "Don't judge a man by his clothes, please. I wasn't spying. If I caught a glimpse, as I did, it was unavoidable. They were talking fast, those two—this man, and the woman."

"Yes. And perhaps—equally unavoidable, do not misunderstand me—you heard what they said?"

Smith hesitated. "Well—as a matter of fact—I did. I heard her tell him——"

With a little cry, Robert Fyfe leaped forward. He pushed the beach-comber aside and stood before Charlie. His face was deathly pale, but his eyes did not falter.

"Drop it," he said hoarsely. "I can put an end to your investigation here and now. I killed Shelah Fane, and I'm willing to pay for it."

A shocked silence greeted his words. Calm, unmoved, quite motionless, Chan stared into the man's face.

"You killed Miss Fane?"

"I did."

"For what reason?"

"I wanted her to come back to me. I couldn't live without her. I pleaded and begged—and she wouldn't listen. She laughed at me—she said there wasn't a chance. She drove me to it—I killed her. I had to do it."

"You killed her—with what?"

"With a knife I carried as one of the props in the play."

"Where is it now?"

"I threw it into a swamp on my way to town."

"You can lead me to the spot?"

"I can try."

Chan turned away.

Alan Jaynes was on his feet. "Eleven-ten," he cried. "I can just make the boat if I hurry, Inspector. Of course, you're not going to hold me now."

"But I do hold you," Charlie answered. "Spencer, if this man makes another move, kindly place him beneath arrest."

"Are you mad?" Jaynes cried. "You have your confession, haven't you——"

"With regard to that," said Charlie, "wait just a moment, please." He turned back to Fyfe, who was standing quietly beside him. "You left the pavilion, Mr. Fyfe, at four minutes past eight?"

"I did."

"You had already killed Shelah Fane?"

"I had."

"You drove to the theater and were in the wings of same at twenty minutes past eight?"

"Yes—I told you all that."

"The stage manager will swear that you were there at twenty minutes past eight?"

"Of course—of course."

Chan stared at him. "Yet at twelve minutes past eight," he said, "Shelah Fane was seen alive and well."

"What's that!" Tarneverro cried.

"Pardon—I am speaking with this other gentleman. At twelve minutes past eight, Mr. Fyfe, Shelah Fane was seen alive and well. How do you account for that?"

Fyfe dropped into a chair and covered his face with his hands.

"I do not understand you," Charlie said gently. "You wish me to believe you killed Shelah Fane. Yet, of all the people in this room, you alone have unshakable alibi."

Chapter IX

EIGHTEEN IMPORTANT MINUTES

No one spoke. Outside what Jimmy Bradshaw had called the silken surf broke once again on the coral sand. The crash died away, and inside that crowded room there was no sound save the ticking of a small clock on a mantel beneath which fires were rarely lighted. With a gesture of despair, Alan Jaynes stepped to a table and, striking a match, applied it to one of his small cigars. Charlie crossed over and laid his hand on Fyfe's shoulder.

"Why have you confessed to a deed you did not perform?" he asked. "That is something I warmly desire to know."

The actor made no answer, nor did he so much as look up. Charlie turned to face Tarneverro.

"So Shelah Fane was seen alive at twelve minutes past eight?" the fortune-teller remarked suavely. "Would you mind telling me how long you have known that?"

Charlie smiled. "If only it happened you understood Chinese language," he replied. "I would not find it necessary to elucidate." He went to the door, and called Jessop. When the butler appeared, Chan asked that he send in Wu Kno-ching at once. "I am doing something now for your benefit alone, Mr. Tarneverro," he added.

"You are a considerate man, Inspector," the fortune-teller answered.

The old Chinese shuffled into the room; he was, evidently, in a rather peevish frame of mind. His carefully prepared dinner had been ruined by the events of this tragic evening, and he was in no mood to accept the philosophy of the patient K'ung-fu-tsze.

Chan talked with him for a moment, again in Cantonese, and then turned to Tarneverro. "I request that he verify story he told me in native language when I interrogated him in this room some while ago," he explained. "Wu, you have said you lingered in kitchen with Jessop and Anna when clock was speaking the hour of eight. You fretted because dinner was seemingly movable feast, and also because bootlegger of your choice had not shown up and was causing you to lose much face. Am I correct so far?"

"Bootleggah velly late," nodded Wu.

"But at ten minutes past hour, erring friend of yours makes panting appearance with hotly desired liquids. While Jessop begins task of making this poison palatable, you wander away in search of mistress." Chan glanced at the fortune-teller. "Wu informal type servant who pops up anywhere on place with great bland look. Characteristic of the race." He resumed his remarks to the Chinese. "You discover Miss Shelah Fane alone in pavilion. Vindicating your honor, you announce bootlegger friend has finally appeared. What did Missie say?"

"Missie look-see watch, say twelve minutes aftah eight plitty muchee time bootleggah come. I say plitty muchee time dinnah gets on table. Mebbe that can happen now if not new cook needed heah *wikiwiki*."

"Yes. Then she ordered you to get out and not annoy her with your bothers. So you went back to kitchen. That's what you told me before, isn't it?"

"Yes, boss."

"All same true, eh, Wu?"

"Yes, boss. Wha' foah my tell lie to you?"

"All right. You can go now."

"My go, boss."

As the old man moved silently away on his velvet slippers, Charlie turned to meet the penetrating gaze of Tarneverro. "All of which is very interesting," the fortune-teller said coldly. "I perceive that when I pointed out to you the matter of the watch, I was merely wasting my breath. You already knew that Shelah Fane had not been murdered at two minutes past eight."

Charlie laid a conciliatory hand on Tarneverro's arm. "Pray do not take offense. I knew Miss Fane had been seen at that later hour, yes; but I was still uncertain of how watch had been manipulated. I listened, curious and then entranced, to your logical explanation. Could I, at its finish, rudely cry thanks for nothing? A gentleman is always courteous. Much better I shower you with well-deserved words of praise, so you go forward with vigorous and triumphant mood of heart."

"Is that so?" remarked Tarneverro, moving off.

Charlie stepped up to the beach-comber. "Mr. Smith," he said.

"Right here, Officer," Smith answered. "I was afraid you were going to forget me. What can I do for you now?"

"A moment ago you began interesting recital of conversation overheard between this gentleman with ribbon-bedecked shirt-front and lady he met in pavilion to-night. At crucial point you suffered very blunt interruption. I am most eager that you return to subject at once."

Fyfe rose to his feet, and stared hard at the derelict in the velvet coat. Smith looked back at him, and a speculative, cunning look flashed into his pale gray eyes.

"Oh, yes," he said slowly. "I was interrupted, wasn't I? But I'm used to that. Sure—sure, I was telling you that I heard them talking together. Well, there's no need to go on with it now. I've nothing to add to what the gentleman has already told you." Fyfe turned away. "He was pleading with her to come back to him—said he loved her, and all that. And she wouldn't listen to him. I felt rather sorry for him—I've been in that position myself. I heard her say: 'Oh, Bob—what's the use?' He went on insisting. Every now and then he looked at his watch. 'My time's up,' he said at last. 'I've got to go. We'll thrash this out later.' I heard the slam of the door——"

"And the woman was alone in the room—alive and well. You are sure of that?"

"Yes—the curtain was flapping—I saw her after he left. She was there alone—moving about."

With a puzzled frown, Charlie glanced at Robert Fyfe. "You are not content with one alibi. You have now a second. I do not understand you, Mr. Fyfe."

The actor shrugged. "I find it hard to understand myself, Inspector. A fit of temperament, perhaps. We stage people are inclined to be overly dramatic."

"Then you withdraw your confession?"

"What else can I do?" Chan did not overlook the glance that passed between the immaculate actor and the battered beach-comber. "Others have withdrawn it for me. I did not kill Shelah—that's quite true. But I thought it would be better if——"

"If what?"

"Nothing."

"You thought it would be better if my investigation went no further."

"Oh, not at all."

"Something came out in that conversation with your ex-wife which you feared this man had overheard. Something you want suppressed."

"You have a keen imagination, Inspector."

"Also, I have a custom to discover facts which some people want to hide. Your move has been to this moment successful—but you and I have not finished with each other, Mr. Fyfe."

"I am at your service at any time, sir."

"Thank you so much, but I hope the next time we meet your service will be of more value to my humble self." He looked at Smith. "As for you, though I am desolated by acute pain to make so rude a remark, I believe you mix plenty falsehood with your truth."

The beach-comber shrugged. "There you go—judging a man by his clothes again."

"Not by your clothes, which are silent, but by your tongue, which speaks," Charlie told him. "Mr. Spencer, will you kindly take this man to station house and make record of his finger-prints."

"So many attentions," Smith put in. "I only hope they don't turn my head."

"After which," Chan continued, "you may release him —for time being."

"All right, Charlie," Spencer said.

"One other thing. Pause a moment while I introduce to you all people in this room." Gravely he went through that somewhat lengthy ceremony. "You have also seen butler and cook. There is in addition a maid, whom I ask that you pause and make note of on your way out. You will speed from station without delay to Pier Seven, from which the boat *Oceanic* sails for coast at midnight. No person you have seen in this house is to sail on that boat. You understand?"

"Sure, Charlie—I'll attend to it," Spencer nodded.

Jaynes stepped forward. "I'd like to remind you that my luggage is aboard that ship—some of it in the hold——"

Charlie nodded. "How fortunate you spoke of that. Mr. Spencer, kindly see that all effects in stateroom belonging to Mr. Jaynes are put ashore in your care. Arrange for such as lie in hold to be guarded for the gentleman at San Francisco dock. Explain he is detained by important business and may be in Honolulu for some time. Is that satisfactory, Mr. Jaynes?"

"It's damned unsatisfactory," the Britisher growled, "but I presume I shall have to make the best of it."

"All you can do," nodded Charlie. "Kashimo, you will accompany Mr. Spencer down-town. Your passionate labors in this house are ended for the night. You retire in glory—and if you come back through unexpected window, you retire for ever. Keep same in mind."

The apprentice detective nodded, and went out after Spencer and the beach-comber. Robert Fyfe stepped forward.

"Is there any necessity for my staying any longer?" he inquired.

Charlie studied him thoughtfully. "I think not. You may go along. You and I will talk together when I have more leisure."

"Any time, Inspector." Fyfe went to the curtains, and held them open. "I am stopping at the Waioli Hotel, on Fort Street," he added. "Drop in at your convenience, won't you? Good night." He went into the hall, where Spencer could be heard talking with the maid. The door slammed behind him, and a second later, the two policemen and Smith also departed.

Charlie stood regarding the tired group in the living-room. "Accept my advice and take heart," he said. "We give Mr. Spencer generous handicap on journey to pier, and then I find great joy releasing this company at last. While we are waiting, there are one or two matters. Since first I spoke with you, it has been found necessary to alter views. Then hour of tragedy was thought certain at two minutes past eight. Now we must advance and say, dreadful event happened some time between twelve minutes past eight and the half-hour. Eighteen minutes there—eighteen important minutes. Each of us must ask himself: What was I doing in those eighteen minutes?"

He paused. His eyes were bright, his manner quite keen and alive—for him. The Chinese are at their best at night; it is their favorite time. But he was alone in his vigor, the others were exhausted and drooping, the make-up of the women stood out, unnatural and far from pleasing, against the pallor of their weariness.

"Eighteen important minutes," Chan repeated. "Miss Dixon, Miss Julie and Mr. Bradshaw disported gaily in breakers, visiting beach occasionally. On that beach Mrs. Ballou sat and idly passed time until dinner. For final ten of those minutes, Mr. Ballou wandered about, no one can say where——"

"I can say where," Ballou cut in. "I came into this room—the butler will verify that. I strolled in here and smoked a cigarette he gave me."

"He remained with you while you smoked it?"

"No—he didn't. He lighted it for me, and went out. When he returned, I was sitting in the same chair——"

"You wish me to note that, eh?" Charlie smiled.

"I don't care whether you note it or not."

Charlie took out a handkerchief and wiped the perspiration from his brow. The tropic night was beginning to live up to its reputation.

"I turn now to the four gentlemen whose alibis have been so rudely shattered. I know where they were at two minutes past eight, but after that——"

"Take me first," said Tarneverro. "You saw me go to join those two people in the lounge of the hotel—they are old friends of mine from Australia. We remained there for a few minutes after you left, and then I suggested that we go out on the lanai that faces the palm court. We did so, and for a time sat and chatted. When I finally looked at my watch, it was precisely eight-thirty. I remarked on the hour and said I was sorry, but I had to go along. We all went inside, I ran up to get my hat, and when I came back to the lobby, I happened on you near the door."

Charlie studied his face. "Your old friends will be willing to swear to all this?"

"I can see no reason why they shouldn't. They know it's true."

Chan smiled. "I congratulate you, Mr. Tarneverro."

"I congratulate myself, Inspector. You may recall that I told you I had another tree."

"Mr. Jaynes," said Chan, turning to the Britisher.

Jaynes shrugged hopelessly. "I have no alibi," he said. "During those eighteen minutes, I was wandering along the beach, alone. Make what you wish of it. I didn't come down here."

"Mr. Van Horn—you did come down here?" Charlie addressed the picture actor.

"I did, worse luck," shrugged Van Horn. "The first time in a long and honorable career that I ever got to a party ahead of the hour set. It will be a lesson to me—I can tell you that."

"It was, I believe, eight-fifteen when Jessop admitted you?"

"About that time—yes. He told me that the party—or what there was of it—had moved to the beach. I went out on the lawn. I saw a light in a building which Jessop told me was a summer-house, and I thought of going there. I wish to heaven I had. But I heard voices down by the water, so I went there instead. I sat down by Rita Ballou—but you know all that."

Chan nodded. "Only one remains. Mr. Martino?"

The director frowned. "Like Huntley and Mr. Jaynes," he said, "I have no alibi worth mentioning. You wrecked me along with them when you smashed that eight-two theory." He took a handkerchief from a side pocket and mopped his forehead. "After Jaynes left me and started down the beach, I sat in one of the hotel swings near the water. I should have been busy getting myself a good alibi, I suppose, but I'm not so clever as Mr. Tarneverro here." He gave the fortune-teller an unfriendly look. "So I just sat alone—the scene looked rather good to me. I wished I could get it into a picture—the purple starry sky, the yellow lamps along the water-front, the black hulk of Diamond Head. A picture in color—we'll have 'em that way before long. I amused myself thinking up a possible story—you can't depend on authors for anything. Presently I looked at my watch. It was eight-twenty-five, so I went to my room to brush up and get my hat. When I came down I met you and Tarneverro here, and heard the news of Miss Fane's murder."

Charlie stood looking thoughtfully at the director. Suddenly he was pushed aside as Tarneverro strode forward.

"That's a nasty scratch on your forehead, Martino," the fortune-teller cried.

Startled, the director put his hand to his brow, and on one finger, as he took it away, he noted a trace of red.

"By jove," he said, "that's odd——"

"You'd better turn over to Inspector Chan the handkerchief you just replaced in your pocket."

"What handkerchief?" Martino produced the one which he had recently passed across his forehead. "Oh, this!"

"I will take it, please," said Charlie. He spread the white

square of silk on a table and brought out his magnifying-glass. For a moment he studied the center of the square, then ran his fingers lightly across it. He looked up.

"A queer thing, Mr. Martino," he remarked. "There exist, caught in mesh of this cloth, a few thin splinters of glass. How would you explain that?"

Martino rose quickly, and with a serious face bent over the table. "I can't explain it," he said. "I can't even explain how that handkerchief came to be in my pocket."

Chan regarded him intently. "It is not your property?" he inquired.

"It certainly isn't," the director replied. "I carry two handkerchiefs with my evening clothes. One here"—he indicated his breast pocket above which the ends of a handkerchief were showing—"and another in my hip pocket." He produced a second. "Certainly I'd have no use for a third. I just happened to reach into my side pocket, my hand touched this, and I used it. But I never put it there, and it isn't mine."

"A likely story," Tarneverro sneered.

"My dear Tarneverro," the director said, "when you've made as many pictures as I have, you'll realize that the truth often sounds less probable than fiction." He picked up the little square of silk and handed it to Charlie. "By the way, there's a laundry mark in one corner of that."

"I know," Chan nodded. He stood for a moment, looking at the tiny letter *B* done with black ink on the silk border. He glanced over at Wilkie Ballou. The planter stared back at him, and taking a handkerchief from his own pocket, casually mopped his brow.

Chapter X

"SHELAH FROM DENNY"

Shrugging his broad shoulders, Charlie turned back to Martino. The director's face was even more crimson than usual, and he was breathing hard.

"Do you wish to make statement," Chan asked, "as to moment when you think this object was placed on your person?"

Martino considered. "When we were leaving the dining-room a while back," he said, "we were all crowded together round the door. I thought then that I felt a little tug at my pocket."

"Just who was near you at that instant?"

"It's hard to say. Everybody was there together. The matter is serious, and I don't like to guess." He paused, and glanced at the fortune-teller. "I do recall that Mr. Tarneverro wasn't far away."

"Is that an accusation?" asked Tarneverro coldly.

"Not precisely. I can't be sure——"

"You'd like nothing better than to be sure," the fortune-teller suggested.

Martino laughed. "You've hit it there, my friend. I haven't much love for you, and you know it. If I'd had my way, you'd have been run out of Hollywood long ago."

"Failing that, you've gone about secretly warning the women against me."

"What do you mean, secretly? I've done it openly, and you know it. I've told them to keep away from you——"

"Why?"

"I don't like the look in your eyes, my friend. What was it you told poor Shelah this morning? What did she tell you?"

"That is something I'd not be likely to discuss with you. So you sat on the beach by the water, did you?"

"Oh, don't get too cocky over that alibi of yours," Martino cried. "How did you happen to have it so pat and ready? Reading the future again, eh?"

"Gentlemen, gentlemen," Charlie protested. "We are arriving precisely nowhere by this. I perceive that nerves are very much up on edge, and I am glad to push open doors and put quick end to investigation. You are all free to depart."

There was an instant dash for the hall. Chan followed.

"Just one word to add," he said, "though I am certain that by now the buzz of my voice in your ears must be most tiresome sound. But please remember—you rest on small island in the midst of broad Pacific Ocean. Attempt by any one of you to go aboard ship will be instantly known to us, and regarded with dark suspicious eye. Stay on, I beg of you, and enjoy beauties of spot, on which subject Mr. Bradshaw will be happy to make oration for you any time, any place."

"That's right," the boy nodded. "Loaf on a palm-fringed shore and forget your troubles. Somewhere winter is raging——"

"In July?" Van Horn inquired.

"Sure—at the South Pole, for example. Put Hollywood out of your thoughts. Remember—Hawaii has the climate California thinks it has."

The door closed behind Ballou and his wife. Van Horn, Martino and Jaynes followed promptly. Bradshaw returned to the living-room, where Julie and Diana had remained, leaving the fortune-teller and Charlie in the hall. Tarneverro picked up his hat.

"Inspector," he remarked, "you have my sympathy. You are up against a puzzling case."

"Also I have your help," Chan reminded him. "The thought consoles me."

Tarneverro shook his head. "I'm afraid you over-estimate my powers. But whatever they are, they are ranged on your side. When am I to see you again?"

"I will call on you to-morrow morning," Chan answered. "We will have good long talk. Perhaps, thinking deeply into matter over night, each of us will have new ideas to offer."

"I shall try to supply my share," nodded Tarneverro,

and went out. For a moment Charlie stood looking at the door through which he had gone, then turning, he went into the living-room.

"Miss Dixon," he said, "may I make further request of you? Will you ascend stairs with me and point out various rooms, naming the persons to whom they have been assigned? I still have a little searching to do before repose."

"Of course," nodded the actress, "and speaking of repose, I hope you'll search my room first. I feel all in after this dreadful evening."

She and Charlie disappeared. With a forlorn gesture, Julie sank into a chair.

"Poor kid!" said Mr. Bradshaw.

"Oh, Jimmy—it *has* been a dreadful evening, hasn't it?"

"It surely has. Think, Julie, think. You were closer to Shelah Fane than any one else. Have you no idea who did—this terrible thing?"

She shook her head. "I can't imagine. Of course, Shelah had enemies—all successful people have—she was envied, perhaps even hated. But I never dreamed any one hated her as much as this. It's just unbelievable, that's all."

The boy sat down beside her. "Let's forget it for a while. How about you? What are you going to do now?"

"Oh—I suppose I'll go back where I came from."

"Where did you come from? You haven't told me."

"From a theatrical boarding-house in Chicago—I was traveling with my mother when she—she left me. Stage people, you see, all my folks—father too. Mother called San Francisco home, though she seldom saw it. But she was born there—so many good actors were, you know. And she——"

"She was one of the best, I guess," said Jimmy Bradshaw.

"I thought so. I've got a grandmother there now—seventy-two, but she goes trouping occasionally—she's such a darling, Jimmy. I think I'll go to her, and get some sort of job—I could make good in an office, I believe. Grandmother would be glad to have me; we're all that's left of—us."

Bradshaw pulled himself together. "If no one else wants to speak, may I say a few words about Hawaii? Everywhere we have poetry and glamour. The climate breeds happiness and laughter, a natural reflection of the sunlight, the rainbows and the purple hills. Here there are no sunstrokes and no snow. Honolulu has its message of beauty for every heart. As for——"

"Jimmy, what in the world——"

"As for the people, where nature is kind man can not help but be. You will find——"

"I don't get you, Jimmy."

"It's simple enough. I've sold this place to fifty thousand tourists, and now I want to sell it to you. As a substitute for grandmother, you see. No doubt she's a darling, as you say. Maybe I'm not, but I'm young yet. For of course it isn't just Honolulu I'm selling. I'm thrown in, you know. How about it, Julie? A little bungalow nestling under two mortgages and a bougainvillea vine——"

"You—you mean you love me, Jimmy?" the girl asked.

"Oh, lord—did I omit that line? I shall have to rewrite the whole darn piece. Naturally, I love you. Who wouldn't? It may not be the most fitting time for me to say all this, but I don't want you to think that I've fallen into the habit of putting things off, just because I live in the lazy latitudes. I'm crazy about you, and before you write grandmother to come down and meet your boat—she might be away trouping anyhow—I want you to give a thought to Hawaii—and to me. Will you do it, Julie?"

She nodded. "I will, Jimmy."

"That's good enough for me," he smiled.

Chan came silently into the room, and the boy stood up. "Well, Charlie, you ready to go along? I let my brother have my car to-night, so I'm honoring you with my presence in that famous flivver of yours."

"You will be remarkably welcome," Chan told him. "Yes—I travel townward almost at once. There remains one little matter——"

Anna, the maid, came hurriedly into the room. "Miss Dixon said you wanted to see me," she remarked to Chan.

He nodded. "A trifling affair. You told me earlier this evening that a certain ring was missing from Miss Fane's finger after the homicide. An emerald ring."

"I did, sir."

Julie O'Neill was leaning forward, breathless, her eyes wide.

"Is this the ring?" Chan suddenly produced a platinum band decorated with a surprising stone that flashed green in the brightly lighted room.

"That is it, sir," Anna nodded.

Chan turned to Julie. "So sorry to drag you in. But will you kindly tell me—how does it happen I find this bauble in the drawer of your dressing-table?" The girl gasped, and Jimmy Bradshaw looked at her in amazement. "I am very sorry this question comes out, which disappoints me sadly," Charlie continued. "But I should say, things need explanation."

"It's very simple," answered Julie in a low voice.

"Naturally," bowed Chan. "Just how simple, according to your story?"

"Well." She hesitated. "There are only a few of us here —I can speak frankly. Shelah was always hard up. Somehow money meant nothing to her, it slipped through her fingers, it was gone a moment after she got it. She came back from the South Seas in her usual state—more or less broke. Every one was always cheating her, stealing from her——"

"Every one?" Chan repeated. "You mean her servants, perhaps?"

"Some of them, yes—when they had a chance. But that doesn't matter. Shelah arrived here in need of money, as always. She'd drawn all the advance she could get from the company—they haven't been as generous of late as they used to be. To-day, just after she reached the house, she sent for me and said she must have ready money at once. She gave me this ring and told me to sell it for her, if I could. I was to make a round of the jewelers immediately— this afternoon. But I put it off. I wasn't keen for the job. However, I fully intended to go in the morning—if this thing hadn't happened to-night. That's how I chanced to have the ring."

Chan considered. "She gave it to you just after she reached house. At what time, precisely?"

"At eight o'clock this morning."

"You have had it ever since?"

"Yes, of course. I put it in that drawer—I thought it would be safe there."

"That is all you wish to tell me?"

"That is all." The girl seemed on the point of tears.

Charlie turned to the maid. "You may go, Anna," he said.

"Very good, sir." Anna glanced at the girl, and then went out.

Charlie sighed heavily. Even though he came of a nocturnal race, the night was beginning to wear on him. He took the ring beneath a light and examined it with his magnifying-glass. There was, he noted, an inscription inside. "Shelah from Denny." So Denny Mayo came back into the case? Chan shrugged.

When he turned about, he perceived that Julie was weeping silently. Bradshaw had put his arm about her shoulder. "That's all right, honey," the boy said. "Charlie believes you. Don't you, Charlie?"

Chan bowed from the waist. "In the presence of so much charm, could I have brutal doubts? Miss Julie, I am sorrowed to perceive your overwrought state. Mr. Bradshaw and I depart at once, leaving to you the solace of slumber. You have youth, and sleep will come. I bid you most sympathetic good night."

He disappeared through the curtains, and with a few whispered words to the girl, Bradshaw followed. Jessop, restraining a yawn but firmly polite as always, saw them out. On the steps Charlie stood for a moment, staring at the sky and drawing in a deep breath of the open air.

"It is something to recall," he said, "that during long painful ordeal in that house, stars were still shining and soft tropic night progressed as usual. What have I not been through? A brief respite will be lovely as soft music in the rain."

They got into his car, waiting alone and lonely in the drive.

"Pretty much up against it, eh, Charlie?" the boy suggested.

Chan nodded. "Dizzy feeling causes my head to circulate. I have upearthed so much, and yet I have upearthed nothing." They bowled along, past the Moana Hotel, in unaccustomed darkness now. The pink walls of the Grand glowed with a new splendor in the moonlight. "When you telephoned me," Chan added, "I was about to begin serious operation on a small fish. One taste I had was excellent. Alas! little fish and I will never meet again."

"A shame to spoil your dinner," Bradshaw replied.

"I will be content if your news does not also spoil my reputation," Charlie told him. "How am I going to emerge from the affair? In shining garments of success, or in sackcloth with ashes?"

"I called up the morning paper," the boy told him. "Used to work there, you know. They were short of men at the moment, and I landed the job of covering the story so far. Got to go back now and write it. I'll say that the police haven't a notion just at present—is that correct?"

Charlie barely avoided a collision with the curb. "Have you no better understanding of your task than that? Say nothing of the sort. Police have many clues and expect early arrest."

"But that's the same old bunk, Charlie. And judging from your talk, it isn't true in this case."

"Seldom true in any case," Chan reminded him. "You should know that."

"Well, I'll say it—to please you, Charlie. By the way, did I hear Tarneverro intimate he was working with you?"

"Yes—he fancies himself as bright assistant."

"He may be bright all right—but are you keen for his help?"

Charlie shrugged. "The bird chooses the tree, not the tree the bird," he remarked.

"Well, Tarneverro's a queer bird, all right. He gives me a funny sensation when I look at him." They rode on in silence for a time. "Anyhow, one thing's certain," the boy said at last.

"Is that really so?" Chan inquired. "Name it, please. I seem to have overlooked it in my haste."

"I mean—Julie had nothing to do with this affair."

Charlie grinned in the dark. "I have recollections myself," he said.

"Of what?"

"Being young—and muddled by love. Since I am now the father of eleven children, it is necessarily some time since I went about with head in clouds and warmly beating heart. But memories remain."

"Oh, nonsense," protested Bradshaw. "I'm looking at this thing coldly—as a rank outsider."

"Then I humbly suggest you have old Hawaii moon overhauled at once," commented Chan. "For it must be losing magic power you write about so glowingly."

He drew up before the newspaper office, the sound of his brakes grating noisily in the deserted street. On the lower floor of the building one lonely light burned dimly, but the up-stairs windows were bright yellow with activity. There men sat sorting the cable news that was flowing in from the far corners of the world, from Europe, Asia, the mainland —brief bits of information thought worthy of transmission to this small island dreaming in the midst of the great Pacific.

Jimmy Bradshaw moved as though to alight, then paused. Out of the corner of his eye he glanced at Charlie. "I don't suppose I can have it now, can I?" he inquired.

"You can not," Chan replied firmly.

"What are you talking about?" asked the boy innocently.

"Same thing you are," Charlie grinned.

"I was referring to that handkerchief you took away from the picture director."

"So was I," answered Charlie blandly.

"Then you knew it was mine?"

"I gathered that, yes. Small initial *B* was on it. Also I perceived you perspiring with no means to quench it. I was greatly moved to admiration by your restraint—not once did you make use of coat sleeve. You are going to tell me that it was taken from your pocket?"

"It must have been—yes."

"At what moment?"

"I don't know, but I suppose some one took it when I was in swimming."

"You are sure of that?"

"Well, it seems the only possible explanation. But I didn't notice it was gone until a long time afterward."

"And a still longer time after that—you mention the affair to me."

"It's my confounded modesty again, Charlie," the boy laughed. "I just couldn't stand the limelight. Let me look at the thing, anyhow."

Charlie handed it over, and Bradshaw examined it carefully in the dashboard light. "Mine all right." He pointed at the mark. "That's my alias at the laundry. This is pretty sinister, if you ask me."

Charlie took back the handkerchief. "I have very good notion to put you in jail," he remarked.

"And trifle with the power of the press?" the boy reminded him. "Think twice, Charlie. I didn't do away with our distinguished visitor. That's not the sort of Hawaiian hospitality I go in for." He hesitated. "I could use that handkerchief to-night."

"So could I," Chan answered.

"Oh, well, then I'll just have to drip perspiration on this immortal story I'm about to write. So long, Inspector."

"So long," Chan returned. "And please keep handkerchief out of that same story, and out of your conversation, or you will hear from me."

"O. K., Charlie. It stays a big secret. Nobody in on it but you and me—and the laundry."

Chapter XI

MIDNIGHT IN HONOLULU

Chan drove slowly on to Halekaua Hale, at the foot of Bethel Street, the home of the police. Parking his car, he ascended the worn stone steps. A light was burning in the detectives' room, and going in, he encountered his Chief.

"Hello, Charlie," that gentleman said. "I've been waiting for you. Drove over to Kalaua to-night, or I'd have been with you down the beach. This is a pretty mix-up, isn't it? Got anything yet?"

Sadly Chan shook his head. He glanced at his watch. "The story has length," he suggested.

"Guess I'd better hear it, anyhow," replied the Chief. In him, there was no lack of vigor. The ride in the moonlight to Kalaua had been restful and refreshing.

Charlie sat down and began to talk, while his Chief listened intently. He took up first the scene of the murder, the absence of any weapon, the unsuccessful attempt of the murderer to fix the moment of the crime at two minutes past eight. Coming to the question of clues, he mentioned the loss of the diamond pin which had held the orchids.

"That's something," nodded the Chief, lighting a cigar.

Chan shrugged. "Something we do not possess," he pointed out. He went on to repeat Shelah Fane's story of her presence at the murder of Denny Mayo—the tale she had told Tarneverro, according to the fortune-teller, that morning.

"Fine—fine," cried the Chief. "That gives you the motive, Charlie. Now if she had only written down the name, as this Tarneverro wanted her to——"

With acute distase, Charlie added the incident of the

letter's loss. His Chief looked at him with surprise and a marked disapproval.

"Never knew anything like that to happen to you before. Losing your grip, Charlie?"

"For a moment, I certainly lost grip and letter too," Chan replied ruefully. "As the matter turned out, it did not have much importance." His face brightened as he added the later discovery of the letter under the rug, proving that it was of no value save as a corroboration of Tarneverro's story. He went on to the destruction of the portrait over which Shelah Fane had been seen weeping bitterly in the afternoon.

"Some one didn't want you to see it," frowned the Chief.

"I arrived at the same deduction myself," Charlie admitted. He pictured the arrival of Robert Fyfe on what was obviously his second visit to Waikiki within a few hours, and then turned to the subject of the beach-comber.

"We took his finger-prints and let him go," put in the Chief. "He hasn't nerve enough to kill a fly."

Chan nodded. "You are no doubt correct in such surmise." His report of Fyfe's subsequent, easily punctured confession, evidently puzzled his superior. He mentioned the handkerchief with the telltale slivers of glass found in Martino's pocket, and Jimmy Bradshaw's somewhat belated claim to its ownership. He was by this time rather out of breath. "So matter stands at present," he finished.

His Chief was looking at him with an amused smile. "Well, Charlie, sometimes I've thought you weren't entirely satisfied here since your return from the mainland," he said. "Pretty quiet, you thought it. No big cases like over there. Just chasing a few scared gamblers down an alley—not very thrilling, was it? Honolulu didn't seem to be big enough for you any more. I guess it's big enough to-night."

"I experience uncomfortable feeling maybe it is too big," Chan admitted. "How will I come out of this? Considerable puzzle, if inquiry is made of me."

"We mustn't let it stump us," replied the Chief briskly. He was an intelligent man, and he knew where to lean. He foresaw that he was going to do some heavy leaning in the next few days. With an appraising glance, he surveyed his assistant. Charlie looked sleepy and somewhat worn—nothing alert, nothing clever in his appearance now. The Chief consoled himself with memories. Chan, he reflected, was ever keener than he looked.

He considered. "This Tarneverro, Charlie,—what sort of fellow is he?"

Chan brightened. "Ah, perhaps you go to heart of the matter. Tarneverro appears dark as rainy night, but it is his business to act so. He owns a quick mind. And he seems fiercely eager to assist poor policeman like me."

"A bit too eager, maybe?"

Charlie nodded. "I have thought of that. But consider—he offers to produce testimony of old couple with whom he sat until moment murder was discovered. Truth of that will be examined to-morrow, but I do not doubt it. No—I am plenty certain he did not visit house of Shelah Fane until I took him there. Other points absolve him."

"What, for example?"

"I have told you he spoke to me before murder was done, hinting we would to-night make arrest in famous case. That would have been strangely foolish move if he contemplated murder himself. And Tarneverro is not foolish—he goes far the other way. Then, too, indicating he has earnest desire to assist he points out the matter of the watch. It was bright act—not very necessary since I already knew facts from Wu Kno-ching—but all same plenty good proof he sincerely aims to help. No, I do not believe him guilty killer, and yet——"

"Yet what, Charlie?"

"I prefer to hold that safe in mind for the present. It may mean much, and it may mean nothing."

"You've got something on Tarneverro?" asked the Chief, looking at him keenly.

"With regard to killing—not one solitary thing. At moment when that took place, I believe he was most decidedly elsewhere. Gazing in another direction—kindly permit that I gaze that way a few hours longer before I divulge my thoughts." The plump detective put one hand to his head. "*Haie,* just now I wander, lost in maze of doubts and questionings."

"You'll have to cut that out, Charlie," his Chief told him in a kindly but somewhat worried tone. "The honor of the force is at stake. If these people are going to come over here to our quiet little city and murder each other at Waikiki, we've got to prove to them that they can't get away with it. I rely on you."

Chan bowed. "I'm afraid you do. Appreciate the distinction, and will do all my humble talents permit. Now I will wish you good night. The evening has worn on me like some prolonged dispute."

He went out into the battered old hall, just as Spencer entered from the street. Chan looked at his watch.

"The *Oceanic* has sailed?" he inquired.

"Yeah—she's out."

"With none of our friends aboard, I trust?" Chan said.

"None that I saw goin' aboard—and I guess I was there first. One of 'em showed up, though."

"Which one?"

"That Alan Jaynes. He came in a car from the Grand Hotel, an' collected his baggage. I heard him swearin' under his breath when the ship backed away from the pier. I helped him load up, an' he went back to the beach. He give me a message for you."

"What was that?"

"He said he was sailing on the next ship, and all hell couldn't stop him."

Charlie smiled. "None the less, I shall see that the province he mentions breaks loose at the dock if he tries it."

He went down the flight of steps to the street. Through the moonlight he saw approaching him the jaunty figure of Smith, the beach-comber.

"This is a pretty idea, Officer," that gentleman said. "You give me a nice ride down to the station, and then you kick me out. How am I going to get back to my bedroom? I've walked it once to-night."

Charlie reached into his pocket and held out one hand in which lay a small coin. "You may make the distance by trolley," he suggested.

Smith looked down at the coin. "A dime," he remarked. "Ten cents. I can't get on a street-car and offer the conductor a dime. A gentleman has to have the prestige of a dollar."

Tired as he was, Chan laughed. "So sorry," he answered. "There may be much in what you say. But I believe it wiser at this time to proffer you the ride and no more. The hour is late, and you should be able to maintain your dignity on very little prestige tonight."

Stubbornly Smith shook his head. "I've got to have the prestige of a dollar," he insisted.

"You mean you've got to have a drink," shrugged Chan.

"If the coin is unsatisfactory, I regretfully withdraw it." He moved toward his car. "So sorry that I travel in opposite direction from your couch beneath the palm."

Smith followed him. "Oh, well," he said, "perhaps I'm a bit too sensitive. I'll take the dime." Charlie gave it to him. "Just a loan, Inspector. I'll make a note of it."

He hurried away down Bethel Street in the direction of King. With one foot on the running-board of his little car, Charlie stared after him. Finally he abandoned the flivver and followed. The empty streets were as bright as day, the risk was great, but Chan was an old hand at the game. Smith's battered shoes flopped noisily on the deserted sidewalk, but the detective moved as though on velvet slippers.

The beach-comber turned to the right on King Street and, dodging in and out of doorways, Chan followed. As his quarry neared the corner of Fort, Charlie waited anxiously in a shadowed nook. Would Smith pause at that corner for a Waikiki car? If he did, this pursuit came to nothing.

But Smith did not stop. Instead he crossed over and hastened down Fort Street. The moon shone brightly on his enormous flapping hat, on the shoulders of his absurd velvet coat. Charlie's interest revived at once. On what errand did the beach-comber set forth at this hour of the night?

Selecting the opposite side of the thoroughfare from that which Smith traveled—it was darker and better suited to his purpose—Chan trailed his man down Fort. Past the principal shops of Honolulu, in each of which a dim light burned, they moved along. Smith came to the entrance of the Waioli Hotel, and stopped there. Hiding in a dark doorway across the street, Chan saw him peer into the hotel lobby. The place was deserted save for a watchman who dozed in a chair behind the great glass window. For a moment the beach-comber hesitated and then, as though changing his mind, turned and retraced his steps. Charlie squeezed his great bulk against the door behind him, in a panic lest he be discovered.

But he was safe. All unsuspecting, Smith hurried back to the corner of King, there to await the Waikiki car. Charlie remained in hiding until the car arrived. He saw the beach-comber mount to a seat and ride away—without the prestige of a dollar.

Slowly Chan walked back to the station house. What did this mean? Evidently when Robert Fyfe announced his address to the detective, he was also proclaiming it to the battered Mr. Smith. And Smith desired to see the actor at once, on urgent business.

Charlie was getting into his flivver when the Chief came down the steps of Halekaua Hale.

"Thought you'd gone home, Charlie," he said.

"I was for a moment delayed," Chan explained.

His superior came up eagerly. "Anything new?"

"I remain just where I always have been," the detective sighed.

"You're not really as much in the dark on this case as you say you are?" asked the Chief anxiously.

Chan nodded. "The man who sits in a well, sees little of the sky."

"Well, climb out, Charlie, climb out."

"I am planning swift ascent," the detective answered, and starting his engine, sped off at last in the direction of his house on Punchbowl Hill.

Chapter XII

NOBODY'S FOOL

The night was breaking, and a gray mist lay over Waikiki. Smith, the beach-comber, shivered slightly and stirred on his bed of sand. He put out his hand, as though to draw up over his thin ill-clad body a blanket that was not there. Turning over, he muttered in his sleep, then lay motionless again.

The gray mist turned to pink. Above the mountains to the east a small segment of sky became a deep gold in color, against which a few scattered clouds stood out, black as the recent night. Smith opened his eyes, and gradually came back to a recognition of his surroundings. He did not choose to sleep on the beach, but for some reason the usual bitterness with which he awoke to the realization that he was broke again was missing to-day. Something pleasant had happened —or was about to happen. Ah, yes. He smiled at the hau tree above him, and the tree showered him with mahogany-red blossoms that had been yellow when he retired for the night. He would have preferred grapefruit and coffee, but flowers were more in keeping with the scene.

He sat up. The gold in the eastern sky was spreading, and now the rim of the sun appeared. The snow-white beach was lapped by water that had in it a glint of gold to match the sky. At his left stood Diamond Head, that extinct volcano. He had always a sort of fellow feeling for Diamond Head, being a bit on the extinct side himself. His mind went back to the events of the preceding night. Good fortune had taken him by the hand and led him to that pavilion window. Too often in these last years he had been blind to opportunity. He was resolved that he would not be blind now.

He got to his feet and, removing his scanty clothing, revealed underneath a frayed pair of bathing trunks. Gathering all his courage, he ran down to the water and plunged in. The shock revivified him. He struck out boldly; one thing at least he had learned on tropic beaches, and that was the art of the swimmer. As he cut through the water the wasted years fell away from him, old ambitions returned, he made plans for the future. He would win back to his former self, he would leave this languorous spot where he had never intended to stay anyhow, he would be a man again. The money that would put his feet back on the highroad was finally within his grasp.

The sun, warm and friendly, crept up the eastern sky. Smith plunged far under the waves, swam there, felt more energetic with every exploit. Finally he returned to shallow water, and walking carefully to avoid the coral, came from his bath back to his bedroom. For a time he sat, leaning against the abandoned hulk of a boat in the shelter of which he had spent the night. The hot sun served as his towel, and he rested, at peace with the world. A delicious feeling of laziness spread over him. But no, no—this wouldn't do.

He donned his clothes, took a broken piece of comb from his pocket, and applied it to his yellow beard and hair. His toilet was completed, and breakfast was now the order of the day. Above him hung clusters of coconuts; often these had been forced to serve. But not this morning, he told himself with a smile. Through a scene of brightness and beauty, he walked slowly toward the Moana Hotel. It was a scene that had, in its way, contributed to Mr. Smith's downfall, for every time he sought to paint it, he threw down his brush in disgust and bemoaned the inadequacy of his talent.

On the sand outside the hotel, an early beach-boy lay strumming a steel guitar and singing a gentle song. Smith went promptly to join him.

"Good morning, Frank," he said.

Frank turned his head. "Hello," he answered dreamily. The beach-comber sat down beside him. Suddenly Frank looked at him, his dark eyes wide and earnest. "I'm not going to sing for tourists to-day," the beach-boy announced. "I'm just going to sing for the blue sky."

Smith nodded. Coming from any other race, this would have been a stilted and theatrical remark, but the beach-comber knew his Hawaiians better than that. He had watched them arrive each morning on their beloved beach, staring at it as though its beauty were brought to their attention for the first time, diving into its familiar waters with cries of delight that betokened a happiness rare in this modern world.

"That's the ticket, Frank," Smith nodded approvingly. He suddenly introduced a more practical note. "Got any money?" he inquired.

The boy frowned. What was this money all the *haoles* seemed so interested in, so vocal about? It meant nothing to him, and never would.

"I guess so," he replied casually. "Dollar in my coat, I think."

Smith's eyes glittered. "Lend it to me. I'll pay it back before night. All the rest I owe you, too. How much do I owe you, anyhow?"

"Can't remember," Frank answered, and sang again.

"I'll have lots of money before the day's out," Smith continued, a note of excitement in his voice.

Frank sang softly. A queer thing to get excited about, money, when the sky was so blue, the water so warm, and there was such a deep satisfaction just in lying on the white beach and humming a song.

"In your coat, you say?" Smith persisted.

Frank nodded. "Go and get it. The locker door's open."

Smith went at once. When he returned he held a dollar bill in one hand, and in the other a small canvas.

"I'm taking that picture I left with you, Frank," he explained. "Something tells me there's a market for my work at last." He stared at the painting critically. A dark-skinned, black-eyed girl stood against a background of cool green. She held a crimson flower between her lips, and she had the look of the tropics, of lazy islands lost in southern seas. "You know," the beach-comber added with almost reluctant admiration, "that's not half bad."

"Yeah," said Frank.

"Not bad at all," Smith continued. "But then, they told me I had talent, Frank. I heard it in New York—and in Paris too. Talent—maybe a touch of genius—but not much else. No backbone—no character—nothing to back it up. You've got to have character, my boy."

"Yeah," repeated Frank idly.

"You know, Frank, painters without half my skill—oh, hell, what's the use? Why should I complain? Look at Corot, Frank. Not one of his pictures was sold during his lifetime. Look at Manet. You know what the critics did to Manet? They laughed at him."

"Yeah," continued Frank. He threw down his guitar, leaped to his feet and, running across the sand, dove like a fish into two feet of water. Smith looked after him. He shook his head.

"No interest in painting," he muttered. "Just music. Well, that's something." He put the bill in his pocket, tucked the canvas under his arm, and went out to the street.

A trolley was approaching, bound for the city, and Smith swung aboard. He offered the dollar proudly—after this, perhaps, the conductor would not judge every one by his clothes. Once or twice, on the way into town, he looked again at his painting. His opinion of it grew even better.

At a lunch room in town he treated himself to a breakfast such as he had not known in several days, then moved on to the Waioli Hotel. His entrance there evoked no great enthusiasm. The clerk stared at him with open disapproval. "What do you want?" he inquired coldly.

"Mr. Fyfe stopping here?" the beach-comber asked.

"He is—but he sleeps late. I can't disturb him."

"You'd better disturb him." There was a sudden note of authority in Smith's voice. "I've an appointment—very important. Mr. Fyfe wants to see me more than I want to see him."

The clerk hesitated, and then took up a telephone. In a moment he turned to the beach-comber. "Be down right away," he announced.

Boldly Smith dropped into a chair and waited. Fyfe appeared almost at once; evidently he had not slept late to-day. There was a worried look in his eyes. He came over to the beach-comber. "You wanted to see me?" he said. "I'm on my way to the theater. Come along."

He left his key at the desk and strode toward the door, Smith struggling to keep up with him. They walked in silence. Finally the actor turned.

"Why be so indiscreet?" he inquired. "You could have telephoned me and I'd have met you."

Smith shrugged. "Telephoning costs money," he replied. "And I haven't much money—yet."

There was a world of meaning in that last word. Fyfe led the way from the more modern quarter of the city into the Oriental district. They moved on past shops crammed with silks, linens, embroideries, jade and porcelains. Bales and baskets filled with the foodstuffs of the Orient encroached upon the sidewalk.

"I take it you expect to have money soon?" Fyfe said at last.

Smith smiled. "Why not? Last night I did you a favor. Oh—I'm nobody's fool. I know why you made that fake confession. You were afraid I was going to repeat what I heard when I was standing outside that window. Weren't you?"

"Just what did you overhear?"

"Enough, believe me. I heard that woman—the woman somebody killed later on—I heard her tell you that she——"

"Never mind!" The actor looked nervously about. Nothing but flat expressionless faces, dark eyes that avoided his.

"I think I fell in with your plan very neatly," Smith reminded him. "When that Chinese detective, after he'd punctured your confession, asked me again what I'd heard—well, I said what you wanted me to, didn't I? I backed up what you'd been saying. I could have exploded a bomb right then and there—but I didn't. Please remember that."

"I do remember it. And I rather expected you'd be around this morning to blackmail me——"

"My dear sir"—Smith raised a thin freckled hand—"you might have spared me that. I have some shreds of respectability left, and—er—what you said is scarcely in my line. It just occurred to me that as an intelligent man, a practitioner of one of the allied arts, you might possibly be interested in my work." He indicated the canvas. "I happen to have a sample with me," he added brightly.

Fyfe laughed. "You're a rather subtle person, Mr. Smith. Suppose I did buy one of your paintings—what would you do with the money?"

Smith licked his lips. "I'd get out of this place for ever. I'm fed up here. For the past year I've been thinking about going home—to my folks in Cleveland. I don't know whether they'd be glad to see me—if I had decent clothes and a bit of money in my pocket—that might help."

"How did you get here in the first place?" the actor inquired.

"I went down to the South Seas to paint. Might be a good place for some people—but for me—well, the first thing I knew I was on the beach. After a long time, my people sent me money to come home. I managed to get aboard a boat, but unfortunately it stopped for a day at this port. And—have you tried any of the *okolehau* they call a drink in this paradise?"

Fyfe smiled. "I understand. You forgot to go back to your ship."

"My dear sir," Smith shrugged, "I forgot the world. When I woke up, my boat was two days out. Oddly enough, my father seemed annoyed. A rather impatient man."

They reached the river and, crossing a narrow stone bridge, entered Aala Park where, because of its convenient location, the dregs of the town congregate. Fyfe indicated a bench. They sat down together, and Smith handed over his canvas.

The actor glanced at it, and a look of surprise crossed his face. "By jove," he cried, "that's damned good."

"Glad to hear you say so," beamed Smith. "A bit unexpected, too, eh? I'm not what you'd call a born salesman, but I can't help pointing out that the thing might be valuable some day. There's just a chance. Think of the pride you could take in saying to your friends: 'Ah, yes—but I recognized his talent long ago. I was his first patron.'"

"Is this your real name—down here in the corner?"

The beach-comber hung his head. "My real name—yes," he replied.

Fyfe laid the canvas on his knee. "Just—what is the price?" he inquired.

"What am I offered?" Smith countered.

"If you're really sincere about wanting to go home," said the actor, "I'll be happy to arrange it for you. Not now, of course—the police wouldn't let you go at present. But when this has blown over a bit, I'll buy you a ticket—and give you something besides. In return for this canvas, you know."

"How much besides?"

"Two hundred dollars."

"Well, I don't know——"

"Make it two fifty. Look here, you're not dealing with a millionaire. I'm an actor on a salary, and it's none too big. I've had a long engagement in Honolulu, and I've saved a bit. I'm offering you about all I've got. If it's not enough, I'm sorry."

"It's enough," said the beach-comber slowly. "I don't mean to be hard on you. I'm not very proud of this, you know. But it's my chance—my chance to get away—lord, I've got to take it. We'll call it a bargain—a ticket to the mainland as soon as they'll let me go, and two fifty in my jeans. But say—how about meantime—I need a small advance now."

"For *okolehau,* eh?"

Smith hesitated. "I don't know," he said frankly. "I hope not. I don't want to touch it. I might talk, and spoil everything. I'm not thinking so much of you—spoil everything for myself, I mean." He stood up. "I won't touch it," he cried suddenly. "I'll fight, and I'll win. I give you my word of honor as a gentleman."

Fyfe looked him over, wondering what that was worth. He took out his wallet.

"I'll have to trust you, I suppose. I'll give you fifty now." Smith's eyes gleamed. "It's all I've got on me. Wait a minute!" He pushed away the beach-comber's eager hand. "Remember—you must be careful. If the police find that you've suddenly got money, they're bound to look into it."

"I was thinking of some new clothes," returned Smith wistfully.

"Not now," Fyfe warned. "Before you sail, yes—we'll attend to that. But now—just as you are for a while—and lie low." The actor was standing too, and he stared hard into the other's face. "I'm depending on you. A man who can paint as you can—don't be a fool. Go straight."

"By heaven, I will!" Smith cried, and hurried off across the park. For a moment Fyfe looked after him, then, with his recent purchase under his arm, walked slowly in the direction of the theater.

Smith went on to Beretania Street, and entered a small low-ceilinged room through a doorway that bore above it the faint sign: "Nippon Hotel." Behind the narrow desk stood a polite little Japanese. On the wall at his back hung the picture of a great liner cleaving the waves, under the words: *"Nippon Yusen Kaisha."*

"Hello, Nada," Smith said jauntily. "My old room vacant?"

"So sorry," hissed the Jap.

Smith threw a bill on to the counter. "Here's ten in advance," he remarked.

"So sorry you stay away such long time," hastily amended the clerk. "Room all ready—yes-s."

"I'll go and brush up a bit," Smith told him. "My baggage will be along later."

"You have money from home, I think," Nada smiled.

"Money from home, nothing," Smith responded airily. "I've sold a picture, Nada. You know, that's more than Corot ever did." He leaned across the counter confidentially. "Poor old Corot, Nada, never got on to himself. It's all in being outside the right window at the right time."

"Mebbe so," agreed Nada. "Much better you go along now. Room numba seven, like always."

"It's great to be home," Smith answered, and went out, whistling a merry tune.

Chapter XIII

BREAKFAST WITH THE CHANS

An hour after Smith took his morning swim, Charlie Chan rose and, stepping to his bedroom window, looked down on the bright panorama of town and sea. From Punchbowl Hill the view was one to stir the heart with beauty: green valleys and gleaming water, at this season the crimson umbrellas of the poinciana, golden shower trees blooming in generous profusion, here and there a brick-red bougainvillea vine. Charlie's lot was cast in a pleasant setting, and he loved to stand thus of a morning and reflect on his good fortune.

To-day, however, he preferred to reflect on the problem that lay before him. Insoluble it had appeared when he went to bed, but he had slept soundly in the knowledge that what is to be will be, and now he felt a new energy stirring within him. Was he, then, a mainland policeman to be stumped and helpless in the face of a question that had, no doubt, some simple answer? It was a matter, however, that called for prompt and intelligent action on his part. He thought of the crane who, waiting for the sea to disappear and leave him dry fish to eat, died of starvation. Chan had no intention of emulating that stupid bird.

It was a far from silent house that lay about him. Eleven children in one family make of early morning something of a bedlam. He heard their voices here, there and all about, shouting, expostulating, laughing and, in one case at least, weeping bitterly. With a comfortable feeling that the day had begun as usual, he prepared himself for his tasks.

In the dining-room he found that his three eldest children were lingering about the table, and as he entered, he saw them regarding him with a keen interest he had not aroused in that quarter for a long time. They all spoke at once, and he realized the cause of their interest. One of their heroines, according to the morning paper, was murdered, and they were going to see the miscreant punished or know the reason why.

"Quiet!" Charlie cried. "Can a man think beneath a tree filled with myna birds?" He turned to his oldest son, Henry, dapper in college-cut clothes and engaged in lighting a cigarette. "You should be at the store."

"Going right along, Dad," Henry replied. "But say—what's all this about Shelah Fane?"

"You have read it in the paper. Some one most unkindly stabbed her. Now, get on to your work."

"Who did it?" said Rose, the oldest girl. "That's what we want to know."

"A few others languish in same fix," her father admitted.

"You're on the case, aren't you, Dad?" Henry inquired.

Charlie looked at him. "In Honolulu, who else would be summoned?" he asked blandly.

"Well, what's the dope?" went on Henry, who had been Americanized to a rather painful extent. "When do you grab the guilty party, and what's his name?"

Charlie again looked at him, and sighed. These children were his link with the future—what sort of future, he often wondered.

"As I have frequent reason to point out, your language is sadly lacking in dignity," he reproved. "I have not yet apprehended the wrong-doer, and as a consequence, I do not know his name."

"But you will, won't you, Dad?" Rose put in. "You're not going to fall down on it, are you?"

"When have I ever so much as stumbled?" he wanted to know.

She was smiling at him mischievously. "Now, Dad——"

"When I was youthful," Chan broke in hastily, "it was regarded deadly sin to question all-pervading wisdom of father. He was honored and respected by children. Such a hint of failure as you have just offered would have been impossible."

She got up and came round to him, still smiling. "Times have changed. You're not going to fail, of course. We all know that. But this is one case your family is really interested in. So move fast, won't you? Don't take too much time out for Oriental meditation."

"Should I pause to think deeply," he replied, "I would be plenty lonesome man in this new world."

Rose kissed him and went out on her way to the bank where she was employed during the summer vacation. Henry stood up languidly.

"Will you be wanting the car to-night, Dad?" he inquired.

"If I ever wanted it, to-night will be the time," his father answered.

Henry frowned. "I guess I'll have to buy one," he said. "I can get a good second-hand bus on the installment plan——"

Charlie shook his head. "Work—and pay your way as you go," he advised. "Then you need fear no midnight knock upon the door."

"Old stuff," replied Henry, and made a leisurely exit.

Chan shrugged, and attacked his breakfast. Evelyn, aged fifteen, was addressing him. "Gee—I thought Shelah Fane was swell. I saw her in some swell parts."

"Enough!" cried Charlie. "Vast English language is spread out before you, and you select for your use the lowliest words. I am discouraged."

His wife appeared with his oatmeal and the tea. She was a jolly-looking woman, nearly as broad as Chan, with a placid smiling face. If her children and her husband had far outdistanced her in the matter of adjustment to a new land, she was, judging from her calm eyes, not at all distressed. "Heah about Shelah Fane," she remarked. "Plitty tellible thing."

"What do you know about Shelah Fane?" Charlie asked, surprised.

"All time chillun make talk, Shelah Fane, Shelah Fane," his wife said. "I think mus' be velly fine woman. I want you catch bad man plenty quick."

Chan choked on his hot tea. "If I do not, I perceive I am expelled from my own household. May I respectfully ask that you give me time. Much work to be done on this case."

"Mebbe you have moah tea," his wife suggested.

He drank a second cup, and then rose from the table. Evelyn brought his hat; they all seemed eager to speed him on his way. At the door he barely avoided falling over a round-faced little boy with keen black eyes that recalled those of his father. "Ah—the small Barry." He lifted the child and gave him an affectionate kiss. "Every day you grow more handsome, like fine namesake, Mr. Barry Kirk. Be good boy, now, and do not eat the plaster."

He went out and got his car, and as he drove down the hill he thought about his children. He had always been proud of the fact that they were all American citizens. But, perhaps because of this very fact, they seemed to be growing away from him—the gulf widened daily. They made no effort to remember the precepts and the odes; they spoke the English language in a manner that grated on Charlie's sensitive ear.

He passed the Chinese cemetery, with its odd headstones scattered down the sloping hillside. There lay his mother, whom he had brought from China to spend her last years in the house on Punchbowl Hill. What would she think if she could see her descendants now: see Henry in his dapper clothes; see Rose, brisk and efficient, planning to go to a university on the mainland in the autumn; hear Evelyn speaking that shabby, out-moded slang she picked up on the school grounds? His mother would not have approved, Charlie knew. She would have mourned for the old ways, the old customs. He mourned for them himself—but there was nothing he could do about it.

Reaching the business district of the city, he turned his attention to the tasks that lay before him. These were many, and he planned in what order he should attack them. Robert Fyfe was uppermost in his thoughts, so he drove at once to the Waioli Hotel.

Mr. Fyfe, the clerk said, had gone out with a man. What man? The description left no doubt as to the identity of Fyfe's caller, and Charlie frowned. What did Smith want of the actor? What had he overheard when he stood outside that pavilion window? Why had Fyfe confessed to a crime he had not committed? He couldn't have committed it, obviously. Not if his story of his actions on the previous night was correct—ah, yes, Charlie reflected, he must look into that.

"I think I heard Mr. Fyfe say he was going to the theater," the clerk remarked.

Chan was not up on the drama. "What theater, please?" he inquired.

"The Royal," the clerk told him, and Charlie went there.

He entered from the street, passing from a tiled lobby into the dark auditorium. On the stage the members of the stock company were rehearsing next week's piece. A few old kitchen chairs represented exits and entrances, and the players stood about, waiting for their cues. At the moment Fyfe was delivering a long speech; he gave it languidly, as though it were something with which he had no personal concern.

Charlie walked down the dim aisle. A man with a green velour hat pulled low over his eyes, who sat at a small table on the stage with the play script in his hand, looked down at the detective with evident annoyance. "What do you want?" he barked.

"Just one word, please, with Mr. Fyfe," Chan replied.

The actor stepped forward and, shading his eyes from the glare of the footlights, peered into the auditorium.

"Oh, yes—Inspector Chan," he said. "Won't you come up, please?"

Panting from the effort, Charlie boosted his heavy bulk on to the stage.

Fyfe was smiling and cordial. "What can I do for you this morning, Inspector?" he inquired.

Charlie regarded him through half-shut eyes. "Not much, I fear, unless maybe mood has altered overnight. You will recall I arranged for you, somewhat against your wish, a very nice alibi. I am here now to verify myself. A mere matter of form."

"Surely," nodded Fyfe. "Oh, Wayne," he called. Reluctantly the man in the green hat got up and came over to them. "This is Mr. Wayne, our stage manager—Inspector Chan, of the Honolulu police. The Inspector is here regarding that affair last night. Wayne—what time was it when you rang up last evening?"

"Eight-twenty," growled Wayne. "Five minutes late."

"I was standing beside you when you rang up?"

"Yes—you were. Though where you were when we were hammering on your door, I'm damned if I know."

"The Inspector, however, does," Fyfe returned. "Was that all you wanted, Mr. Chan?"

"One other thing." Chan addressed the stage manager. "In play which you perform this present week, does Mr. Fyfe in actor capacity indulge in use of knife?"

"A knife?" repeated Wayne. "Why, no—there's no knife in this play. It's a polite drawing-room comedy."

"Thank you so much," Charlie said, bowing. "That is all." He turned on Robert Fyfe a speculative eye. "Will you come with me, please?"

He led the way down into the auditorium, thinking deeply as he did so. Shelah Fane was seen alive at eight-twelve. Robert Fyfe was in the wings of the theater, ready to go on, at eight-twenty. Just eight minutes—no one could possibly travel the distance from Waikiki to town in that time. Fyfe's alibi was perfect. And yet——

In the darkened foyer back of the last row Charlie paused, and the two leaned on the rail.

"I am still wondering, Mr. Fyfe," the detective remarked, "why you made false confession that you killed Shelah Fane."

"I'm inclined to wonder a bit myself, Inspector."

"Obviously you did not kill her."

"I'm afraid you must think me a fool," Fyfe said.

"Other way about, I think you very smart man."

"Do you, really? That's flattering, I'm sure."

"There was reason for that confession, Mr. Fyfe."

"If there was, it has quite escaped my memory at this time, Inspector."

"Much better you tell me. Otherwise you place obstacle in path of justice."

"I must be the judge of that, Mr. Chan. I do not wish to hinder you. On the contrary I am eager for your success."

"Under such a circumstance, I find that difficult to believe." Chan was silent for a moment. "You have seen our friend the beach-comber this morning?"

Fyfe hesitated. He regretted more than ever the public nature of his meeting with Smith. Then he threw back his head and laughed—a laugh too long delayed, as Charlie noted.

"I certainly have," the actor admitted. "He called on me almost before I was up."

"For what purpose?"

"To get money, of course. I imagine he is making the rounds of the people he met last night. He seemed to think that the mere meeting gave him a sort of claim on us all."

"You are too busy with plural words," Chan protested. "His claim, I think, was on you alone." The actor said nothing. "You gave him money?" Charlie persisted.

"Why—yes—a few dollars. I was rather sorry for him. He is not a bad painter——" Fyfe stopped suddenly.

"How do you know he is not a bad painter?" Chan was quick to ask.

"Well—he—he left a canvas with me——"

"This canvas?" Charlie stepped down the aisle, and picked up something from a vacant seat. "I noted it as we came back here together," he explained. "If you do not mind, I will take it to light and examine it."

"By all means," the actor agreed.

Charlie walked to the door, and pushing it open, gazed for a moment at the painting. The eyes of that girl, posed against green shrubbery, seemed strangely alive. He came back to Fyfe's side.

"You are correct," he remarked, dropping the canvas into one of the chairs. "The man has talent. Pity such a one must resort to—blackmail."

"Who said it was blackmail?" demanded Fyfe.

"I say so. Mr. Fyfe, I could place you beneath arrest——"

"Isn't my alibi satisfactory?"

"Quite. But you hamper my work. For the last time—what was it Smith, the beach-comber, heard your ex-wife say to you?"

The stage manager came to the footlights, and called.

"I'm so sorry," said Fyfe, "but I'm keeping the company. I really must go along——"

Chan shrugged. "The inquiry is young, as yet. Before I am through, I will know, Mr. Fyfe."

"Drop in any time," said Fyfe blandly, holding out his hand. "Too bad I must leave you now, but an actor's life, you know——"

Chan gravely shook hands, and the actor hurried up the aisle. As he returned to the bright street, Charlie wore a puzzled frown. He knew that behind Fyfe's suave manner there lurked something of vital importance—something that might, indeed, solve his problem. Yet he would never get it from Fyfe. The beach-comber—ah, perhaps. He made a mental note of the beach-comber.

Climbing back into his flivver, Chan drove over to King Street and turned in the direction of Waikiki. As he passed the public library, set well back from the street amid great trees, he was tempted to stop. It occurred to him that he ought to read, in a Los Angeles paper, the story of Denny

Mayo's murder. Buried in the yellowed columns describing that spectacular moment in the movie colony's history, he might discover a line that would at once put him on the true scent in his search for Shelah Fane's assailant.

With quick decision he swung about and returned to the library. In another moment, he was addressing the woman at the library desk.

"Is it possible that I obtain at once Los Angeles paper for June, three years ago?" he inquired.

"Certainly, Mr. Chan," she answered. "Just fill out the card."

He filled it hastily, and saw it passed to a young assistant. The girl started to move toward the files, glancing at the card as she did so. She turned and came back.

"I'm sorry," she said. "I just happened to remember. That volume of the *Los Angeles Times* is in use just now."

"In use?" Chan was surprised.

"Yes. A gentleman took it out half an hour ago."

"Can you describe this gentleman?"

The girl nodded toward the reading-room. "He's still there. By that farther window."

Chan went over and peered round the corner of a bookcase. Seated bent over a huge gray-bound volume, he saw Huntley Van Horn. The picture actor did not look up; he seemed grimly intent on what he was doing. With a gesture toward the desk, meant to convey the fact that he dropped the whole matter, Chan walked softly out of the building.

Chapter XIV

THE PAVILION WINDOW

Charlie went to the street, got into his flivver, and in another moment was traveling rapidly toward Waikiki. It was good to feel the faithful little car shuddering under him again; so often in the past it had carried him along on the trail of innumerable clues. Many of these clues had led him, as he put it, "into presence of immovable stone wall." Thereupon he had swung the car about, seeking a new road. And the road that ended in victory had, in most cases, stretched before him at last.

As he sped through the brilliant morning, he thought of Huntley Van Horn. He pictured the cinema actor on the night before, walking across the lawn at the very moment when the black camel must have been kneeling at Shelah Fane's gate. No one was with the actor, no one saw him; he could easily have stepped into the pavilion, silenced the woman for ever and then calmly joined the two people on the beach.

What sort of man was Van Horn? Charlie wished he had read a few of the movie gossip magazines his children were always bringing into the house. Not the sleek, pretty boy type of film favorite, that was evident. Cynical, aloof, well-poised, he was the type who could keep his own counsel and turn an expressionless face on any one who sought to pry into his affairs. Ah, yes—Mr. Van Horn would bear thinking about. Such thinking might yield a rich reward.

But it was not with Van Horn that Chan was immediately concerned. He was on Kalakaua Avenue now, and though the sun was still shining above him, he had entered a zone where rain was falling. He saw, as he approached the hotels, tourists who wore rain-coats and carried umbrellas; evidently they took this liquid sunshine with a seriousness that amused a *kamaaina* like Charlie. He turned sharply to the right and, moving on past the lovely gardens of the Grand Hotel, parked his car in the drive at the rear. Walking unconcerned through the drizzle, he went over and ascended the hotel steps.

The head bell-man, a Chinese boy with a winning smile, greeted him in Cantonese. Chan paused to chat for a moment. No, he explained, he was not looking for any one in particular; he would, with kind permission, stroll about a bit. He crossed the high cool lobby, returning the jovial greeting of a young assistant manager.

He walked down the long corridor, toward the lounge. Unlike many of his fellow citizens of Honolulu, he had no feeling of somewhat resentful awe in this impressive interior. Having been to the mainland he regarded himself as a traveled man, a judge of hotels, and he approved heartily of this recent addition to the charms of Waikiki. He nodded affably at the flower girl, and stood for a moment in the entrance to the lounge. This room always inspired him. Through the great archways opening on the terrace he caught the shimmer of the sea, breath-taking fragments of a scene no coast in the world can surpass.

The huge room was empty of guests, but a few silent Oriental servants were busy arranging the floral decorations for the day. On tiny slivers of bamboo stuck in bowls of sand, they mounted innumerable hibiscus flowers, beautiful and fragile blossoms that would fade when evening came. Chan passed through to the terrace facing the ocean, and luck was with him. The only occupants of the place at that moment were the two old people with whom he had seen Tarneverro talking the previous evening. He stepped over to the Hongkong chairs where they sat, and stood looking down at them. The man put aside his morning paper; the woman glanced up from her book.

Chan bowed low. "May I wish you good morning," he said.

"Good morning, sir," the old man replied courteously. There was a pleasant Scotch burr to his words, and his face, lined by hard work under a hot sun, was as honest as any Charlie had ever seen.

Chan pushed back his coat. "I am Inspector Chan of the Honolulu police. You have, I think, perused in the morning paper story of quick finish of noted actress. I am sorry to intrude my inspeakable presence between you and this charming view, but gentleman you know was friend of the departed lady. It therefore becomes inevitable that I speak to you for short moment."

"Happy to meet you," said the old gentleman. He rose, and pulled up a chair. "Be seated, Inspector. I am Thomas MacMaster, of Queensland, Australia, and this is Mrs. MacMaster."

Chan achieved a notable bow, and the old lady gave him a quick kindly smile. A bit of idle chatter seemed in order.

"You are enjoying nice holiday?" the detective inquired.

"That we are," returned MacMaster. "And we've earned it, eh, Mother? Aye, after long years on a sheep ranch, we're off to revisit old Scotland at last. A very leisurely journey, Inspector; we mean to miss nothing along the way. And delighted we are"—he waved toward the beach—"that we did not miss this bonny spot."

His wife nodded. "Aye, bonny it is. We're very much afraid we'll no have the strength of character to move on."

"Speak for yourself, Mother," MacMaster said. "When the moment comes, I'm sure I'll have strength for two. Do not forget that Aberdeen is waiting."

"In behalf of Honolulu," beamed Chan, "my warmest thanks for all these treasured compliments. I recognize they come from honest lips, and my heart feels itself deeply touched. But reluctantly I must approach subject of last night's homicide. May I open my remarks by pointing out that some *malihini*—some stranger—must be responsible for this cruel event? Here people are kind, like climate. We seldom murder," he added feelingly.

"Of course," murmured the old lady.

Looking up, Charlie saw Tarneverro in the doorway. The fortune-teller's dark face lighted with satisfaction when he saw the group on the terrace, and he came rapidly down the steps. Chan sighed. He would have preferred to do this thing himself.

"Ah, good morning, Inspector," Tarneverro said. "Good morning, Mrs. MacMaster. And how are you, sir?"

"A wee bit lost," answered the old man. "I can not feel just right and not be at my work. But Mother tells me I must learn to rest."

"You certainly must—you have it coming to you," Tarneverro smiled. "Inspector, I am happy to see you on the job at this early hour. You are no doubt here to verify my alibi, and that is quite fitting and proper. Have you asked these two friends of mine the important question?"

"I was approaching it with suitable preparation."

"Ah, yes," the fortune-teller continued. "Mr. MacMaster, in the matter of that unfortunate affair last night—I happen to have been one of the few people in the Islands acquainted with the poor girl, and it is important that I establish to the Inspector's satisfaction the fact that I was elsewhere at the moment of her death. Luckily I can establish it—with your help." He turned to Charlie. "After I left you in the lounge last night, you saw me return to my conversation with Mr. and Mrs. MacMaster. Mr. Macaster will tell you what happened after that."

The old man frowned thoughtfully. "Mr.—er—Tarneverro suggested that we go out on the veranda—I believe you call it a lanai—that looks across the palm court. We did so, and for the matter of a half-hour sat talking about the old days in Queensland. Finally Mr. Tarneverro had a look at his watch. He said it was thirty minutes after eight and that he must leave us, as he had a dinner engagement down the beach. We stood up——"

"Begging humblest pardon," Chan cut in, "did you by any chance consult own timepiece?"

"Aye, that I did," returned the old man. His manner was very earnest and there was an unmistakable ring of truth to his words. "I took out my watch——" He removed an old-fashioned timepiece from his pocket. "'I'm a wee bit fast,' I said. 'Eight-thirty-five, I make it. Mother, it's time old folks like us went up-stairs.' You see, on the ranch we were always early abed, and well-established habits are hard to break. So we came into the hotel. Mother and I stopped at the elevators, and Mr. Tarneverro went round the corner to his own room on the first floor. While we waited for the lift, I stepped to the desk to set my watch the correct time. Eight-thirty-two it was then, and I made the change. Those are the facts, Inspector, and Mother and I will swear to them."

Chan nodded. "The speech of some is like wind in empty space," he said. "But blind man could see your word is good."

"Aye, it always has been. From Aberdeen to Queensland no one has ever questioned it, Inspector."

"You have known Mr. Tarneverro long time?" Charlie asked.

Tarneverro answered. "Ten years ago," he remarked, "I was playing in a Melbourne theater. I was an actor in those days, you know. Our company stranded, and I went out to Mr. MacMaster's ranch, a few miles from Brisbane, to work for him. I stayed a year—the happiest year of my life. For as you may see by looking at them, these two are the kindest people in the world, and they were like father and mother to me——"

"We did nothing," the old lady protested. "It was a joy to have you and——"

"Alone and lonely as I was," Tarneverro interrupted, "it was great luck to come upon people like these. You can imagine my delight when I ran across them again at this hotel the other day." He rose. "I take it that is all you wanted to know, Mr. Chan. I'd like to have a talk with you."

"That is all," remarked Chan, rising too. "Lady,—sir,— may vacation continue as happy as it is this bright morning on undescribably lovely beach. I am so pleased that our paths met here at famous crossroads."

"We share that pleasure, sir," MacMaster replied. His wife nodded and smiled. "We'll be thinking of ye as we travel on to Aberdeen. Our very best wishes for success."

Charlie and the fortune-teller went inside, and sat down on a sofa. "You are favorite of the gods," Chan remarked. "If I needed alibi I would ask nothing better than word from honest people such as those."

Tarneverro smiled. "Yes—they're a grand pair. Simple and wholesome and addicted to all the old virtues." He paused. "Well, Inspector, you know where I was during those vital eighteen minutes. How about the others?"

"I know also where Robert Fyfe was," Charlie replied, "though much about his actions puzzles me. Speaking of the rest, they have no such luck. Not one has offered alibi."

Tarneverro nodded. "Yes—and one among them may need an alibi badly before this affair is ended. You had, I take it, no flash of inspiration in the night?"

Chan sadly shook his head. "I had nothing but plenty good sleep. And you?"

The other smiled. "I'm afraid I weakly fell into a dreamless slumber too. No—I have thought hard, but I'm afraid I can't help you much. There are so many possibilities. Shall we go over them? Rita and Wilkie Ballou. Both in Hollywood at the time of Denny Mayo's death. Mayo was said to be a bit careless with the ladies—and it is clear that Ballou is a notably jealous man."

"I think about Ballou," remarked Chan slowly.

"It might pay," Tarneverro agreed. "He was wandering about—came into the living-room to get a cigarette—claims he stayed there. Turning from him for the time being, there's Alan Jaynes. His state of mind was rather emotional last night. Who knows anything about him? Suppose that like that of Ballou, his is a wildly jealous nature. He saw those flowers—not his—on the shoulder of the woman he loved. We found them trampled under foot, as though in rage. The Mayo affair, as I believe you pointed out, may have had nothing to do with Miss Fane's murder, after all. Perhaps it was just a case of mad unreasoning jealousy——"

"Perhaps," answered Chan calmly. "There is also Martino."

"Yes—Martino," repeated the fortune-teller. A black look swept across his handsome face. "It would give me great pleasure to help you pin this thing on him. He has made some very rude remarks about me——"

"What sort of man you call him?" Charlie asked.

"Oh, he seems to have brains," Tarneverro admitted. "And a kind of rude strength—a queer combination, the esthete and the brute in one package. He wasn't in Hollywood when Mayo was killed, but once again—perhaps we are on the wrong trail there. Martino's been a bit of a ladies' man—there may have been some unsuspected relationship between him and Shelah Fane. Certainly that handkerchief in his pocket had a fishy look to me. Of course he denied he owned it—who wouldn't? But if any one placed it on Martino's person, he was taking a tremendous and unnecessary risk. Why not throw it into the bushes—drop it on the lawn? Why attempt the difficult, the dangerous? The handkerchief, Inspector, may have been Martino's own property. He may have gone on carrying it after the murder, quite innocent of the fact that it contained those splinters of glass. Unless"—the fortune-teller paused—"unless you have evidence that it belonged to some one else?"

Chan regarded him with sleepy eyes. "I have so little evidence," he sighed. "Languishing in such a state, how gladly I hear you talk. Continue, please, to dispense logic and eloquence, those twin blossoms of speech. I now bring up the name of Huntley Van Horn."

Tarneverro regarded him keenly. "Have you anything on Van Horn?"

"I regret to note that he has no alibi. Also, he was at proper place at proper time to do the deed." Chan paused, and decided he would keep some matters to himself. "Aside from that, I have nothing of importance. Deign to state your opinion of the man."

"Well," said Tarneverro, "I haven't thought much about Van Horn. He's an odd, rather bitter sort of chap—a notorious bachelor—the despair of all the women. No breath of scandal has ever touched him. I have always admired the fellow, though heaven knows he has never been any too friendly to me. He's an intelligent chap, with excellent taste—a bit conceited, perhaps, but no man could receive the adulation he does, and escape that." He considered a moment. "No, Inspector," he added with sudden decision, "in spite of the fact that his opportunities were excellent, as you point out, I can not see Huntley Van Horn as our quarry in this affair."

Charlie rose. "Thank you for this little conversation." He glanced at his watch. "Now I must haste to home of Shelah Fane. You will accompany me?"

"I'm sorry," Tarneverro replied, "but I am not at liberty to do so just at present. You'll let me know of any new developments, won't you? It isn't mere curiosity on my part. If we are to work together I must, of course, know what you are doing."

"We will encounter from time to time," Chan assured him. They walked to the hotel door.

The head bell-man said something to Tarneverro in Cantonese, and the fortune-teller regarded him with a blank uncomprehending look. "What does he say?" he inquired of Charlie.

"He makes most respectful inquiry after your health this splendid morning," Chan translated.

"Oh, I'm fine, Sam," Tarneverro smiled. There was a puzzled expression on Sam's broad face. "So long, Inspector," the fortune-teller continued. "Ring me up if you strike anything new. I'll be hunting about myself—anything I can do—well, I'm with you to the finish, as I told you."

"You are so extremely kind," bowed Chan, and returned to his car.

The front lawn of Shelah Fane's house, when Charlie arrived there, lay peaceful and serene in the shade of its ancient banyan tree. Jessop answered the door, perfect in manner and attire, as always.

"How are you, Constable?" he said. "The morning is rather on the gorgeous side, is it not?"

"Presume so," agreed Chan. "It is matter we do not notice here. All mornings much the same."

"Which must, if I may say so, sir, grow a trifle monotonous in time." The butler followed Chan into the living-room. "Now in England, Constable, drawing back the curtains of a morning is something of a sporting proposition."

Charlie stood looking about the great room, where so much had happened the night before. It was calm, quiet and sunny now.

"Miss Julie and Mr. Bradshaw are in the neighborhood of the beach, sir," Jessop remarked. "One of your officers—a Mr. Hettick, I believe—is busily engaged in the pavilion."

"Ah, yes—Hettick is our finger-print expert," Charlie explained. "I will go outside at once." On the lawn he encountered the two young people, who greeted him warmly. "So sorry to develop into pest," he said to Julie. "But path of duty is often rocky one."

"Why, you could never be that," she smiled. "We've been expecting you."

He glanced at her, so fresh and lovely, her blue eyes wide and innocent. He thought of the emerald ring.

"Well, how did you like my story in the paper this morning?" Bradshaw wanted to know.

"My perusal was of a necessity hurried," Chan replied. "Imagine it covered the ground."

"Is that the best you can say for it?" the boy complained.

Charlie shrugged. "Always think twice before you scatter tributes," he answered. "If no one had praised the donkey's song, he would not still be singing." He grinned. "The comparison is, of course, unhappy one. I take it you enjoy a pleasant morning?"

"Oh, I just ran out to help Julie," the boy told him. "I've been acting as a shock-absorber between her and the reporters. The fellows on the evening paper weren't very polite. They seem a bit miffed the story didn't break right for them."

"A natural feeling," Chan replied.

"What are you going to do now?" asked Bradshaw.

"Propose to look about in bright light of day," Charlie answered.

"I'll help you," Bradshaw said. "Julie you just sit down and relax. Close your eyes and try not to think. Nobody ever has at Waikiki and you can't tell—it might be dangerous."

The girl smiled at him and dropped on to a beach chair.

"Want to keep the poor kid cheered up," Bradshaw explained, as he and Chan walked toward the pavilion. "This has been a pretty tough shock for her. But in time I think I can convince her that all her troubles are over. That is—if she'll marry me."

"You possess excellent opinion of yourself," Charlie smiled.

"Why shouldn't I? I know myself so well."

As they reached the pavilion, Hettick came out. He had been brought over from the mainland at the time of the reorganization to strengthen the force, and he had never been very cordial to Charlie, whom he had replaced in the rôle of finger-print expert.

"Good morning, Mr. Hettick," Chan said politely. "Have you had successful time of it?"

"Not very," the man replied. "Plenty of prints, but mostly those of the murdered woman. All the others can be accounted for, I guess. Come inside, and I'll show you——"

"One little moment," interrupted Charlie. "First I take careless stroll about outside of place."

Followed by Bradshaw, he made his way through some bushes at the side of the cottage, and came out on the public beach that bounded the grounds on the west. Beneath the single pavilion window which opened on that beach—the one under which Smith had stood the previous night—he paused.

A great many footprints were there now, and those of the beach-comber barely distinguishable. Charlie stooped down and carefully sifted the sand. With a little cry of satisfaction, he stood erect again.

"Important discovery," he announced.

Bradshaw came nearer. He saw in Charlie's palm the remains of a small cigar, the size of a cigarette.

"Trampled into the sand," Charlie added. "I would never have expected to find this here."

"Why—I know only one man who smokes these," the boy cried. "I saw him—last night——"

"You are quite correct," Chan beamed. "One man, and who would believe he could act so careless? I am consumed with wonder. When did Mr. Alan Jaynes stand outside this window—and why?"

Chapter XV

"TWO JUICES OF THE ORANGE"

Charlie took an empty envelope from his pocket and carefully placed his latest discovery inside it. He and the boy again penetrated the bushes and entered the pavilion. Hettick was sitting idly by the dressing-table, with the paraphernalia of his calling spread out before him.

Dropping down on a wicker chair, Chan glanced around the room where, only the night before, he had encountered tragedy. The detective's face was placid and serene; he might have been awaiting the luncheon bell untroubled by any problem. Through an enormous plate-glass window he watched a liner from the coast move slowly into port.

"You have enjoyed no luck here, Mr. Hettick?" he inquired.

"Not much," replied Hettick. "The things on the table are covered with prints—all those of the murdered woman herself. I got her record at the mortuary this morning. By the way, the coroner asked me to tell you he has postponed the inquest until to-morrow. He expects you to have something by then."

Chan shrugged. "Thank him for the compliment. Also inform him I will exchange places with him at any moment." His gaze returned to the room; the woodwork, he noted, had recently been painted white. Suddenly he rose and stepped to the small window opening on the beach. "You have not tested this sill, I believe," he remarked.

"No—as a matter of fact, I haven't," Hettick answered. "I meant to, but it slipped my mind."

Chan grinned. "Mind gets so slippery in warm climate. May I humbly suggest you do so now?"

Hettick came over and covered the sill with his lamp black. With practised hand he applied the camel's-hair brush.

Charlie and the boy crowded close. "Ah!" cried Chan. On the smooth white surface of the sill were the marks of some one's fingers and thumb.

"These were not made by Shelah Fane?" Charlie inquired.

"No," answered Hettick. "Those were left by a man's hand."

Chan stood, deep in thought. "Recent, too. We achieve some progress now. A man's hand. A man opened that screen, climbed up on sill. Why? To enter room, of course. When? Last night, when murder was in atmosphere. Yes, we move, we advance." He paused. "What man?" In his coat pocket, his fingers touched the envelope containing the cigar stub. He turned with sudden decision. "One thing is certain. I must without delay obtain thumb prints of Alan Jaynes." Smiling at Jimmy Bradshaw, he added: "Police have fine clue and promise early arrrest. But if you publish one word of this, I recall matter of your laundry and put you in jail at once."

"I won't use it, Charlie," promised the boy. "What are you going to do now?"

"I propose to leave you with nobody for company—except Miss Julie. And who is she?"

"Wait a minute, and I'll tell you. She's the most——"

"Later," cut in Chan. "Much later. Mr. Hettick, I request that you remain here until my return. Your keen eye will be required. I am off for session at Grand Hotel."

He left the pavilion, and the boy followed. As Charlie passed out of sight around the corner of the house, Bradshaw went over to where Julie sat. He dropped down beside her.

"Has that funny policeman gone?" she asked eagerly.

"For a few minutes. He'll be back before he's missed." Looking up at her, the boy thought he saw an expression of fear cross her delicate face. He wondered. "Charlie has just made an important discovery outside the pavilion window," he added.

"W-what?" she inquired.

"I don't believe he'd like to have me tell you," Bradshaw answered. Not just yet, at any rate. But—what about this Alan Jaynes? You don't know him very well, do you?"

"Scarcely at all," the girl replied. "I never saw him

until yesterday morning. Shelah met him in Tahiti—I believe she was very fond of him. But Shelah was fond of—so many people. She was even—fond of me." Without warning Julie turned away her head and burst into tears.

Bradshaw got up and laid a hand on her heaving shoulder. "Now—now," he said uncomfortably. "You mustn't do that. You're ruining all my press stuff. Waikiki, the abode of peace, the crescent beach where happiness rules supreme. Suppose one of these tourists who took me at my word should see you."

"I—I'm sorry," she sobbed. "I'm not happy; I can't be."

"No, of course you can't—not at this moment, I mean. But why not look ahead to all the happiness that's coming, and draw a little advance on that?"

"I'll—I'll never be happy again," she told him.

"Nonsense. I'm going to make the world as glamorous for you as I've made this town in the Tourist Bureau ads. When we're married——"

She pushed him away. "We'll never be married. Oh, it's terrible. I'm horrid, really—and you don't suspect. You'll hate me—when you know."

"Do tell! Look at me." He leaned over and kissed her.

"You mustn't," she cried.

"I've got to," he smiled. "It's my duty. I've advertised this place for its romance, and romance there must be if I have to attend to it myself. Now listen to me—inside a week or less all this will be over, and you can begin to forget. Charlie Chan is going to solve the puzzle at any minute——"

"Oh—do you think so?"

"He's sure to. You can't keep anything from Charlie."

"I wonder," said the girl.

"I know," Bradshaw replied firmly.

Scarcely sharing Bradshaw's confidence, Chan was at that moment entering the lobby of the Grand Hotel. He waved a hand toward the bell-man, and went at once to the desk.

"I arrive again," he remarked to the clerk. "For a non-paying guest, I am plenty much in evidence around this place. Will you give me number of room occupied by Mr. Alan Jaynes, if you will be so good?"

The clerk smilingly gave it to him, and pointed out the house telephones at the right of the desk. Charlie was relieved to hear the Britisher's answering voice. He politely requested a moment's conversation, and Jaynes replied that he would come down immediately.

Charlie walked with unaccustomed speed to the lounge. A small Filipino bell-boy was there alone, and the detective summoned him.

"I wish to be served with two of your delicious orange-juice drinks," he announced.

"Yes, sir," replied the boy.

"I will also accompany you while you secure same." The boy appeared taken back, but it was not his rôle to argue. From out of the jungle he had come to learn that the guest is always right.

Charlie followed his small guide to the serving pantry, where they encountered a man in a white apron.

"Inspector Chan, of the Honolulu police," Charlie explained briefly. "I have just engaged to purchase two juices of the orange. Will you hand me the glasses in which you propose to place same, please?"

The servant was too weary to be surprised. The climate, as he often explained to his wife, had got him. He produced the glasses and Charlie, removing an immaculate handkerchief from his pocket, began to polish them briskly.

"This action, I hasten to say, involves no criticism of you," he remarked. "But I am reading lately about germs." He grinned. "A very dangerous form of animal life." It could be noted, however, that it was only the outside of the tumblers that concerned him. He completed the task, set the objects of his attention carefully down on the tray the boy had brought, and reaching into his pocket, handed a quarter to the serving man. "You will do me great favor if you will fill these receptacles without placing fingers on same." He turned to the boy. "That also applies to you. Do you understand? You are not to touch those glasses. Set tray on table as it is. Otherwise, when moment arrives for your tip, I develop far-away look in eye and can not see you."

Returning to the lounge, Charlie found the Britisher already there. "Ah—Mr. Jaynes," he said. "I am happy to see you again. You had good night's rest, I hope?"

Jaynes stared at him. "No," he replied, "I didn't; but what of it?"

"So sorry," Chan cried. "Waikiki is famous sleeping place, and being old resident of Honolulu, I experience deep pain when it fails to live up to reputation. Will you do me the honor to join me on this sofa?"

He dropped down on the seat, which creaked protestingly beneath him.

"Harsh voice of furniture proclaims to world my excessive avoirdupois," he continued affably. "I diet and I fast, but to no avail. What is to be, will be. Man—who is he to fix own weight upon the scales? All that is determined elsewhere."

Jaynes sat down beside him. "What can I do for you this morning, Inspector?" he inquired.

"You can accept, if you will be so kind, renewed apologies for detaining you on this island. Some people pronounce it Paradise, but even Paradise, I can appreciate, looks not so good when one is panting to travel elsewhere. Again my warm regrets. I assure you I apply myself with all possible speed to task of clearing up mystery, so that you may make quick exit."

"I'm glad to hear that," nodded Jaynes. He took out a case and offered Charlie one of his little black cigars. "No?" He lighted one himself. "You are making progress, I hope?"

"I encounter difficulties," Charlie admitted. "Those who know, don't talk; those who talk, don't know. But that is always to be expected in my work. Within last hour I think I see faint glimmer of light ahead. Ah——" The Filipino boy had arrived with the tray; he set it down on a small table before them. "I should have said, Mr. Jaynes, that I am on orange-juice diet, and the hour of the drink is here I have ventured to order same for you."

"Oh, no, thanks," replied the Britisher. "I don't believe——"

"Same is all prepared," Charlie protested, and a note of imminent offense crept into his voice. "The beverage is harmless. You are not going to refuse?"

"Well—thank you," said Jaynes. At the moment he wanted nothing less, but he knew how easily the feelings of a Chinese may be hurt, and he could not risk any further offense to this particular representative of the race. "You are very good." He reached for a glass.

Beaming, Charlie lifted his own. "We will drink to my quick success, since you desire it equally with me." He imbibed heartily, and set the glass down. "Presume mild nature of the liquid gives you hearty pain. I have noted how bitterly men from your country resent this prohibition."

"What prohibition?" Jaynes inquired.

"Ah, you mock and jeer. Well, it is noble experiment, but it is not new, as many think. The Emperor Yü, who came to the throne of China in year 2205 B. C., said when he tasted liquor for the first time, this will do my people much harm, and forbade its use. His edict had good effect for a while, but later got lost in dim pages of history. China," added Chan, drinking again, "like the purse of a generous man, has endured much. But it still survives."

Jaynes was looking at him with a deep curiosity. Had this odd policeman dropped in merely to discuss prohibition? Charlie noted the look.

"But to return to our mutton broth," he said. "I desire to make inquiries of you regarding last night. You are most unfortunate man not to possess nice alibi for motions during time of homicide. You were, as I understand things, wandering about plenty mad at fatal hour?"

"I'm afraid I was," Jaynes admitted.

"From the moment when you left Martino on beach until he went out and found you with announcement of murder, you exist quite alone?"

"Yes."

"Making your walk, how far down beach did you penetrate?"

"Only as far as the Moana Hotel. I sat there under the banyan tree and tried to think what I had better do."

"You did not—will you join me in another quaffing—ah, yes—you did not travel on to property of Shelah Fane?"

"I've just told you," replied Jaynes, "that I went only as far as the Moana. As I say, I sat down there to try to figure things out. When I had grown a bit calmer, it occurred to me that perhaps I was making a big row about nothing. A woman who could be so easily influenced by a silly fortune-teller—I asked myself whether she would, after all, make a satisfactory wife. Her life was far removed from mine—I began to feel that the whole affair might turn out to have been a mere passing infatuation with both of us. I resolved to take the boat at midnight and, if possible, forget the entire business. After that was decided, I felt better. I came back here, past the Outrigger Club, and just outside the hotel Martino met me with the appalling news of the poor girl's murder."

"No one noted you at Moana under banyan tree?"

"I fancy not. I sat in a dark corner."

"Were you ever in pavilion where Shelah Fane encountered finish?"

"No—I never saw the place."

"Then you could not have been in the neighborhood at any time? Hovering about window, for example?"

"Well, hardly." Without prompting, Jaynes took up his glass and drained it. Suddenly he stared at Charlie. "I say—why do you ask me that?"

"I seek only to narrow search," Chan explained. "That will be all, thank you. Can you name hour of next boat to mainland?"

"I certainly can," answered the Britisher. "There's one to-morrow at noon. I hope to heaven——"

"I will extend myself to the utmost," smiled Chan. "Though, to look at me, many might remark that I had already done so."

Jaynes laughed. "Don't let that thought deter you," he said. "You'll do your best, I know. By the way, I'm afraid I was a bit rude to you last night—but I was very anxious to get away. For many reasons—not only my business in the States—but this whole terrible affair—I wanted to be out of it. I still do. You understand?"

"I understand," nodded Chan gravely. His left hand, in the side pocket of his coat, touched a certain envelope. "I will say good morning," he added.

He stood watching the Britisher cross the terrace and stroll toward the sea. Sensing some one at his back, he turned just in time. An old bent Chinese who continually paraded the lounge in his native costume, armed with a brush and dust-pan, was reaching out for the glasses.

"Haie!" Chan seized the withered hand. "Do not touch, or the wrath of the seven watchful gods descends upon you." He took out his handkerchief and tenderly wrapped it round the glass from which Jaynes had drunk. "I am removing this, and the affair does not concern you."

But evidently the old man thought it did concern him, for he followed Charlie to the desk. There Chan encountered one of the managers. "I should like to purchase this object," he said, revealing what the handkerchief held. "Kindly name price."

The manager laughed. "Oh, that's all right. Take it along. What are you doing, Charlie? Collecting finger-prints from our harmless guests?"

"You are close to truth," nodded Chan. "Save perhaps

with that word harmless. Thank you so much. And now will you kindly call off this aged gentleman who thinks he has captured one of the forty thieves?"

The manager said something to the servant, who moved away, muttering to himself. His comments, Chan knew, were not complimentary, but he gave no heed. He hurried through the door to his car.

Deep in thought, he drove back to Shelah Fane's house. Were the finger-prints on this glass identical with those on the window-sill in the pavilion? If they were, then he was approaching journey's end.

Hettick was waiting, and to him Charlie entrusted his precious cargo, still redolent of orange juice. The expert set quickly to work. Presently he stood by the window, the tumbler in one hand, a magnifying-glass in the other. Chan came close, awaiting the verdict.

Hettick shook his head. "Nothing like it," he announced. "You've been on the wrong trail this time, Inspector."

Keenly disappointed, Chan sat down in a chair. So it had not been Alan Jaynes who entered this room last night? It had all seemed to fit in so neatly that up to this minute he had not had a doubt of it. On the wrong trail, eh? He hadn't cared for the way in which Hettick had said that. The men at the station had been in a rather unfriendly mood since Charlie's return from the mainland. They had expected to find him in a haughty and triumphant state of mind since his exploits there, and the fact that he had shown no trace whatever of such an attitude, had done nothing to lessen their envy. He had been forced to endure many joking remarks that held an undercurrent of hostility.

On the wrong trail, eh? Well, who didn't take the wrong path occasionally in this business? Where was the superman so good that he never erred?

On the wrong trail. Chan sat deep in thought Jaynes had been outside that window—the stub of the small cigar, which he had evidently forgotten, was proof enough. But it was not he who had pushed up the screen and entered, leaving the imprint of fingers on the white sill. Some one else had done that. Who? Who else had been——

Suddenly Charlie smote his forehead a resounding blow. "*Haie*—I have been complete and utter idiot. I move too fast, without proper thought. Everybody seeks to hurry me—even my own family. And I was not built for hurry.

Hurry is the wind that destroys the scaffolding." He turned to Hettick. "What has become of finger-print record of beach-comber, taken at station last night?"

"Oh," replied Hettick. "I've got that here." He produced a manila envelope from his pocket and removed a glass plate. "Do you think——"

"I think, yes—a little late, but still I think," said Charlie. He took the plate from the unresisting hand of his brother officer and hurried to the window. "Come quickly," he called. "Your glass—look! What is your decision?"

"They are the same," Hettick announced.

Triumph shone brightly in Charlie's little eyes. "At last I arrive somewhere," he cried. "Smith, the beach-comber, was in this room last night! Am I forever on wrong trail or do I have my lucific moments?"

Chapter XVI

A WORD OF WARNING

Chan's air of calm detachment had vanished for the moment, and he walked the floor as though inspired by his latest discovery.

"Smith, the beach-comber," he said once more. "Dreary bit of human wreckage cast up on shore of splendid island. Ragged remnant of a man—how busy he was around this building last night. A big evening, I think, in the life of Smith."

Hettick was gathering up the tools of his trade. "Well, I believe I'll go back to the station now," he remarked. "I've given you boys something to work on. Go out and make the most of it."

"Ah, you are clever detective," Chan grinned. "Things slip from mind sometimes, but when humble fellow worker recalls them, then you move on like avenging demon. You have given us material indeed. Yes, please return to station at once. I will arrive later, and in meantime I respectfully suggest that you send out alarm call for Smith. Tell Chief beach-comber must be pulled into station with no delay. Let all low dives be explored. Put Kashimo on it. He is our most passioned searcher, and what is better, he knows all cracks and crannies of modest little underworld."

Hettick promised he would deliver the message, and departed. Charlie followed at his heels. He saw Julie and Bradshaw on the lawn, and paused beside them. "You wish ride to town?" he inquired of the latter.

"No, thanks," Bradshaw replied. "I've got my car today. Besides Julie has just persuaded me to stay for lunch."

"May life hold for her no sterner task than such persuasion," smiled Chan. "I do not wish to cloud your future, Miss Julie, but must warn you that I return here soon."

He was skirting the house when Jessop appeared at the lanai door. "Ah—er—Constable," he said. "May I ask you to step inside just a moment?"

Struck by the seriousness of the butler's manner, Charlie passed through the door which the servant held open. "You have something to say to me?" he asked.

"I have, sir. Kindly come with me." Jessop led the way into a small reception-room near the front of the house. He entered it first—evidence of unusual abstraction on his part. "Oh—I beg your pardon, sir. I'll just close this door, so we may have an undisturbed tête-à-tête."

"Time is none too plentiful with me——" Chan began, somewhat surprised by these elaborate preparations.

"I know that, Constable, I will—er—plunge in at once." In spite of this promise, he hesitated. "My old father, who was for more than forty years the trusted employee of a rather exacting duke, remarked to me in my youth: 'A good servant, Cedric, sees all, knows all, but tells nothing.' It is only after prolonged and mature consideration, Constable, that I have determined to ignore that excellent counsel."

Chan nodded. "Circumstances," he remarked, "upset cases."

"Precisely, sir. I have always been a law-abiding man, and what is more, I am eager to see you get to the bottom of this matter without—if I may say so—further delay. Last evening I chanced to be busy in the hall at the moment when you were engaged in interviewing Miss Julie regarding the emerald ring. This may suggest to you that I was eavesdropping, but I can assure you that such duplicity was farthest from my thoughts. I heard the young lady tell you that Miss Fane had given her that ring early in the morning, and that she—Miss Julie, I mean—had held it in her possession from that moment on, until you discovered it in her room."

"Such was Miss Julie's story," Charlie agreed.

"I am at a complete loss to understand it, sir. I don't know what she meant by her testimony—but I do know this. At about seven last night, Miss Fane called me to her room and gave me the letter which I was to deliver to Mr. Tarneverro immediately on his arrival at the house. As she passed over the missive, I distinctly saw, gleaming on her right hand, the ring in question. I am positive on that point,

Constable, and prepared to offer a sworn statement along those lines."

Chan was silent for a moment. He thought of Julie O'Neill, so young, so innocent-looking. "Thank you very much," he said at last. "What you say seems of vast importance."

"I only hope it may not be so important as it appears," Jessop replied. "I tell you this, Constable, with considerable reluctance. I have nothing against Miss Julie—a charming young woman—indeed she is, sir. I was tempted for a long time to remain silent, but it struck me that my duty lay, most decidedly, in the opposite direction. Like yourself, I desire to see the miscreant in this affair adequately punished. Miss Fane was always extremely kind to me."

Chan moved toward the door. "I shall act upon your information at once," he announced.

Jessop looked uncomfortable. "If my name could only be kept out of it, sir——"

"Same may not be possible," Charlie told him.

Jessop sighed. "I recognize that, Constable. I can only say again that I am quite positive I saw the ring. My eyesight is excellent, which, to a man of my age, is a matter of deep satisfaction."

They went out into the hall. Anna, the maid, was slowly coming down the stairs. Chan turned to Jessop.

"Thank you again," he said. "You may go now."

The butler disappeared toward the kitchen, and Charlie waited for Anna at the foot of the stairs.

"Good morning," he remarked pleasantly. "I desire one word with you, please."

"Of course," replied Anna, and followed him into the living-room.

"You recall story of Miss Julie regarding the ring?"

"Naturally, sir."

"Same was given her by Miss Fane in early morning and remained in her possession. Have you anything to say regarding that?"

"Why—why what do you mean, sir?" the maid returned.

"You did not yourself see the ring on Miss Fane's finger during the day? Or when she came to you to procure pin for orchids?"

"If I did, it made no impression on me, sir."

"You see things, yet they make no impression?"

"You know how it is, sir. Things become familiar and

you don't really notice. What I mean is—the ring may or may not have been there. I'm afraid I can't say, sir."

"You wish the matter to stand at that?"

"I fear it must, as far as I am concerned."

Chan bowed. "Thank you—that is all."

He stepped through a French window, and walked slowly across the lanai. He had no heart for the task that faced him now, but many such tasks had confronted him in the past, and he had never faltered. Stepping out on the lawn, he went over to a beach swing where Bradshaw and the girl were sitting.

"Miss Julie," he began. The girl looked up at him, and at sight of his grave face, her own paled.

"Yes, Mr. Chan," she said in a low voice.

"Miss Julie, you have told me Miss Fane gave you that emerald ring soon after her arrival yesterday morning. Why did you tell me that?"

"Because it's the truth," Julie answered bravely.

"Then how do you account for fact that ring was seen on her finger last evening at seven?"

"Who says it was?" the girl cried.

"Is that important?"

"It is very important. Who says it was?"

"I learn it from what I think reliable source."

"You have no means of knowing how reliable, Mr. Chan. Who made that statement? Not Miss Dixon—she isn't up yet. It must have been one of the servants. Jessop, perhaps. Was it Jessop, Mr. Chan?"

"What does it matter——"

"But I assure you it matters very much. Because, you see, I don't stand very well with Jessop. There's an old grudge between us—on his part, at least."

"You will, please, explain what you mean by that?"

"Of course. As I told you last night, Miss Fane's servants were always cheating her. When I first became her secretary I shut my eyes to it, because I'm no tale-bearer. But about a year ago, her finances became terribly involved, and I began an investigation. I discovered that Jessop had a most shameless arrangement with the tradespeople—all the bills were padded outrageously and Jessop was getting a share of the profits.

"I said nothing to Miss Fane—I knew what that would mean—a temperamental outburst, tears and recriminations, and probably a grand scene of forgiveness in the end. She was always so kind-hearted. Instead I went to Jessop, told him I knew what he was doing and that the thing must stop. He was most indignant. All the other servants in Hollywood, he told me, were doing the same, and he seemed to consider it a sort of royal prerogative. But when I threatened to tell Miss Fane, he backed down and agreed to put an end to the practice. I fancy he did, too, but since that time he has always been very cool to me, and I know that I have never been forgiven. So you see why I asked you if it was Jessop who told that—falsehood about the ring."

"Just where do you stand—as you say it—with Anna?"

"Oh, Anna and I have always been on the most friendly terms," Julie answered. "A good steady girl who saves her money and buys bonds with it. It's money honestly come by—I'm sure of that because"—Julie smiled faintly—"the poor thing has never had a chance to pad bills. None of them passes through her hands."

Chan looked at Julie's flushed face for a long moment. "Then you desire to repeat that Miss Fane herself gave you the ring yesterday morning?"

"I certainly do. It's the truth, Mr. Chan."

Charlie bowed. "I can only accept your word, Miss Julie. It is quite possible—the person who told me of seeing the ring last night may have been moved by ancient grudge—I thought of it at the time. Miss Julie, I say to myself, too fine and sweet for underhand work. You will note, Jimmy, that you and I have tastes in common."

"Which does you credit," smiled Bradshaw.

"Which credits us both," amended Chan. "I will no longer hang about, a blot on this lovely scene. My kindest good-by—until we meet again."

He walked thoughtfully to his car, and drove away through the hot noon sunshine. "So many roads that wind and wind——" He had read that somewhere. He sighed. So many roads—would the little car finally leap down the right one?

As he approached the Grand Hotel, Huntley Van Horn was again in his thoughts. He was reluctant to reappear so soon at the hotel's main entrance so, parking his car in the street, he entered the grounds and walked toward the palm court. A group of excited tourists was gathered beneath the tallest of the cocopalms, and looking aloft, Charlie saw one of the beach-boys, in a red bathing-suit, climbing the tree with the agility of a monkey. He stood for a moment, admiring the boy's skill.

"The kid's clever, eh, Inspector?" remarked a voice at his elbow.

He turned and looked into the smiling gray eyes of Van Horn. They were standing a little apart from the others, and the picture actor was the recipient of many awed, adoring glances from young women who were ostensibly there to watch the beach-boy.

"Ah, Mr. Van Horn," Chan said. "This meeting is indeed most fortunate. I am calling here for the sole purpose of seeing you."

"Really?" The actor looked up at the tree. "Well, he seems to have traveled as far as he can on that one. Shall we go on the veranda—pardon me, the lanai—and have a chat?"

"The idea is most suitable," Charlie agreed. He followed Van Horn and they sat down in a secluded corner. The boy had descended the coco-palm and stood now the center of an admiring group, hugely enjoying the limelight. Chan watched him.

"Sometimes in my heart," he remarked, "arouses hot envy of the beach-boys. To exist so happily—to have no cares and troubles, no worries—ah, that must be what men mean by Paradise. All they ask of life is one bathing-suit, slightly worn."

Van Horn laughed. "You have worries, I take it, Inspector?"

Charlie turned to him; he had decided to be frank. "I have." He paused. "You are one of them," he added suddenly.

The picture actor was unperturbed. "You flatter me," he answered. "Just how am I worrying you, Inspector?"

"You worry me because in this matter of Miss Shelah Fane's murder you are quite defenseless. Not only do you possess no alibi, but of all those concerned, you were nearest to the scene of her death. You walked across lawn at very important moment, Mr. Van Horn. I could not worry about you more if you were own son."

Van Horn grinned. "That's kind of you, Inspector. I appreciate it. Yes—I am rather badly cast in the story of the crime. But I rely on you. As an intelligent man, you must realize that I could have had absolutely no motive for killing the poor girl. Until I joined her company to make this picture, I scarcely knew her, and all through our journey and the work together, we were on the friendliest terms."

"Ah, yes," Chan watched the actor's face eagerly. "Were you likewise on friendly terms with Denny Mayo?" he inquired.

"Just what has Denny Mayo to do with all this?" Van Horn asked. Despite his best efforts, his expression was not quite so casual as he wanted it to be.

"May have much to do with it," Charlie told him. "I seek to upearth facts. Maybe you assist me. I repeat—were you on friendly terms with Denny Mayo?"

"I knew him fairly well," Van Horn admitted. "A most attractive chap—a wild Irishman—you never could tell what he was going to do next. Every one was very fond of him. His death was a great shock."

"Who killed him?" Charlie asked blandly.

"I wish I knew," Van Horn replied. "Last night, when I heard you asking everybody about three years ago last June, in Hollywood, I sensed that you thought his death involved in this somehow. I'm curious to know the connection."

"That, no doubt," said Charlie, "is why you haste to library early this morning to do hot reading about Mayo case?"

Van Horn smiled. "Oh—so you found me among my books, eh? Well, Inspector, as my press-agent will tell you, I'm of rather a studious type. There's nothing I like better than to curl up in a corner with a good book—real literature, mind you——"

Charlie raised a protesting hand. "The wise man, knowing he is under suspicion," he remarked, "does not stoop to tie his shoe in a melon patch.

Van Horn nodded. "An old Chinese saw, eh? Not bad either."

"You will," said Chan sternly, "before we leave these chairs, tell me the reason for your visit to library this morning."

Van Horn did not reply. He sat for a moment with a frown on his handsome face. Then he turned with sudden decision.

"You've been frank with me, Inspector. I'll be the same with you. Though when you've heard my reason for that visit, I fear you'll be more puzzled than ever." He took from his pocket an envelope bearing the crest of the Grand Hotel, and drew out a single sheet of note-paper. "Will you please read that?"

Chan took the paper. It bore a brief note, type-written and unsigned. He read:

> *"Just a word of warning from a friend. You should go at once to the Honolulu Public Library and remove from the bound volumes of all Los Angeles papers carrying the Denny Mayo murder story, certain rather damaging references to your own part in that affair."*

Charlie looked up. "Where did you get this?"

"I found it under my door when I awoke this morning," the actor told him.

"You went to library at once?"

"Directly after breakfast. Who wouldn't? I couldn't recall that I'd ever been mentioned in connection with the case—there was no reason why I should have been. But naturally—my curosity was aroused. I went down and read every word I could find regarding Mayo's murder in the *Los Angeles Times*—the only paper they had. And oddly enough——"

"Yes?" Chan prompted.

"It was just as I thought. My name wasn't mentioned anywhere. I've had a rather puzzled morning, Inspector."

"Natural you should," nodded Charlie. "A queer circumstance, indeed. Have you any idea who wrote this note?"

"None whatever," returned Van Horn. "But the purpose of it seems to be clear. Somebody has sought to cast suspicion in my direction. It's a delicate little attention, and I appreciate it. He—or possibly she—figured that I would go to the library and sign for that volume, and that of course you would soon find it out. After that, you would fancy me deeply involved in this affair, and would spend precious time sleuthing in the wrong direction. Fortunately, you took the unusual course of coming to me at once with your suspicion. I'm glad you did. And I'm damned glad I kept the letter."

"Which, after all, you may have written to yourself," Chan suggested.

Van Horn laughed. "Oh, no—I'm not so deep as all that, Mr. Chan. The letter was under my door when I rose. Find out who wrote it, and you may find the murderer of Shelah Fane."

"True enough," agreed Charlie. "I will keep it now, of

course." He stood up. "We have had a good talk, Mr. Van Horn, and I am grateful for your confidence. I go my way with one more puzzle burning in my pocket. Add a few more, and I collapse from mental strain. I trust I have not held you away from luncheon."

"Not at all," the actor replied. "This has been a very lucky interview for me. Good-by, and all my best wishes for success."

Chan hastened through the palm court, and at last set his flivver on the road to the city. As he moved along, he thought deeply about Huntley Van Horn. Despite his airy manner, the actor had seemed to be open and sincere. But could he, Charlie wondered, be sure of that? Could he ever be sure in this world? Deceit sprouted everywhere and thrived like a weed.

Suppose Van Horn was sincere? Who put that note under his bedroom door while he slept? Chan began to realize that he was engaged in a duel—a duel to the death. His opponent was quick and wary, cleverer than any person he had yet encountered in a long career. How many of these clues were false, dropped but to befuddle him? How many real?

An inner craving told him that lunch would be a pleasant diversion; he was never one to put such promptings aside. But as he approached the public library an even greater craving assailed him—a keen desire to read for himself the story of Denny Mayo's murder. With a sigh for the business man's lunch that must languish without him a little longer, he stopped the car and went inside.

The desk was deserted for the moment, and he turned into the reading-room at his right. There was just a chance that the big volume taken out by Van Horn early that morning was not yet restored to its place on the shelves. Yes—there it lay, on the table at which he had seen the picture actor sitting. Save for one or two children, the place was deserted. Charlie rapidly crossed the room and opened the book.

It happened that he knew the date of the Mayo tragedy, and he sought immediately the issue of the subsequent morning. His eyes opened wide. Under an eight-column head, "Movie Actor Found Murdered in Home," a great torn gap stared up at him.

Quickly he examined the pages, and then sat back, dazed and unbelieving. Every picture of Denny Mayo had been ruthlessly cut from the book.

Chapter XVII

HOW DENNY MAYO DIED

Chan sat motionless for a long time, deep in thought. Some desperate person was determined that he should not look upon the likeness of Denny Mayo. The captions to the pictures were for the most part intact. "Denny Mayo When He First Came to Hollywood." And here again: "Denny Mayo as He Appeared in *The Unknown Sin.*" But in every instance the reproduction of the actor's face was destroyed.

Who had done this thing? Huntley Van Horn? Perhaps. Yet if that were so, Van Horn's methods were crude and raw for so suave a gentleman. To go boldly to the library, ask for this volume, sign his name to the slip as he claimed to have done, and then mutilate the yellowed page, would be unbelievably naive. It invited swift and inevitable detection. It certainly did not sound like Van Horn.

With a ponderous sigh, Charlie applied himself to the story that had surrounded Denny Mayo's pictures. The actor had come to Hollywood from the English stage, and had won immediate success. He had lived with one servant in a detached house on one of the best Los Angeles streets. On the night of the murder the servant, after completing his usual duties, took the evening off. He went out at eight o'clock, leaving Mayo in excellent spirits.

Returning at midnight, the man let himself in through the kitchen door. Seeing a light in the living-room, he went there to ask if anything further was required of him before he went to bed. On the floor of the room he discovered the actor, dead some two hours. Mayo had been shot at close range with his own revolver, a delicate weapon which he was accustomed to keeping in the drawer of his desk. The revolver was lying at his side, and there were no finger-prints on it

—neither his own nor those of any unknown person. No one had been seen entering or leaving the house which occupied a dark position under its many trees.

Unfortunately, the following morning—and Charlie's eyebrows rose at this—the police had permitted the general public to swarm through the house. Actors, actresses, directors, producers—all friends, they claimed, of the dead man—had paraded through the rooms, and if any vital clue was still lying about it could easily have been destroyed. In any case, no vital clue was ever found. Those the police discovered led nowhere.

Little was known about Mayo's past; he had come from far away, and no member of his family stepped forward during the investigation. It was rumored that he had a wife in England, but he had not seen her for several years, never mentioned her to his friends—might, possibly, have been divorced. His life in Hollywood had not been spectacular; women admired him, but if he returned this admiration in any instance, he had been most discreet about it. If any one had a grudge against him——

Further along in the story, a name caught Charlie's eye, and he sat up with sudden interest. Hastily he read on until he came to it. Mayo had been working in a picture, and as his leading woman he had had an actress named Rita Montaine. Miss Montaine was engaged to marry a certain Wilkie Ballou, a prominent figure in Honolulu, scion of an old family there. Some obscure person testified that he had overheard a quarrel between Mayo and Ballou—it concerned a party to which Mayo had taken Miss Montaine. But the witness had heard Ballou make no threats against the actor.

Nevertheless, Ballou had been questioned. His alibi was complete, sworn to by Miss Montaine herself. On the night of Mayo's death the actress said that she and Ballou had been together from six o'clock until after midnight. They had taken a long ride in Ballou's car and danced together at a roadhouse far from the scene of the crime. She admitted that she was engaged to Ballou and intended to marry him soon.

These two faded from the limelight. Charlie read on, through the helpless meanderings of a completely baffled police. He turned page after page, no new developments arose, and amid a frantic sputtering on the part of the reporters, the story gradually died out.

How about that alibi of Ballou's? Sworn to by the

woman who was going to marry him. Was she also ready to lie for him?

Chan picked up the heavy volume and returned to the main room of the library. He laid his burden down on the desk, behind which stood a bright young woman. Without speaking, he opened the book and indicated the mutilated pages.

If his aim had been to annoy the young woman, he could have found no better means. Her cry of dismay was immediate and heartfelt. "Who did this, Mr. Chan?" she demanded.

Charlie smiled. "Thanks for touching faith in my ability," he remarked. "But I can not tell you."

"It was taken out by Mr. Van Horn, the actor. This soft of thing is prohibited by law, you know. You must arrest him at once."

Chan shrugged. "It was also lying on table from time Mr. Van Horn left it, early to-day, until well past noon. What proof have we that Van Horn mutilated it? I know him well, and I do not think him complete fool."

"But—but——"

"I will, with your kind permission, speak to him over wire. He may be able to cast little light."

The young woman led him to the telephone, and Chan got Van Horn at the hotel. He explained at once the condition in which he had found the book.

"What do you know about that!" Van Horn remarked.

"Alas! very little," Charlie returned. "The volume was in the intact state when you saw it?"

"Absolutely. Perfectly O. K. I left it on the table about nine-thirty and went out."

"Did you see any one known to you about place?"

"Not a soul. But I say, Inspector, this throws new light on that note I got this morning. Perhaps the intention of my unknown friend was not so much to involve me, as to get that volume out of the files. He—if it was a he—may have hoped that the thing would happen just as it has happened—that I would take it out and leave it where he could find it without himself signing a slip. Have you thought of that?"

"So much to think of," Chan sighed. "Thank you for the idea." He went back to the desk. "Mr. Van Horn left the volume in original state. He is certain of that. Was it noted that any one else examined it this morning?"

"I don't know," the young woman replied. "The librarian in charge of that room is out to lunch. Look here, Mr. Chan, you've got to find who did this."

"Plenty busy with murder just now," Charlie explained.

"Never mind your murder," she answered grimly. "This is serious."

Chan smiled, but the young woman was in no mood to join him. He promised to do his best and departed.

A glance at his watch told him that he had no time for his usual leisurely lunch. He had instead a sandwich and a glass of milk, then went to the station. The Chief was pacing the floor of the detectives' room.

"Hello, Charlie," he cried. "I've been wondering where you were. Pretty busy this morning, I take it?"

"Like fly on hot griddle," Chan answered. "And just as eager to get off."

"Haven't got anything yet, eh?"

"Have so much I am worn out," Charlie told him. "But no idea who killed Shelah Fane."

"That's what we want," the Chief insisted. "The name—the name. Good lord, we ought to get somewhere pretty soon."

"Maybe we will," replied Chan, with just the slightest inflection on the "we." He sat down. "Now I will relate morning's adventures, and it can happen that your keen brain will function where mine wanders lonely in the dark."

He began at the beginning: his visit to the theater, Robert Fyfe's cast-iron alibi, his admission that he had given the beach-comber money in exchange for a painting. He mentioned his call at the library and his discovery there of Huntley Van Horn, then went on to the two old people on the terrace of the hotel, who had accounted so readily for Tarneverro's actions on the previous night.

"They may be lying," said the Chief.

Charlie shook his head. "You would not say that if you saw them. Honesty gleams like unceasing beacon from their eyes."

"I'll judge of that for myself," remarked his superior. "What was their name? MacMaster? I'll talk with them later. Go on."

Charlie continued. He told of finding the stub of the small cigar of a sort smoked only by Alan Jaynes, beneath the pavilion window.

"Oh, lord," sighed the Chief. "They can't all be in it. Somebody's kidding you, Charlie."

"You go back to singular pronoun," smiled Chan. "A moment ago it was we. But that was only in regard to approaching moment of success, I think."

"Well, somebody's kidding us, then. Have it your own way. You got Jaynes' finger-prints?"

"I slyly obtained same. But it was print of Smith, the beach-comber, we discover on window-sill."

"Yes—that was something we can really act on. I sent out the word to pick him up right away. They'll bring him in any minute now. What have you been doing since then?"

Charlie repeated Jessop's story about the ring, which, he pointed out, might mean merely the repayment of an old grudge. He showed his Chief the letter which Van Horn had offered in explanation of his visit to the library. Finally he told of the mutilation of the bound volume of the newspaper, and ended with the mention of Ballou and his wife in the story of the Denny Mayo murder case.

For a long time, when he had finished, his Chief sat in silence. "Well," he said at length, "according to your investigation, they're all in it, I guess. Good heavens, can't you draw any deductions from all this?"

"Kindly state what are your deductions," answered Chan with gentle malice.

"Me? I don't know. I'm stumped. But you—the pride of the force——"

"Kindly recall—I have never been demon for speed. While I stumble about this way, I am fiercely thinking. Large bodies arrive late. Grant me time."

"What do you propose to do now?"

"I consider a little social visit with Mrs. Ballou."

"Great Scott, Charlie,—watch your step. Ballou's an important man in this town, and he's never been very friendly to me."

"I plan to use all possible diplomacy."

"You'll need it, and then some. Don't offend him, whatever you do. You know—these old families——"

Charlie shrugged. "I have not lived in Honolulu all these years in state of blindness. Do not worry. I move now on feet shod with velvet, and my voice drips oil and honey."

Kashimo came in. He walked with dragging step and had a discouraged air.

"Well, where's this fellow Smith?" demanded the Chief.

"No place, sir," said Kashimo. "Melted like ice."

"Melted, hell! You go out again, and don't come back without him."

"Look everywhere," Kashimo complained. "All funny joints, up-stair, in cellar. Comb town. No Smith."

Charlie went over and patted him on the back. "If at first you have drawn blank, resume the job," he advised. He took a slip of paper from a desk and began to write. "I give you a list of unsavory places," he explained. "Maybe you overlook some. Perhaps, after all, I have better knowledge of city's wickedness than honored member of Young Men's Buddhist Association like yourself."

He handed his list to the Japanese, who took it and left, followed by Charlie's kindly encouragement.

"Poor Kashimo," Chan remarked. "When there is no oil in the lamp, the wick is wasted. In dealing with such a one, friendly words bring best results. Now I go forth to wallow some more in bafflement."

I'll be waiting to hear from you," his Chief called after him.

Charlie set out for the Manoa Valley home of the Ballous. The business district disappeared behind him, and he traveled a street lined with great houses set on rolling lawns. Above his head flamed flowering trees, now in the last weeks of their splendor. He sped past Punahou Academy, and as he penetrated farther into the valley, he left the zone of sunshine for one of darkness. Black clouds hung over the mountains ahead and suddenly, borne on the wind, came a wild gust of rain. It beat fiercely on the top of the little car and blurred the windshield. Yet a mile away, at Charlie's back, Honolulu sparkled in the midday sun.

He reached the handsome house of Wilkie Ballou, and Rita received him in the dark drawing-room. Her husband, she explained, was up-stairs dressing for his afternoon golf. In Honolulu a real golfer pays no attention to rain; it may be pouring on his street, but bright and sunny round the corner. Rita's manner was cordial, and Chan took heart.

"I am so sorry to obtrude my obnoxious presence," he apologized. "If you never saw me again, I feel sure you would like it well enough. But—mere matter of form—I must inflict little talk on every one present at sad affair last night."

Rita nodded. "Poor Shelah! How are you getting on, Inspector?"

"I make splendid progress," he informed her blithely. There was, he felt, no occasion to go into that. "Would you speak with me little while about days when you were famous Hollywood figure?"

With bored eyes, Rita looked out at the rain lashing against the window. "I certainly will," she said.

"May I add that you broke heart of my eldest daughter, who is great film fan, when you retired from silvery sheet? No one, she moans, is ever so good as you were."

Rita's face brightened. "She remembers me? That's sweet of her."

"Your fine skill will never be forgotten anywhere," Chan assured her, and knew that he had made a friend for life.

"How can I help you?" she inquired.

Chan considered. "You knew Miss Fane in Hollywood?"

"Oh, yes, quite well."

"It is wisely forbidden to speak ill of those who have ascended the dragon, but sometimes we must let old rules go down the board. Was there at any time scandal in the lady's life?"

"Oh, no, none whatever. She wasn't that sort, you know."

"But she had what you call love-affairs?"

"Yes, frequently. She was emotional and impulsive—never without a love-affair. But they were all harmless, I'm sure."

"Did you hear that once she loved a man named—Denny Mayo?" Charlie watched Rita's face closely, and he thought she looked a little startled.

"Why, yes—Shelah was rather wild about Denny at one time, I believe. She took it rather hard when he was—killed. You knew about that, perhaps?"

"I know all about that," answered Chan slowly. But to his disappointment, the words seemed to leave the woman quite calm. "You had acquaintance with this Denny Mayo yourself, I think?"

"Yes—I was in his last picture."

Chan had an inspiration. "It may be you have photograph of Mayo somewhere among possessions?"

She shook her head. "No—I did have some old stills, but Mr. Ballou made me burn them. He said he wouldn't have me mooning about over the dear, dead past when I was——" She stopped, her eyes on the door.

Charlie looked up. Wilkie Ballou, in a golf suit, was in the doorway. He strode grimly into the room.

"What's all this about Denny Mayo?" he demanded.

"Mr. Chan was simply asking me if I knew him," Rita explained.

"Mr. Chan should mind his own business," her husband growled. He walked over and faced Charlie. "Denny Mayo," he said, "is dead and buried."

Chan shrugged. "I am so sorry, but he does not stay buried."

"He stays that way as far as my wife and I are concerned," Ballou answered, and there was a certain dignity about him as he said it.

For a moment Chan looked sleepily into the hostile eyes of the millionaire. "Your alibi for the night of Mayo's murder," he ventured, "seems to have enjoyed a fine success."

Ballou flushed. "Why not? It was the truth."

"So naturally, it prevailed." Chan moved toward the door. "I am sorry if I have disturbed you——"

"You haven't disturbed me in the least," Ballou snapped. "Just what did you expect to find here, anyhow?"

"I thought I might chance upon photograph of Denny Mayo."

"And why should you want his photograph?"

"Some unknown person objects to my looking at it."

"Is that so?" said Ballou. "Well, you won't find Mayo's picture here. Or anything else that will interest you, for that matter. Good day, Inspector; and I must ask you not to call again."

Charlie shrugged. "I travel where duty takes me. Would much prefer to loll in station house—but can you study swimming on a carpet? No—you must go where waters are deep. Good day, Mr. Ballou."

Rita followed him into the hall. "I'm afraid we haven't been able to help you," she remarked.

"Thanks all same," bowed Chan.

"I'm so sorry," the woman said. "I want to see you succeed. If there was only something I could do——"

Chan's eyes caught the flash of rings on her fingers. "There might be," he remarked suddenly.

"Anything," she replied.

"Last night you saw Miss Shelah Fane after long separation. Quick glance of women catches points men despise to notice. You recall all she was wearing, no doubt?"

"Why, of course. She had on a stunning gown—ivory satin, it was——"

"I speak mostly of jewels," Chan told her. "What woman is so blind she fails to note other woman's jewelry?"

Rita smiled. "Not I. She had on a gorgeous string of pearls, and a diamond bracelet——"

"And her rings?"

"Only one. A huge emerald I remember seeing in Hollywood. It was on her right hand."

"This was when you last encountered her? The young people were already in the water enjoying warm swim?"

"Julie and that boy were—yes."

Charlie bowed low. "My gratitude has no bounds. Now I must go on with my work. Good-by."

He went out into the perpetual valley rain, and turned his car toward the sunlit beach.

Chapter XVIII

THE BELL-MAN'S STORY

Julie and Jimmy Bradshaw sat on the white sand of Waikiki and gazed at an ocean that stretched, apparently empty of life, from this curving shore all the way to the atolls of the South Seas.

"Well, I suppose I'd better be getting along downtown," remarked the boy. He yawned, and dropping on his back, watched the white clouds drift lazily across a cobalt sky.

"Picture of a young man filled with pep and energy," Julie smiled.

He shuddered. "Very poor taste, my girl, introducing words like that into a conversation at Waikiki beach. It must be that, after all, I have given you a very imperfect idea of the spirit of this place. Here we loaf, we dream——"

"But you'll never get anywhere," Julie reproved.

"I'm there already," he answered. "Why should I bestir myself? When you're in Hawaii you've no place to go—you've reached heaven, and a change couldn't possibly be an improvement. So you just sit down and wait for eternity to end."

Julie shrugged. "Is that so? Well, I'm afraid I'm not built that way. Great for a vacation, yes—this place is all you say of it. But as a permanent residence—well——"

He sat up suddenly. "Good lord, you mean I haven't sold you on it? Me—the greatest descriptive writer in history—and I've failed to put over the big deal of my life. James J. Bradshaw strikes a snag—meets failure face to face—it seems incredible. Where have I slipped up, Julie? Haven't I made you feel the beauty of this island——"

"Beauty's all right," the girl replied. "But how about

its effect on character? It seems to me that when you've stopped moving, you're going back."

"Yeah," he smiled. "I went to a Rotary Club luncheon once myself—over on the mainland. Boys, we gotta progress or perish. Last year we turned out ten million gaskets, this year let's turn out fifteen. Make America gasket-conscious. Take it from me——"

"What were you saying about getting back to the office?"

He shook his head. "I thought I'd cast you for the rôle of Eve in this paradise, and what a serpent you turn out to be. Getting back to the office is something we never do over here. We don't want to wake the poor fellows who didn't go out."

"That's just what I've been saying, Jimmy."

"But dear Mrs. Legree, you don't need to be chained to an office desk in order to accomplish things. You can work just as well lying down. For instance, a minute ago I was well started on a new appeal to tourists. 'Come—let the laughing lei girl twine her garlands of flowers about your shoulders. Try your skill at riding Waikiki's surf, or just rest in lazy luxury——' "

"Ah, yes—that's what you prefer to do——"

" 'Under the nodding coco-palms.' Don't you like our coco-palms, Julie?"

"They're interesting, but I think I prefer the redwoods. You draw a deep breath in a redwood forest, Jimmy, and you feel like going out and licking the world. Can't you see what I mean? This place may be all right for people who belong here—but you—how long have you been in Hawaii?"

"A little over two years."

"Did you intend to stay here when you came?"

"Well, now—let's not go into that."

"You didn't, of course. You just took the line of least resistance. Don't you ever want to go back to the mainland and make something of yourself?"

"Oh—at first——" He was silent for a moment. "Well, I've failed to make the sale on Hawaii, I guess. That will always leave a scar on my heart, but there's something more important. Have I sold myself? I'm keen about you, Julie. If you'll say the word——"

She shook her head. "Don't let's go into that, either, Jimmy. I'm not what you think me—I'm horrid, really—

I—oh, Jimmy, you wouldn't want to marry a—a liar, would you?"

He shrugged. "Not a professional one—no. But a clumsy amateur like you—why, you do it as though you'd had no experience at all."

She was startled. "What do you mean?"

"All that about the ring. Why, in heaven's name, do you go on with it? I've been wise ever since this morning, and as for Charlie Chan—say, I admire the polite way he's treated you. I don't believe you've fooled him for a minute."

"Oh, dear—I thought I was rather good."

"What's it all about, Julie?" the boy inquired.

Tears were in her eyes. "It's about—poor Shelah. She took me in when I was broke and without a friend—she was always so good to me. I'd—I'd have done anything in the world for her—let alone tell a little lie."

"I won't ask you to continue," Bradshaw remarked. "I don't have to. Don't look around. Inspector Chan of the Honolulu police is approaching rapidly, and something in his walk tells me that this is the zero hour for you. Brace up. I'm with you, kid."

Charlie joined them, amiable and smiling. "Not too welcome, I think. But anyhow I attach myself to this little group." He sat down, facing the girl. "What is your opinion of our beach, Miss Julie? Here you are deep in the languid zone. How do you like languor, as far as you have got with it?"

Julie stared at him. "Mr. Chan, you have not come here to talk to me about the beach."

"Not precisely," he admitted. "But I am firm believer in leading up. Suitable preparation removes the sting of rudeness. Making an example, it would have been undecently abrupt for me to stride up and cry: 'Miss Julie, why do you lie to me about that emerald ring?' "

Her cheeks flushed. "You think I have been—lying?"

"More than think, Miss Julie. I know. Other eyes than Jessop's saw the ring on Miss Fane's finger long after you immersed in waters of Waikiki last night."

She did not reply. "Better own up, Julie," Bradshaw advised. "It's the best way. Charlie will be your friend then—won't you, Charlie?"

"Must admit feeling of friendship would suffer a notable increase," Chan nodded. "Miss Julie, it is not true that

Miss Fane gave you that ring yesterday to obtain cash for it?"

"Oh, yes, it is," the girl insisted. "That much is true."

"Then she took it back later?"

"Yes—just after she returned from her interview with Tarneverro, about noon."

"Took it back, and wore it when she died?"

"Yes."

"After the tragedy, you again obtained possession?"

"I did. When Jimmy and I found her, I went in and knelt beside her. It was then I took the ring."

"Why?"

"I—I can't tell you."

"You mean you won't."

"I can't, and I won't. I'm sorry, Mr. Chan."

"I also get deep pain from this." Charlie was silent for a moment. "Can it happen you removed the ring because name of 'Denny' was engraved inside?"

"Wh—what do you know about Denny?"

Chan sat up with sudden interest. "I will tell you, and perhaps you will grow frank. I have learned that Shelah Fane was in Los Angeles house the very night Denny Mayo was murdered there. Consequently, she knew name of killer. It was scandal in her past she was eager to conceal. Perhaps, to aid that concealment, you yourself wished name of Denny Mayo kept out of all discussions. A natural desire to shield your friend's reputation. But as you see, your actions have not availed. Now you may speak, with no injury to your dear benefactor."

The girl was weeping softly. "Yes, I guess I might as well tell you. I'm so sorry you know all that. I'd have given anything to keep Denny Mayo out of this."

"You were aware, then, of that scandal in Miss Fane's past?"

"I suspected that something was terribly wrong, but I didn't know what. I was quite young—I had just come to Shelah—at the time of Denny's—accident. On the night it happened, Shelah arrived home in a state of hysteria, and I was there alone with her. I took care of her the best I could. For weeks she wasn't herself. I knew that in some way she was connected with Mayo's murder, but until this moment, I never learned the facts. I was young, as I say, but I knew better than to ask questions."

"Coming to yesterday——" Chan prompted.

"It was just as I told you—yesterday morning she said she must get hold of money at once, and she gave me the ring to sell. Then she went down to the Grand Hotel to see Tarneverro, and when she came back she was sort of hysterical again. She sent for me to come to her room—she was walking the floor. I couldn't imagine what had happened. 'He's a devil, Julie,' she cried. 'That Tarneverro's a devil—I wish I had never sent for him. He told me things about Tahiti and on the boat—how could he know—he frightened me. And I've done something terribly foolish, Julie—I must have been mad.' She became rather incoherent then. I asked her what it was all about. 'Get the emerald,' she told me. 'We mustn't sell it, Julie. Denny's name is inside it, and I don't want any mention of that name now.' "

"She was hysteric, you say?"

"Yes. She was often that way, but this was worse, somehow. 'Denny Mayo won't die, Julie,' she said. 'He'll come back to disgrace me yet.' Then she urged me to get the ring, and of course I did. She told me we'd find something else to sell later. Just then she was too upset to discuss it. In the afternoon, I saw her crying over Denny Mayo's picture."

"Ah," cried Chan, "that was portrait of Denny Mayo mounted on green mat?"

"It was."

"Continue, please."

"Last night," Julie went on, "when Jimmy and I made our terrible discovery in the pavilion, I thought at once of what Shelah had said. Denny would come back to disgrace her yet. Somehow, I thought, his death must be connected with Shelah's. If only his name could be kept out of it—otherwise I didn't know what scandal might be revealed. So I slipped Denny's ring from her finger. Later, when I heard mention of the photograph, I ran up-stairs and tore it into bits, hiding them under a potted plant."

Chan's eyes opened wide. "So it was you who performed that act? And later—when pieces of photograph scattered into wind—was it you who concealed large number of them?"

"Oh, no—you've forgotten—I wasn't in the room when that happened. And even if I'd been there, I wouldn't have been clever enough to think of that. Some one came to my aid at a critical moment. Who? I haven't the least idea, but I was grateful when I heard about it."

Chan sighed. "You have made everything a delay," he remarked, "and caused me to waste much precious time. I can admire your loyalty to this dead woman——" He paused. *"Haie,* I would enjoy to know such a woman. What loyalty she inspired. An innocent girl obstructs the police in defense of her memory, a man who could not have been guilty pleads to be arrested as her murderer, doubtless from same motive."

"Do you think Robert Fyfe took those lost bits of the photograph?" Bradshaw inquired.

Charlie shook his head. "Impossible. He had not yet arrived on scene. Alas! it is not so simple as that. It is not simple at all." He sighed. "I fear I will be worn to human skeleton before I disentangle this web. And you"—he looked at the girl—"you alone have melted off at least seven pounds."

"I'm so sorry," Julie said.

"Do not fret. Always my daughters tell me I am too enormous for beauty. And beauty is, of course, my only aim." He stood up. "Well, that is that. Jimmy, do not let this young woman escape you. She has proved herself faithful one. Also, she is most unexpert deceiver I have ever met. What a wife she will make for somebody."

"Me, I hope," Bradshaw grinned.

"I hope so, too." Charlie turned to the girl. "Accept him, and all is forgiven between you and me. The seven pounds is gladly donated."

She smiled. "That *is* an offer. Oh, Mr. Chan, I'm so happy that everything is settled between us. I didn't like to deceive you—you're so nice."

He bowed. "Even the aged heart can leap at talk like that. You give me new courage to go on. On to what? Alas! the future lies hidden behind a veil—and I am no Tarneverro."

He left them standing together beneath a hau tree, and walked slowly to his car. Emerging from the drive, he narrowly escaped collision with a trolley. "Wake up, there!" shouted the motorman in rage, and then, recognizing a member of the Honolulu police force, sought to pretend he'd never said it. Charlie waved to him and drove on.

The detective was lost in a maze of doubt and uncertainty. The matter of the emerald ring was clear at last—but still he was far from his goal. One point in Julie's story interested him deeply. It had been Denny Mayo's picture that he had sought to put together the previous night.

Up to now he had thought himself balked in that purpose by some one who did not wish him to know the identity of the man over whose portrait Shelah had wept so bitterly. But might the motive not have been the same that prompted the destruction of the pictures at the library? The same person, undoubtedly, had been busy in both instances, and that person was bitterly determined that Inspector Chan should not look upon the likeness of Denny Mayo. Why?

Charlie resolved to go back and relive this case from the beginning. But in a moment he stopped. Too much of a task for this drowsy afternoon. "Much better I do not think at all," he muttered. "I will cease all activity and put tired brain in receptive state. Maybe subconscious mind sees chance and leaps on job during my own absence."

In such a state of suspended mental effort he turned his car into the drive of the Grand Hotel and, parking it, walked idly toward the entrance. A stiff breeze was blowing through the lobby, which was practically deserted at this hour of the day.

Sam, the young Chinese who rejoiced in the title of head bell-man, was alert and smiling. Charlie paused. There was a little matter about which he wished to question Sam.

"I hope you are well," he said. "You enjoy your duties here, no doubt?" Leading up, he would have called it.

"Plenty fine job," beamed Sam. "All time good tips."

"You know man they call Tarneverro the Great?"

"Plenty fine man. Good flend to me."

Charlie regarded the boy keenly. "This morning you spoke to him in Cantonese. Why did you do that?"

"Day he come, he say long time ago he live in China, knows Chinese talk plitty well. So he and I have talk in Cantonese. He not so good speaking, but he knows what I say allight"

"He didn't seem to understand you this morning."

Sam shrugged. "I don't know. This moahning I speak all the same any othah day he has funny look an' say don' unnahstand."

"They are peculiar, these tourists," Chan smiled.

"Plenty funny," admitted Sam. "All same give nice tips."

Charlie strode on to the lounge, and through that to the terrace. He sat down there.

His vacation from thinking had been brief indeed, for now he was hard at it again. So Tarneverro understood the Cantonese dialect. But he did not wish Charlie Chan, whom he was so eager to assist in the search for Shelah Fane's murderer, to know that he understood it. Why was that?

A smile spread slowly over Charlie's broad face. Here at last was a fairly simple question. Tarneverro's initial act in helping to solve the murder had been the pointing out of the fact that the watch had been set back, and that the alibis for two minutes past eight were consequently worthless.

But would he have done that if he had not first overheard and understood Charlie's conversation with the cook—if he had not known that Wu Kno-ching had seen Shelah Fane at twelve minutes past eight and that the gesture with the watch was, accordingly, useless? His prompt display of detective skill had seemed, at the time, to prove his sincerity. But if he understood Cantonese, then he was simply making a virtue of necessity and was not sincere at all.

Charlie sat for a long time turning the matter over in his mind. Was his eager assistant, Tarneverro the Great, quite so eager as he appeared to be?

Chapter XIX

TARNEVERRO'S HELPING HAND

Val Martino, the director, came down the steps from the hotel lounge, a dashing figure in his white silk suit and flaming tie. He might have been the man on the cover of some steamship folder designed to lure hesitating travelers to the tropics. His gaze fell on Charlie, lolling at ease in a comfortable chair and looking as though he had not a care in the world. The director came over immediately.

"Well, Inspector," he remarked, "I scarcely expected to see you in such a placid mood just now. Unless you have already solved last night's affair?"

Chan shook his head. "Luck is not so good as that. Mystery still remains mystery, but do not be deceived. My brain moves, though my feet are still."

"I'm glad of that," Martino replied. "And I hope it gets somewhere soon." He dropped into a chair at Charlie's side. "You know that thing last night just plain wrecked two hundred thousand dollars' worth of picture for me, and I ought to hurry to Hollywood on the next boat and see what's to be done about it. Whoever killed Shelah certainly didn't have the best interests of our company at heart, or he'd have waited until I finished my job. Oh, well—it can't be helped now. But I must get away as soon as possible, and that's why I'm plugging for you to solve the problem at once."

Chan sighed. "Everybody seems to suffer from hurry complex. An unaccustomed situation in Hawaii. I am panting to keep in step. May I ask—what is your own idea on this case?"

Martino lighted a cigarette. "I hardly know. What's yours?" He tossed the match on to the floor, and the old

Chinese with the dust-pan and brush came at once, casting a look at Charlie which seemed to say: "This is exactly the sort of person I would expect to find in your company."

"My ideas do not yet achieve definite form," Chan remarked. "One thing I do know—I am opposed in this matter by some person of extreme cleverness."

The director nodded. "It looks that way. Well, there were several clever people at Shelah Fane's house last night."

"Yourself included," Charlie ventured.

"Thanks. Naturally, that had to come from you. But it's true enough." He smiled. "I am speaking, of course, in confidence when I say there was another man present of whose cleverness I have never had the slightest doubt. I don't like him, but I've always thought him pretty smooth. I refer to Tarneverro the Great."

Chan nodded. "Yes, he is plenty quick. One word with him, and I had gathered that."

The director flicked the ash from his cigarette on to the floor. The old Chinese brought an ash-tray and set it close beside him on the small table.

"There are all kinds of seers and crystal-gazers fattening on the credulity of Hollywood," Martino continued. "But this man is the ace of the lot. The women go to him; and he tells them things about themselves they thought only God knew. As a result——"

How does he discover these things?" Charlie asked.

"Spies," the diector answered. "I can't prove it, but I'm certain he has spies working for him night and day. They pick up interesting bits of news about the celebrities, and pass them along to him. The poor little movie girls think he's in league with the powers of darkness, and as a result they tell all. That man knows enough secrets to blow up the colony if he wants to do it. We've tried to run him out of town, but he's too smart for us. You know, I'm rather sorry I stopped Jaynes last night when he wanted to beat Tarneverro up. I believe it would have been a grand idea. But on the other hand, Shelah's name would have been dragged into it, and remembering that, I broke up the row. The pictures are my profession, there are lots of fine people in the colony, and I don't like to see them suffer from harmful publicity. Unfortunately the decent ones must share the disgrace when the riffraff on the fringe misbehaves."

"Was it your intention," Chan inquired, "to hint that Tarneverro the Great may have killed Shelah Fane?"

"Not at all," responded Martino hastily. "Don't get me wrong. I was only trying to point out that if you sense a clever opponent in this affair, you should remember that there are few men cleverer than the fortune-teller. Further than that, I say nothing. I don't know whether he did it or not."

"For the time between eight and eight-thirty last night," Chan informed him, "Tarneverro has most unshakable alibi."

Martino stood up. "He would have. As I told you, he's as slick as they come. Well, so long. Good luck to you—and I mean that with all my heart."

He strolled off toward the glittering sea and left Chan to his thoughts. In a few moments the detective arose with sudden decision and went to the telephone booth in the lobby. He got his Chief on the wire.

"You very much busy now?" he asked.

"Not especially, Charlie. I've got a date with Mr. and Mrs. MacMaster here at five-thirty, but that's an hour away. Is anything doing?"

"Might be," Chan answered. "I can not tell. But I will shortly require backing of your firm authority for little investigation at Grand Hotel. Pretty good idea if you leaped into car and rode out here at once."

"I'll be right with you, Charlie," the Chief promised.

Going to the house phone, Charlie called the room of Alan Jaynes. The Britisher answered in a sleepy tone. The detective informed him that he was coming up immediately to talk with him and then stepped to the hotel desk.

"Without calling room, can you ascertain if Mr. Tarneverro is in residence?" he asked.

The clerk glanced at the letter box. "Well, his key isn't here," he said. "I guess that means he's in."

"Ah, yes," nodded Chan. "If you will be so kind, do this big favor for me. Secure Mr. Tarneverro on wire, and say that Inspector Chan passed through here in too great rush to bother himself. But add that I desire to see Mr. Tarneverro soon as can be in lobby of Young Hotel downtown. Say it is of fierce importance and he must arrive at once."

The clerk stared. "Down-town?" he repeated.

Chan nodded. "The idea is to remove him from this hotel for a brief space of time," he explained.

"Oh, yes," smiled the clerk. "I see. Well, I suppose it's all right. I'll call him."

Charlie went up to the room occupied by Alan Jaynes. The Britisher admitted him, yawning as he did so. He was in dressing-gown and slippers, and his bed was somewhat disheveled.

"Come in, Inspector. I've just been having forty winks. Good lord—what a sleepy country this is!"

"For the *malihini*—the newcomer—yes," Chan smiled. "We old-timers learn to disregard the summons. Otherwise we would get nowhere."

"You are getting somewhere, then?" Jaynes asked eagerly.

"Would not want to say that, but we are traveling at good pace—for Hawaii," responded Charlie. "Mr. Jaynes, I have come to you in spirit of most open frankness. I am about to toss cards down flat on table."

"Good," Jaynes said heartily.

"This morning you told me you had never been in pavilion, never even loitered in neighborhood of place?"

"Certainly I did. It's the truth."

Charlie took out an envelope, and emptied on to a table the stub of a small cigar. "How, then, would you explain the fact that this is found just outside window of room in which Shelah Fane met sudden death?"

Jaynes looked for a long moment at this shabby bit of evidence. "Well, I'll be damned," he remarked. He turned to Chan, an angry light in his eyes. "Sit down," he said. "I can explain it, and I will."

"Happy to hear you say that," Chan told him.

"This morning, when I was in my bath," the Britisher began, "about eight o'clock, it must have been, some one knocked on my door. I thought it was the house-boy, and I called to him to come in. I heard the door open, and then the sound of footsteps. I asked who it was, and—why the devil didn't I break his neck last night?" he finished savagely.

"You have reference to the neck of Tarneverro the Great?" Charlie inquired with interest.

"I have. He was here in this room, and said he wanted to see me. I was rather taken aback, but I told him to wait. I stood up in the tub and began a brisk rub-down—will you come with me to the bathroom, Mr. Chan?"

Surprised, Chan rose and followed.

"You will observe, Inspector, that there is a full-length mirror affixed to the bathroom door. With the door slightly ajar—like this—a person standing in the bath has a view of a portion of the bedroom—the portion which includes the desk. I was busy with my rub-down when I suddenly saw something that interested me keenly. A box of those small cigars was lying on the desk, with a few gone. I saw, in the mirror, Mr. Tarneverro walk over and help himself to a couple of them. He put them in his pocket."

"Good," remarked Chan calmly. "I am much obliged to the mirror."

"At first I thought it was merely a case of petty pilfering. Nevertheless, I was deeply annoyed, and I planned to go out and order him from my room. But as I finished drying myself and got into my dressing-gown, it occurred to me that something must be in the air. I decided to say nothing, lie low, and try to find out, if possible, what the beggar was up to. I didn't guess—I'm a bit dense, I'm afraid—it never popped into my mind that he wanted to involve me in Shelah's murder. I knew he had no love for me, but somehow —that's not the sort of thing——

"Well, I came out and asked him what he wanted. He looked me boldly in the eye and said he had just dropped in to urge that I let bygones be bygones, and shake hands on it. No reason why we shouldn't be friends, he thought. Felt that Miss Fane would wish it. Of course, I was aching to throw him from the window, but I controlled myself. Out of curiosity, I invited him to have one of my cigars. 'Oh, no, thanks,' he said. 'I never use them.'

"He ran on about Miss Fane, and how it would be best if we dropped our enmity of last night. I was cool but polite —I even shook hands with him. When he had gone, I sat down to think the thing out. What could have been his purpose in taking those cigars? As I say, I couldn't figure it. Now, of course, the matter is only too clear. He proposed to scatter a few false clues. By gad, Inspector—why should he take the trouble to do that? There's just one answer, isn't there? He murdered Miss Fane himself."

Chan shrugged. "I would be happy to join you in thinking that, but first several matters must be wiped away. Among others—an air-tight alibi."

"Oh, hell—what's that?" Jaynes cried. "A clever man always has an alibi." His heavy jaws snapped shut. "I appreciate what Mr. Tarneverro tried to do for me—I do, indeed. When I see him again——"

"When you see him again, you will make no noise," Charlie cut in. "That is, if you wish to be of help."

Jaynes hesitated. "Oh—very good. But it won't be easy. However, I'll hold my tongue if you say so. Was there anything else you wanted?"

"No, thanks. You have supplied me with plenty. I go on my way with renewed energy."

Waiting for the elevator, Chan thought about Jaynes' story. Was it true? Perhaps. It seemed a rather glib explanation, but was the Britisher clever enough to concoct such a tale on the spot? He appeared to be a stolid, slow-thinking man—always going somewhere to be by himself and figure things out. Could such a man—Charlie sighed. So many problems!

He stepped cautiously from the elevator and peered round the corner. The coast seemed to be clear and he went to the desk. "Has Mr. Tarneverro departed?" he inquired.

The clerk nodded. "Yes—he went out a moment ago, in a great hurry."

"My warmest thanks," Charlie said.

His Chief was coming up the hotel steps, and he went to greet him. Together they sought out a secluded corner.

"What's up?" the Chief wanted to know.

"Number of things," Chan replied. "Mr. Tarneverro bursts into investigation and demands our strict attention."

"Tarneverro?" The Chief nodded. "That fellow never has sounded good to me. What about him?"

"For one point," Charlie answered, "he understands Cantonese." He told of making that discovery, which had served to turn his thoughts toward the fortune-teller. "But since I called you, even more important evidence leaps up," he added. Briefly he repeated Jaynes' story about the cigars.

The Chief whistled. "We're getting there, Charlie," he cried.

Chan shrugged. "You overlook Tarneverro's alibi——"

"No, I don't. I'll attend to that later. By the way, if you see that old couple from Australia about, keep out of their way. I've arranged for them to come to my office, as I told you, and I don't want to talk with them here. We can handle them better amid the proper surroundings. Now, what is it you want to do?"

"I desire," Chan answered, "to make complete search of Tarneverro's apartment."

The Chief frowned. "That's not quite according to Hoyle, Charlie. I don't know. We have no warrant——"

"Which is why I asked you to come. Big man such as

you are can arrange it. We leave everything as we found it, and Tarneverro will not know."

"Where is he?"

Charlie explained the fortune-teller's present whereabouts. The Chief nodded. "That was a good idea. Wait here, and I'll have a talk with the management."

He returned presently, accompanied by a tall lean man with sandy hair. "It's all fixed," the Chief announced. "You know Jack Murdock, don't you, Charlie? He's going with us."

"Mr. Murdock old friend," Chan said.

"Well, Charlie, how you been?" Murdock remarked. He was an ex-policeman, now one of the house detectives for the hotel.

"I enjoy the usual good health," Charlie replied, and with the Chief, followed Murdock.

After the house detective had unlocked the door and admitted them to Tarneverro's sitting-room, he stood looking at Chan with a speculative eye.

"Not going to rob us of one of our most distinguished guests, are you, Charlie?" he inquired.

Chan smiled. "That is a matter yet to be determined."

"Quite a little affair down the beach last night," Murdock continued. "And you're in the limelight, as usual. Some people have all the luck."

"Which they pay for by having also all the worry," Chan reminded him. "You are in soft berth here. Fish course last night was excellent. Did you taste it?"

"I did."

"So did I—and that was as far as I got," sighed Chan. "Limelight has many terrible penalties." He glanced about the room. "Our object is to search thoroughly and leave no trace. Fortune favors, however, for we have plenty time."

He and the Chief went to work systematically, while the house detective lolled in a comfortable chair with a cigar. The closets, the bureau drawers and the desk were all gone over carefully. Finally Charlie stood before a trunk. "Locked," he remarked.

Murdock got up. "That's nothing. I've a skeleton key that will fix it." He opened the trunk, which was of the wardrobe variety, and swung it wide. Chan lifted out one drawer, and gave a little cry of satisfaction.

"Here is one thing we seek, Chief," he cried, and produced a portable typewriter. Placing it on the desk, he inserted a sheet of note-paper and struck off a few sentences. "Just a word of warning from a friend. You should go at once to the Honolulu Public Library and——" He finished the note, and taking another from his pocket, compared the two. With a pleased smile he carried them to his Chief.

"Will you kindly regard these missives and tell me what they suggest to you?" he said.

The Chief studied them for a moment. "Simple enough," he remarked. "Both were written on the same machine. The top of the letter *e* is clogged with ink, and the letter *t* is slightly out of alignment."

Chan grinned and took them back. "Long time confinement in station house does not cause you to grow rusty. Yes—it is just as you say. Two notes are identical, both being written on this faithful little machine. Happy to say our visit here is not without fruit. I must now put typewriter in place so our call will go unsuspected. Or would go that way, if it was not for lingering odor of good friend Murdock's cigar."

The house detective looked guilty. "Say, Charlie—I never thought of that."

"Finish your weed. Damage is now done. But take care luxury of present job does not cause brain to stagnate."

Murdock did not smoke again, but let the cigar go out in his hand. Charlie continued to explore the trunk. He had about completed his search without further good fortune, when in the most remote corner of the lowest compartment, he came upon something which seemed to claim his interest.

He walked up to his Chief. In the palm of his hand lay a man's ring, a large diamond in a heavy setting of gold. His superior stared at it. "Take good look," Chan advised, "and fix same in your mind."

"More jewelry, Charlie?"

Chan nodded. "Seeking to solve this case, it seems we wander lost in jewel store. Natural, perhaps, since we deal with Hollywood people." He restored the ring to its place, closed the trunk and locked it. "Mr. Murdock, that will end business here."

They returned to the lobby, where the house detective left them. Chan accompanied the Chief out to the drive.

"What did you mean about the ring, Charlie," asked the latter.

"Little story which I have been perhaps too reluctant to repeat," smiled Chan. "Why? Perhaps because it concerns most distasteful moment of my long career. You will recall that last night, in house down the beach, I stood in middle of floor with letter written by Shelah Fane held firmly in my hand. Suddenly light goes out. I am most rudely struck in the face—struck and cut on the cheek, proving the assailant wore a ring. Lights go on, and the letter is gone."

"Yes, yes," cried the Chief impatiently.

"Immediately I make a survey—of the men in the room, who wears ring? Ballou and Van Horn—yes. Others do not. Mr. Tarneverro, for example, does not. Yet yesterday morning, when I visited him in room, I noted that ring I have called to your attention, on his finger. What is more, when we rode down to Shelah Fane's house after news of murder, I perceived the diamond gleaming in the dark. I saw it again when he helps me make investigation in pavilion. Yet when lights flash on after theft of letter, ring is no longer in evidence. What would be your reaction to that, Mr. Chief?"

"I should say," the Chief returned, "that Tarneverro struck that blow in the dark."

Charlie was thoughtfully rubbing his cheek. "Oddly enough," he remarked, "such was my own reaction."

Chapter XX

ONE CORNER OF THE VEIL

They went over and stood by Charlie's car. A puzzled frown wrinkled the Chief's brow. "I don't get this, Charlie."

"On which point," returned Chan placidly, "we are like as two reeds bending beside stream."

"Tarneverro hit you. Why?"

"Why not? Maybe he feels athletic."

"He'd just been telling you about that letter—hoping that the two of you would run across it somewhere—and when you got it he knocked you down and took it away from you."

"No doubt he wished to examine it in private."

The Chief shook his head. "Beyond me—way beyond me. He stole a cigar from Jaynes, hurried down and dropped the butt outside the pavilion window. He wrote a note to Van Horn, sending him off to the library on a fool's errand. He—he—what else has he done?"

"Perhaps he has murdered Shelah Fane," Charlie suggested.

"I'm sure he did."

"Yet he owns fine alibi."

The Chief looked at his watch. "Yes—I'll attend to that alibi at five-thirty, if those old people show up as they promised. What are you going to do now?"

"I follow you to join in that interview, but first I make stop at public library."

"Oh, yes, of course. Come as soon as you can. I—I think we're getting somewhere now."

"Where?" inquired Chan blandly.

"Lord knows—I don't," replied the Chief, and hurried

to his own car. He got away first, and Charlie followed him through the big gates to Kalakaua Avenue.

It was nearly five o'clock, the bathing hour at Waikiki was on, and along the sidewalk passed a perpetual parade of pretty girls in gay beach robes and stalwart tanned men in vivid dressing-gowns. Other people had time to enjoy life, Charlie reflected, but not he. The further discoveries of the afternoon baffled him completely, and he had need of all his Oriental calm to keep him firmly on the pathway of his investigation. Tarneverro, who had sworn that his dearest wish was to assist in finding the murderer of Shelah Fane, had been impeding the search from the start. The fortune-teller's dark face, with its deep mysterious eyes, haunted Chan's thoughts as he flivvered on to town.

Stopping at the public library, he again appeared at the desk.

"Would you kindly tell me if the young woman in charge of reading-room is now on scene?" he asked.

The girl appeared, upset and indignant over the morning's events. She would never again leave a newspaper file idle on a table, but the Japanese boy whose work it was to return such items to the shelves was taking the day off. She remembered Van Horn, of course; she had seen him in the films.

"Were other striking personalities present in reading-room during the morning?" Charlie inquired.

The girl thought. Yes—she remembered one. A rather peculiar-looking man—she recalled especially his eyes. Chan urged her to a further description, and was left in no doubt as to whom she referred.

"Did you perceive him examining newspaper file left by actor?"

"No, I didn't. He came in soon after Mr. Van Horn left, and stayed all morning, reading various papers and magazines. He seemed to be trying to pass the time."

"When did he leave?"

"I don't know. He was still here when I went out to lunch."

"Ah, yes," Chan nodded. "He would be."

"You think he cut the book?"

"I have no proof, and never will have, I fear. But I am sure he mutilated the volume."

"I'd like to see him in jail," said the girl warmly.

Charlie shrugged. "We have tastes in common. Thank you so much for significant information."

He drove quickly to the police station. The Chief, alone in his room, was gruffly talking over the telephone. "No—no—nothing yet." He slammed the receiver on to its hook. "Good lord, Charlie, they're hounding me to death. The whole world wants to know who killed Shelah Fane. The morning paper's had over a hundred cables. Well, what about the library?—Wait a minute."

The telephone was ringing again. The Chief's replies were none too gentle.

"That was Spencer," he announced, hanging up. "I don't know what's got into the boys—they seem to be helpless. They can't find a trace of that confounded beachcomber anywhere. He's of vital importance, Charlie; he was in that room last night——"

Charlie nodded. "He must assuredly be found. I am plenty busy man, but it seems I must go on his trail myself. As soon as interview with old people is ended——"

"Good! That's the ticket. You go out the first chance you get. What was I saying?—Oh, yes—the library. What did you find there?"

"No question about it," Charlie replied. "Tarneverro is man who destroyed pictures of Denny Mayo."

"He is, eh? Well, I thought so. Doesn't want you to know what this Mayo looked like. Why? I'll go mad if this keeps up. But there's one thing sure, and I'm clinging to it. Tarneverro's our man. He killed Shelah Fane, and we've got to pin it on him." Chan started to speak. "Oh, yes—I know—his alibi. Well, you watch me. I'll smash that alibi if it's the last act of my life."

"I was going to name one other objection," Chan told him gently.

"What's that?"

"If he contemplated killing of Shelah Fane, why did he announce first to me that we are about to arrest killer of Denny Mayo? Why, as my boy Henry would say, bring that up?"

The Chief put his head in his hands. "Lord, I don't know. It's a difficult case, isn't it, Charlie?" A plain-clothes man appeared at the door, announcing Mr. Thomas MacMaster and wife. "Show them in," cried the Chief, leaping to his feet. "We can do one thing, anyhow, Charlie," he said. "We can smash that alibi, and when we've done that, maybe things will clear up a bit."

The old Scotch couple entered, and at the guileless and

innocent look of them, the Chief received a severe shock. The old man approached Chan with outstretched hand.

"Ah, good evening, Mr. Chan. We meet again."

Charlie got up. "Would you kindly shake hands with the Chief of Detectives. Mrs. MacMaster, I would also present my superior officer to you. Chief desires to ask a few polite questions." He stressed the polite ever so slightly, but his superior got the hint.

"How do you do, madam," he said cordially. "Mr. MacMaster—I am sorry to trouble you."

"No trouble at all, sir," replied the old man, with the rolled *r* of Aberdeen. "Mother and I have never had much to do wi' the police, but we're law-abiding citizens and glad to help."

"Fine," returned the Chief. "Now, sir, according to what you told Inspector Chan here, you are both old friends of the man who calls himself Tarneverro the Great?"

"Aye—that we are. It was in his younger days we knew him, and a splendid lad he was. We're deeply fond of him, sir."

The Chief nodded. "Last night you say you sat with him on one of the lanais of the Grand Hotel from a few minutes after eight until half past the hour."

"That is what we said, sir," MacMaster returned, "and we will swear to it in any court you put us in. It is the truth."

The Chief looked him firmly in the eye. "It can't be the truth," he announced.

"Why—why, what do you mean, sir?"

"I mean there's a mistake somewhere. We have indisputable evidence that Mr. Tarneverro was elsewhere during that time."

The old man drew himself up proudly. "I do not like your tone, sir. The word of Thomas MacMaster has never been questioned before, and I have not come here to be insulted——"

"I don't question your word. You've made a mistake, that's all. Tarneverro left you at eight-thirty, you claim. Did you verify that by your own watch?"

"I did."

"The watch might have been wrong."

"It was wrong."

"What!"

"It was a wee bit fast—a matter of three minutes. I

compared it with the hotel clock, which stood at eight-thirty-two."

"You're not—pardon me—a young man, Mr. MacMaster?"

"Is that also forbidden by law in the States, sir?"

"What I mean is—your eyes——"

"My eyes, sir, are as good as yours, and better. Mr. Tarneverro left us at eight-thirty—the correct time. He had been with us since we came out from our dinner, save for a brief period when he talked with a gentleman at the far end of the lounge. And during that time he did not leave our sight. That I say—and that I'll stand by"—he banged a great fist on the desk—"until hell freezes over!"

"Father—don't get excited," put in the old lady.

"Who's excited?" cried MacMaster. "You have to be emphatic wi' a policeman, Mother. You have to talk his language."

The Chief considered. In spite of himself, he was impressed by the obvious honesty of the old man. He had planned to bully him out of his testimony, but something told him such tactics would be useless. Hang it all, he reflected, Tarneverro did have an alibi, and a good one.

"You second what your husband says, madam?" he inquired.

"Every word of it," the old lady nodded.

The Chief made a helpless gesture, and turned toward MacMaster. "All right," he remarked. "You win."

Charlie stepped forward. "May I have honor to address few remarks to these good friends of mine?" he inquired.

"Sure. Go ahead, Charlie," replied the Chief wearily.

"I make simple inquiry," Chan continued gently. "Mr. Tarneverro was young man starting career when he visited your ranch, I believe?"

"He was that," agreed MacMaster.

"An actor on theatrical stage?"

"Aye—and not a very successful one. He was glad of the work wi' us."

"Tarneverro very odd name. Was that what he called himself when he worked with you?"

The old man glanced quickly at his wife. "No, it was not," he said.

"What name did he offer at that time?"

MacMaster's jaw shut hard, and he said nothing.

"I repeat—what name did he offer when he worked with you?"

"I'm sorry, Inspector," the old man replied. "But he has asked us not to refer to the matter."

Chan's eyes flashed with sudden interest. "He requests that you do not mention his real name?"

"Yes. He said he had done wi' it, and asked us to think of him as Mr. Tarneverro."

Charlie felt his way carefully. "Mr. MacMaster, a serious situation looks us hard in the face. Murder was done last night. Tarneverro is not guilty man. You prove same yourself by offer of alibi, which is accepted by us in sincere spirit, because we know it is spoken same way. You have performed that favor for him. You do it gladly because you love truth. But more even dear friend has no right to ask of you. You have said you are law-abiding, and no one exists who is stupid enough to doubt that. I wish to know Mr. Tarneverro's name when he was with you in Australia."

The old man turned uncertainly to his wife. "I—I don't know. This is a difficult position, Mother."

"You will not prove him murderer by giving it," Charlie continued. "Already you have saved him from that. But you will impede our work if you withhold same—and I am plenty certain you are not kind of man to do that."

"I don't understand," the Scotchman muttered. "Mother, what do you think?"

"I think Mr. Chan is right." She beamed upon Charlie. "We have done enough when we swear to his alibi. If you won't tell, Father, I will. Why should a man be ashamed of his real name?—And it was his real name, I'm sure."

"Madam," said Chan. "You have proper view of things. Deign to mention the name."

"When we knew Tarneverro on the ranch," continued the old lady, "his name was Arthur Mayo."

"Mayo!" cried Chan. He and the Chief exchanged a triumphant glance.

"Yes. He told you this morning he was alone when he came to work for us. I can't think why he said that—it wasn't true. You see, he and his brother came to us together."

"His brother?"

"Yes, of course—his brother, Denny Mayo."

Chapter XXI

THE KING OF MYSTERY

Chan's breath came a little faster as he listened to this unexpected bit of news. Tarneverro was Denny Mayo's brother! No wonder, then, that the fortune-teller had been so eager to learn from Shelah Fane the name of Mayo's murderer. No wonder he had offered to help Chan to the limit of his ability in the task of finding out who had silenced Shelah just as she was, supposedly, on the point of telling.

And yet—had he carried out that promise to assist? On the contrary, he had evidently been placing in Chan's way every obstacle possible. Puzzles, puzzles—Charlie put his hand to his head. This man Tarneverro was the king of mystery.

"Madam, what you say is very interesting," the detective remarked. His eyes brightened. On one point, at least, light was breaking. "Will you be kind enough to tell me—was there resemblance in features between those two men?"

She nodded. "Aye, there was, though many people might not have noticed, because of the difference in age and coloring. Denny was blond, and Arthur very dark. But the first time I saw them, standing side by side in my kitchen, I knew they were brothers."

Chan smiled. "You have contributed something to our solution, madam, though up to moment of present speaking, only the gods know what. I think that is all we now require of you. Do I speak correctly, Chief?"

"Yes, that's right, Charlie. Mr. MacMaster, I'm obliged to your wife and you for this visit."

"Not at all, sir," the old man answered. "Come, Mother.

I—I'm not quite comfortable about this. Perhaps you've talked a wee bit too much."

"Nonsense, Thomas. No honest man is ashamed of his name—and I'm sure Arthur Mayo is honest. If he's not, he's sore changed from what he was when we knew him." The old lady rose.

"As for the alibi," her husband said stubbornly, "we stick to that—through thick and thin. Tarneverro was with us from eight to eight-thirty, and if the murder was done in that half-hour, he didn't do it. To that I'll swear, gentlemen."

"Yes, yes—I suppose you will," the Chief replied. "Good evening, sir. Madam—a great pleasure to meet you."

The old couple went out, and the Chief looked at Charlie. "Well, where are we now?" he inquired.

"Tangled in endless net, as always," Chan answered. "One thing I know—Tarneverro waits for me at Young Hotel. I will call him at once and request his presence here."

When he had done so, he came back and sat down beside his superior. His brows were contracted in thought.

"The case spreads itself," he remarked. "Tarneverro was Denny's brother. That ought to give us big boost toward our solution, but other way about, it only increases our worry. Why did he not tell me that? Why has he, as matter of fact, fiercely struggled to keep it from me? You heard what lady said about resemblance. That explains at once why all pictures of Mayo were torn to bits. Tarneverro was willing to travel long length to make sure we do not discover this fact just related to us." He sighed. "Anyhow, we have learned why portraits were destroyed."

"Yes, but that doesn't get us anywhere," the Chief replied. "If it was his brother who was killed, and he was on the point of asking you to arrest the murderer as soon as Shelah Fane revealed the name, I'd think that he would naturally tell you of his connection with Mayo—especially after the news of Miss Fane's death. It would have been a logical explanation of his interest in the case. Instead of telling you, he tries desperately to keep the relationship hidden." The Chief paused. "Strange none of these Hollywood folks ever noticed a resemblance between Mayo and the fortune-teller."

Chan shook his head. "Not likely they would. The two visit town at widely separated times, and were not seen together there. Many people, Mrs. MacMaster said, would not note the resemblance, but Tarneverro flatters me by assuming I am one who would. As for others, he knows well it is the kind of likeness almost no one sees until it is pointed out. Then everybody sees it. Human nature is like that."

"Human nature is getting to be too much for me," growled the Chief. "What course do you propose to take with this fortune-teller when he gets here?"

"I plan to walk softly. We will say nothing about his many misendeavors, but we will speak of this thing we have just learned. What reasons will he give for his silence? They may have vast significance."

"Well, I don't know, Charlie. It might be better to keep him in the dark even on that point."

"Not if we pretend we hold no suspicion whatever. We will assume instead a keen delight. Now we know he has every reason to help us, and the skies brighten above our weary heads."

"Well, you handle him, Charlie."

A few moments later Tarneverro strode debonairly into the room. His manner was aloof and a bit condescending, as though he found himself in quaint company but was man of the world enough to be at home anywhere. He nodded at Charlie.

"Ah, Inspector, I waited for you a long time. I'd about given you up."

"A thousand of my humblest apologies," Chan returned. "I was detained by heavy weight of business. May I present my honored Chief?"

The fortune-teller bowed. "A great pleasure. How are you getting on, Inspector? I've been very eager to know."

"Natural you should be. Only a moment ago did we upearth fact which makes us realize how deep your interest is."

Tarneverro glanced at him keenly. "What do you mean by that?"

"I mean we discover that Denny Mayo was your brother."

Tarneverro stepped over and laid his walking-stick on a desk. The act, it seemed, gave him a moment for thought.

"It's true, Inspector," he remarked, facing Chan again. "I don't know how you found it out——"

Charlie permitted himself a quiet smile of satisfaction. "Not many things remain buried through investigation such as we are making," he remarked gently.

"Evidently not." Tarneverro hesitated. "I presume you are wondering why I didn't tell you this myself?"

Chan shrugged. "Undoubtedly you possessed good reason."

"Several reasons," the fortune-teller assured him. "For one thing, I didn't believe that such knowledge would help you in any way in solving the case."

"Which is sound thinking," Chan agreed readily. "Still—I must confess slight hurt in my heart. Frankness between friends is like warm sun after rain. The friendship grows."

Tarneverro nodded and sat down. "I suppose there's a great deal in what you say. I'm rather sorry I kept the relationship to myself, and I apologize most humbly. If it's not too late, Inspector, I will give you the whole story now——"

"Not at all too late," Chan beamed.

"Denny Mayo *was* my brother, Inspector, my youngest brother. The relationship between us was more like that of father and son. I was intensely fond of him. I watched over him, helped his career, took pride in it. When he was brutally murdered, the shock was a terrible one for me. So you can easily understand why I say"—his voice trembled with sudden passion—"that to avenge his death has been for three years my chief aim—indeed my only aim. If the person who killed Shelah Fane is the same man or woman who murdered Denny—then, by heaven, I can not rest until justice is done."

He rose and began to pace the floor.

"When I heard the news of Denny's murder, I was playing in a London production. There was nothing I could do about it at the moment—I was too far away. But at my earliest opportunity I went to Hollywood, determined to solve the mystery of his death. I thought that the chances of my doing so would be better if I did not arrive in the picture colony as Denny's brother, but under an assumed name. At first I called myself Henry Smallwood—it was the name of a character I had lately played.

"I looked around. The police, it was evident, were completely at sea on the case. Gradually I became impressed by the number of seers and fortune-tellers of various sorts in Hollywood. They all seemed to be prospering, and it was rumored that they were the recipients of amazing confidences and secrets from the lips of the screen people.

"A big idea struck me. In my younger days I had been

an assistant to Maskelyne the Great, one of a long line of famous magicians, and a man of really remarkable powers. I had some talent in a psychic way, had told fortunes as an amateur and had the nerve to carry the thing through. Why not, I thought, take an impressive name, set myself up as a crystal-gazer, and by prying into Hollywood's secrets, seek to solve the mystery of poor Denny's death? The whole thing looked absurdly simple and easy."

He sat down again.

"So for two years, gentlemen, I have been Tarneverro the Great. I have listened to stories of unrequited love, of overwhelming ambition, of hate and intrigue, hope and despair. It has been interesting, many secrets have been whispered in my ear, but until recently the one big secret I longed to hear was not among them. Then, out of a blue sky, yesterday morning at the Grand Hotel, my moment came. I finally got on the trail of Denny's murderer. It took all my will power to control myself when I realized what was happening. Shelah Fane told me she was in Denny's house that night—she saw him murdered. I had difficulty restraining myself—I wanted to leap upon her then and there and wring the name of his killer from her reluctant lips. Three years ago I would have done it—but time—well, we grow calmer with the passage of time.

"However, once I discovered she knew, I would never have left her until she told. When you saw me last night, Inspector, my hopes were running high. I proposed to take you with me to her home after the party, and between us I felt certain we could drag out that name at last. I intended to hand the guilty person over to you immediately, for"—he looked at the Chief—"I need hardly tell you that I have never thought of avenging the crime in any other manner. From the first, I proposed to let the courts deal with Denny's killer. That was, of course, the only sane way."

The Chief nodded gravely. "The only way, of course."

Tarneverro turned toward Chan. "You know what happened. Somehow this person discovered that Shelah was on the verge of telling, and silenced her for ever. On the very threshold of triumph, I was defeated. Unless you find out who killed poor Shelah, my years of exile in Hollywood will very likely go for nothing. That's why I'm with you—that's why I want"—his voice trembled again—"the murderer of Shelah Fane more than I've ever wanted anything in all my life before."

Charlie looked at him with a sort of awe. Was this the man who had been scattering all those false clues about the place?

"I am glad of this frankness, lately as it arrives," the detective said, with an odd smile.

"I should have told you at once, I presume," Tarneverro continued. "I was, as a matter of fact, on the point of explaining my relationship to Denny as we rode down to Shelah's house. But, I reflected, the information would not help you in the least. And I did not want it to become known why I was telling fortunes in Hollywood. If it did, of course my career there would be ended. Suppose, I said to myself, Inspector Chan fails to find Shelah Fane's murderer. In that case I must go back to Hollywood and resume my quest. They are still coming to me with their secrets. Diana Dixon consulted me to-day. That is why, until Denny's murderer is found, I do not want my real name made public. I rely on you gentlemen to be discreet."

"You may do so," Chan nodded. "Matter remains buried as though beneath Great Wall of China. Knowing how firmly you are with us in this hunt adds on new hope. We will find Shelah Fane's murderer, Mr. Tarneverro—and your brother's all same time."

"You are making progress?" asked the fortune-teller eagerly.

Charlie regarded him fixedly. "Every moment we are approaching nearer. One or two little matters—and we are at journey's end."

"Good," said Tarneverro heartily. "You know now my stake in the affair. I hope you will forgive me that I didn't reveal it fully at the start."

"Explanation has been most reasonable," smiled Chan. "All is forgiven. I think you may now be excused."

"Thank you." Tarneverro glanced at his watch. "It is getting on toward the dinner hour, isn't it? I'm sorry that what I have told you is of no vital importance in your search. If there were only some really valuable contribution that I could make——"

Chan nodded. "Understand your feeling plenty well. Who knows? Your opportunity may yet arise." He escorted Tarneverro from the room, and out the front door of the station house.

When he returned, the Chief was slumped down in his

chair. He looked up with a wry smile. "Well," he remarked, "what was wrong with that picture?"

Charlie grinned. "Pretty much everything," he responded. "Tarneverro plenty queer man. He wants to help—so he robs cigar from Mr. Jaynes and drops same outside pavilion window. He thirsts for my success—so he writes note that causes me to waste time on innocent Mr. Van Horn. He has mild little reason, of no importance, for not telling me he is Denny Mayo's brother—but he rages about destroying pictures of Denny as though he would keep matter from me or die in the attempt. He beholds letter in which may be written name of Denny's killer, and when I am about to open it, he kicks out light and smashes me in face." Chan rubbed his cheek thoughtfully. "Yes, this Tarneverro plenty peculiar man."

"Well, where do we go from here?" the Chief inquired. "It begins to look like one of your stone walls, Charlie."

Chan shrugged. "In which case, we circle about, seeking new path. Me, I get renewed interest in beach-comber. Why was he in pavilion room last night? More important yet, what was conversation he overheard between Shelah Fane and Robert Fyfe, for suppression of which Fyfe pays handsome sum?" He moved toward the door. "Kashimo has now played his game of hide-and-seek long time enough. I go to bestow inside small quantity of provisions, and after that I myself will do a little scouring of this town."

"That's the talk," his Chief cried. "You go after that beach-comber yourself. I'll eat down-town too, and come back here as soon as I've finished. You'll find me here any time after seven."

Charlie went to the telephone and called his house, getting his daughter Rose on the wire. He announced that he would not be home for dinner. A sharp cry of protest answered him.

"But, Dad,—you must come home. We all want to see you."

"Ah—at last you begin to feel keen affection for poor old father."

"Sure. And we're dying to hear the news."

"Remain alive a small time longer," he advised. "There are no news as yet."

"Well, what have you been doing all day?" Rose wanted to know.

Chan sighed. "Maybe I should put my eleven children on this case."

"Maybe you should," she laughed. "A little American pep might work wonders."

"That is true. I am only stupid old Oriental——"

"Who says you are? I never did. But Dad, if you love me, please hurry."

"I will speed," he answered. "If I do not, I perceive I can not come home to-night."

He hung up the receiver and went to a near-by restaurant, where he ate a generous dinner.

Refreshed and fortified, he was presently strolling down King Street toward Aala Park. Dusk was falling over that littered stretch of ground, the campus of the undergraduates in the hard school of experience. They lolled about on the benches, some of them glancing up at Charlie with hostile eyes under discreetly lowered lids. There was muttering as he passed, an occasional curse from the lips of some one who had met the detective under circumstances none too pleasant. He paid no attention to any of them—he was seeking a man in a velvet coat and duck trousers that had once been white.

The Park yielded nothing. He crossed to a street of mean shops and shabby business. Above his head, on a fragile balcony, an enormous Filipino woman in a faded kimono puffed on an after-dinner cigar. Charlie moved along into a section of Honolulu quite unknown to tourists who breathed the pure air of the beach and raved about the beauty of these islands.

There was no beauty in the River District, only squalor and poverty; seven races jumbled together in an international slum. He heard voices raised in bitter argument, the weeping of children, the clatter of sandals, and, even here, the soft whine of Hawaiian music. *The Song of the Islands* floated lazily on the fetid air. Over a doorway that led to a dark and dirty stair, he saw the sign: "Oriental Cabaret."

He paused for a moment in the glare of the lights that formed this sign. A girl was approaching, dark-skinned, slender, graceful. He stood aside to let her pass, and saw her face. The tropics, lonely islands lost in vast southern seas—a lovely head against a background of cool green. Quickly he followed her up the stairs.

He came into a bare room with a sagging roof. There were many tables with blue and white checkered cloths; painted girls were eating at the rear. A suave little proprietor came forward, rubbing his hands with outward calm, but somewhat disturbed inside.

"What you want, Inspector?"

Charlie pushed him aside and followed the girl he had seen below. She had taken off her hat and hung it on a nail; evidently she worked here.

"Begging your pardon," Chan began.

She looked at him, fear and defiance mingling in her smoldering eyes. "What you want?"

"You are acquainted with *haole*—white man—Smith, the beach-comber?"

"Maybe."

"He painted your portrait—I have seen it. A beautiful thing."

The girl shrugged. "Yes, he come here, sometimes. I let him make the picture. What of it?"

"Have you seen Mr. Smith lately?"

"Not for long time—no."

"Where does he live?"

"On the beach, I think."

"But when he has money—where then?"

The girl did not reply. The proprietor came forward. "You tell him, Leonora. Tell Inspector what he asks you to."

"Oh, well. Sometimes he live at Nippon Hotel, on Beretania Street."

Chan bowed. "Thank you so much." He wasted no time in that odorous cluttered room, but hastened down the dark stair. In a few moments he entered the Nippon Hotel. The sleek little Japanese behind the desk greeted him with a cordiality Chan knew was rankly insincere.

"Inspector, you honor my house."

"Such is not my purpose. *Haole* named Smith—he stops here?"

The clerk took a register from beneath the desk. "I look see——"

Charlie reached out and took the book from his slightly resisting hands. "I will see. Your eyes are notably bad. Archie Smith, room seven. Lead me there."

"Mr. Smith out, I think."

"We will discover if he is. Please make haste."

Reluctantly the Japanese led him across an open courtyard, filled with a neglected tangle of plants and flowers. The Nippon Hotel was a cluster of shabby sheds, antiquated outbuildings. They stepped on to a lanai; a Japanese woman porter, bent low under a heavy tin trunk, staggered by. The clerk moved on into a musty hallway, and pointed to a door. The numeral seven—or what was left of it—hung by one nail on the panel.

"In there," said the Jap, and with a hostile look, disappeared.

Chan opened the door of number seven, and entered a dim low-ceilinged room. One dirty bulb was burning over a pine table, and at that table sat Smith, the beach-comber, with a canvas on his knees. He looked up, startled.

"Oh," he said. "So it's you?"

Chan regarded him sleepily. "Where you been all day?"

Smith indicated the canvas. "The evidence is right here, Inspector. I've been sitting in my palatial studio painting that courtyard outside. Glad you dropped in—it's been a bit dull since I finished." He leaned back in his chair and critically surveyed his work. "Come and look at this, Inspector. Do you know, I believe I've got something into it—a certain miasmic quality. Did you ever realize before that flowers can look mean and sinister? Well, they can—in the courtyard of the Nippon Hotel."

Chan glanced at the painting and nodded. "Yes, plenty good, but I have no time to be critic now. Get your hat and come with me."

"Where are we going—to dinner? I know a place on the Boulevard St.-Germain——"

"We go to the station house," Charlie replied.

"Wherever you say," nodded Smith, and putting aside the canvas, picked up his hat.

They crossed Aala Park to King Street. Chan regarded the derelict with an almost affectionate gaze. Before he and Smith parted company again, the beach-comber was going to tell him much—enough, perhaps, to solve his problem and put an end to all his worries.

The Chief was alone in the detectives' room. At sight of Charlie's companion, he brightened visibly. "Ah, you got him. I thought you would."

"What's it all about?" Smith asked jauntily. "I'm flattered, of course, by all these attentions, but——"

"Sit down," said the Chief. "Take off that hat." Thank heaven, here was some one who needn't be handled any too gently. "Look at me. A woman was killed last night at Waikiki, in a separate building on the grounds of her home. What were you doing in the room where she was killed?"

Beneath the yellow beard, Smith's face paled. He wet his lips with his tongue. "I was never in that room, Chief."

"You lie! We found your finger-prints on the window-sill. Look at me. What were you doing in that room?"

"I—I——"

"Come on, brace up. You're in a tight place. Tell the truth, or you'll swing for this. What were you doing——"

"All right," said Smith in a low voice. "I'll tell you about it. Give me a chance. I didn't kill anybody. It's true, I was in that room—in a way——."

"In a way?"

"Yes. I opened the window and climbed up on the sill. You see——"

"Kindly start at beginning," Chan cut in. "We know you arrived at window of pavilion to hear man and woman talking inside. What was said we pass over for the minute. You heard the man leaving the room——"

"Yes—and I went after him. I wanted to see him—but he got into a car and drove away down the avenue. I couldn't catch him. So I ambled back and sat down on the beach. Pretty soon I heard a cry—a woman's cry—from that pavilion. I didn't know what to do. I waited a while, and then I went over and looked through the window. The curtain was down, but it flapped about. Everything was quiet—I thought the place was empty. And then—well, really—I'm a little embarrassed about this. I'd never done such a thing before. But I was desperate—strapped—and when you're that way you get the feeling, somehow, that the world owes you a living——"

"Get on with it," barked the Chief.

"Well, just inside the window I caught a glimpse of—of a diamond pin. I thought there was no one inside, so I pushed up the screen and climbed on to the sill. I stooped over and picked up the pin—and then I saw her—the woman—lying over there by the table—stabbed, dead. Well, of course I realized at once that was no place for me. I lowered the screen, hid the pin in a little secret safety-deposit box of mine on the beach, and strolled as casually as I could to the avenue. I was still moving when that cop picked me up, an hour later."

"Is pin still on beach?" Chan inquired.

"No—I got it this morning." Smith reached into his trousers pocket and produced it. "Take it quick—I don't want it—don't let me ever see it again. I must have been crazy, I guess. But as I say—when you're down and out——"

Charlie was studying the pin. It was a delicate affair, a row of fine diamonds set in platinum. He turned it over. The pin itself was broken midway, and the end of it was lost.

The Chief was looking sternly at the beach-comber. "Well," he said, "you know what this means. We'll have to lock you up——"

"One moment, please," broke in Charlie. "Finding of pretty pin is good enough, but it is not vital to us. Vital matter is, what did this man hear Shelah Fane and Robert Fyfe saying to each other while he lingered outside pavilion window? Something of great importance—something Mr. Fyfe made false confession to quiet—something he has paid Mr. Smith nice sum to conceal. But now Mr. Smith changes mind. He will not conceal it any longer."

"Oh, yes, I will," cried Smith. "I mean—it was nothing—nothing——"

"We hold you for theft," cut in Charlie. "Do you enjoy prisons? I think not. Neither does territory enjoy supporting you there. Under a certain circumstance, memory of theft might fade from our minds for ever. Am I speaking correctly, Chief?"

The Chief was dubious. "You think it's as important as that, Charlie?"

"It is of vast importance," Chan replied.

"All right." He turned to the beach-comber. "Tell us the truth of what you heard last night, and you can go. I won't press the charge. But—it's got to be the truth, this time."

Smith hesitated. His rosy dream of the mainland, decent clothes, respectability, was dying hard. But he shuddered at the thought of Oahu Prison.

"All right," he said at last. "I'll tell you. I hate to do it, but—oh, well—there's Cleveland. My father—a punctilious man. Easily annoyed—growing old, you know. I've got to get out of this jam for his sake, if not for my own. When I came up to that window, Inspector——"

Chan raised his hand. "A moment, please, I have keen desire to see Robert Fyfe in this room when you tell the story." He looked at his watch. "I can reach him at hotel, I think. Excuse me." He took up the telephone and summoned Fyfe. Then he went over and sat down in a chair at the beach-comber's side. "Now we will rest as comfortable as may be. You, Smith, explore your mind and arrange story in advance. Kindly remember—the truth."

The beach-comber nodded. "You're on, Inspector. The truth this time." He looked down at his battered shoes. "I knew it was too good to last. Got a cigarette? No? Neither have I. Oh, well, life's like that."

Chapter XXII

WHAT THE BEACH-COMBER HEARD

They sat in silence, and the minutes dragged by. Smith's pale gray eyes stared hopelessly into the future, a future where he walked for ever, broke and forlorn, along a curving beach. Lighting a big cigar, the Chief picked up the evening paper. Charlie Chan took the diamond bar pin from his pocket and studied it, deep in thought.

Ten minutes passed, and then Robert Fyfe entered the room. He came in as though he were stepping on to a stage: suave, smiling, sure of himself. But as his gaze fell upon Smith the smile faded suddenly, and a frown replaced it.

"Good evening," the actor said. "I can give you about twenty minutes, Mr. Chan, and then I must run. It wouldn't do to be late at the theater again to-night."

"Twenty minutes will be ample plenty," nodded Charlie. "Mr. Smith and yourself have met before. Over here sits my Chief."

Fyfe bowed. "Ah, yes. I take it you have called me here for some important reason, Inspector?"

"Seems important to us," Chan answered. "I will squander no words. Last night you hold famous conversation with ex-wife in beach pavilion. The true contents of that talk have not yet been revealed. First when matter is discussed, you confess to crime you did not do, in order to change subject. Then, this morning, you discover yourself sudden lover of art, and buy picture from Smith, hoping to keep him quiet." He looked fixedly at the actor. "I rejoice you got nice painting, Mr. Fyfe. Because that will be all you get. Smith can not longer keep quiet. Smith is about to speak."

A look of distress crossed the actor's face, and was succeeded by one of anger. He wheeled about and faced the beach-comber. "You contemptible——"

Smith raised a protesting hand. "I know—I know. What a broken reed I've turned out to be. I'm as sorry about this as you are, old man. But these keen lads here have got something on me—something rather serious—it means prison unless I ditch you. And I've slept in the pure open air so much—somehow a prison cot doesn't appeal to me. Frightfully sorry, as I said, but I'm going to throw you over. By the way, have you got a cigarette?"

Fyfe glared at him for a moment, and then, shrugging his shoulders, opened a silver case and held it out. Smith helped himself.

"Thanks. It's a wretched affair, Mr. Fyfe, and—no, that's all right, I've got a match—the sooner we get it over with, the better." He lighted the cigarette, and took a long pull at it. "To return to our favorite subject—last night on the beach—I went up to that pavilion window and they were in there together—this man and Shelah Fane. She was doing most of the talking—got a look at her—lovely, even more so than in the films. I'd rather like to have painted her —wearing that cream-colored gown——"

"Come, come," cried the Chief. "Get on with it."

"That's what I'm trying to do. I just wanted to point out how beautiful she was—a woman like that ought to be allowed at least one—shot."

Chan stood up. "What is your meaning now?"

"I mean she'd taken it, anyhow. She was telling Mr. Fyfe all about it—how three years ago, in Hollywood, she killed a man——"

With a groan Fyfe sank into a chair, and covered his face with his hands.

"Killed what man?" the Chief demanded.

"Ah, yes—the name." Smith hesitated. "Denny, I think she called him. Yes, that was it—Denny Mayo."

There was a moment's tense silence, and then Fyfe leaped to his feet. "Let me tell this," he cried. "It will sound dreadful, if he tells it. Let me explain about Shelah—she was emotional, impetuous. I'll try to make you understand——"

"I don't care who tells it," said the Chief. "But I want it told, and quick."

Fyfe turned to Chan. "You heard, Inspector, how she called me at the theater—a distracted, pitiful call—and said she must see me at once. I answered that I'd come after the show, but she said no, that might be too late. If I'd ever loved her, I must come at once. She had something to tell me, she wanted my advice, she was desperate. So—I went.

"I met her on the lawn; she seemed overwhelmed with anxiety and fear. We went to the pavilion and she burst at once into her story. Some years after our divorce, she told me, she met this Denny Mayo—she fell madly in love with him—I could picture it. I knew how Shelah loved. Wildly, unreasonably. Mayo seemed to care for her; he had a wife in London, a dancer in musical comedies, but he promised to divorce her and marry Shelah. For a time Shelah was happy—and then one night Mayo asked her to come to his house.

"That was three years ago—a night in June. She went to his place at the hour he had suggested. He told her that he was through; that his wife had had an accident and was unable to work any longer; that he believed he owed a duty to this woman—at any rate he was going to write her to join him in Hollywood. Poor Shelah went a little mad then. Quite out of her senses. There was a revolver in the drawer of Mayo's desk, she got it, pointed it at him, threatened to kill him and herself. I have seen her in such moments; she was not responsible, I know. They struggled over the weapon, it went off in her hand. She stood looking down at Mayo, dead at her feet.

"She came to her senses then, I fancy. At any rate, she took her handkerchief and removed her fingerprints from the gun. She stole out of the house and went home unobserved. She was safe. Not once did the investigation point to her. Safe—but never happy again. From that day she lived in torment.

"A few weeks ago, in Tahiti, she met Alan Jaynes. She wanted to marry him, but she was haunted by that memory of the past. She'd fallen into the habit of consulting this fellow Tarneverro about everything; he had impressed her deeply with his cleverness. She sent for him to meet her here, and yesterday morning she went to his apartment.

"When she went there, she had no intention of telling him anything about Denny Mayo. She merely wanted him to read her future, to advise her as to whether a marriage with Jaynes would turn out happily. But he—he seemed to exert some mysterious power over her. Perhaps he hypnotized her. In any case, the first thing she knew, she found herself confessing the whole terrible story to the fortune-teller——"

"Stop!" cried Chan, with unaccustomed bruskness. "Ah, pardon me—one moment, please. You mean to say she told Tarneverro that she herself killed Denny Mayo?"

"Of course she did. I——"

"But Tarneverro relates different story."

"Then he lies. Shelah confessed to him that she had killed Denny—don't you understand—that's why she was so frightened, why she sent for me. I was the only one she could turn to, she said. She hadn't liked the light she saw in Tarneverro's eyes when she made her confession. She was deathly afraid of the man. She was sure he planned to use that confession in some way that would do her infinite harm. She clung to me, pleaded for my help. But what could I do? What was there to be done?"

Fyfe sat down as though exhausted by his story. "I tried to reassure her, promised to help her all I could—but I pointed out to her that I must get back to the theater at once. She begged me to stand by, stay with her—but you know, gentlemen, the show must go on. I had never disappointed an audience in my life—I refused to do it then. I left her and returned to town."

Again Fyfe buried his face in his hands. "If I had only stayed with her—but I didn't. The next thing I heard, poor Shelah was—murdered. I intended to tell the police the whole story at once, but somehow—when it came right down to it—I couldn't. Shelah, who had always been so straight and fine, such a good pal, so generous and kind. I pictured that blot on her past, that wild thing she had done in one irresponsible moment, cabled to the ends of the earth. She was gone. To find her murderer would never bring her back. No, I thought, keep Shelah's name unsullied. That's your job now.

"Then this accursed beach-comber came in and started his story. I went a little mad myself. I'd always loved Shelah—I loved her still—more than ever when I saw her last night. So I made my melodramatic confession to shut off the investigation. I don't know whether I'd have gone through with it or not—this morning when I woke up it seemed that I had carried chivalry a bit too far. Fortunately for me, I didn't have to go through with it—Mr. Chan disproved my confession on the spot. But I had succeeded in my purpose, I had given Smith here a tip, and when he came to me to-day I was ready and willing to pay all I had to keep him quiet. I couldn't bear the thought of Shelah disgraced before the world that had so greatly admired her."

Charlie got up and laid his hand on the actor's shoulder. "You have caused me much trouble but I forgive freely, for you are gallant gentleman. Pardon me if I grow tiresome with much pounding on one point, but it is of vast importance. You are quite sure that Miss Fane told her story to Tarneverro exactly as she told it to you?"

"Absolutely," Fyfe replied. "And if you can find any connection between Tarneverro and Denny Mayo, then the fortune-teller killed her. That's certain."

Charlie exchanged a long look with his Chief. The latter turned to Smith. "You can go along," he said. "And don't let me see you here again."

The beach-comber rose quickly. "You won't—not if it's left to me," he remarked. "Of course, if you keep dragging me in——" He walked over to Fyfe. "I really am sorry, old man. I want you to know—in one respect at least I kept my word—I haven't had a drink all day. I sat in my room—money in my pocket—sat there and painted a lot of wicked-looking flowers, with my throat as dry as the Sahara. It was a tough assignment, but I came through it. Who knows—maybe I've got a chance yet. Here"—he took a roll of bills from his pocket—"this is yours."

"Why, what is it?" Fyfe asked.

"Thirty-two bucks—all I've got left of the fifty. Sorry it isn't more, but I bought a bit of canvas and some brushes—a chap can't just sit in a room, you know."

Fyfe stood up, and pushed the money away. "Oh, that's all right. It was a rather good painting—that's how I feel about it. Keep the money and get yourself some decent clothes."

Smith's pale gray eyes shone with gratitude. "By heaven—you're a gentleman. It does a fellow good to meet you. I feel something stirring within me—can it be a great resolve? They tell me there's a scarcity of stewards on the boats. To-morrow morning I'll buy myself some new things, and sign on for the trip to the coast. San Francisco—it's only a short walk from there to Cleveland. Yes—by the lord—I'll do it."

"Good luck to you," Fyfe answered.

"Thanks. May I trouble you—one more cigarette?

You're very kind." He moved to the door, stopped and came back. "Somehow, Chief, I don't like to leave you. Will you do me a favor?"

The Chief laughed. "I might," he said.

"Lock me up until morning," the beach-comber went on. "Don't let me go into the street with all this money on me. I might be held up, or possibly—possibly—— What I mean is, put me in a safe place overnight, and the chances of getting rid of me tomorrow will be a lot better than they look right now."

"With pleasure," nodded the Chief. "Come with me."

Smith waved a hand at Charlie Chan. "Remind me in the morning, Inspector, I owe you a dime—ten cents." He followed the Chief from the room.

Charlie turned to Fyfe. "You are now in demand at playhouse. I am deeply grateful for all you have told."

"Mr. Chan—if you could only keep this thing about Shelah from reaching the public——"

Charlie shook his head. "I am so sorry, but I fear same can not be done. The matter has vital connection with her murder."

"I suppose it has," Fyfe sighed. "Well, anyhow, you've been mighty decent to me, and I appreciate it."

Chan bowed him out.

Left alone, the detective stared thoughtfully into space. He was standing thus when the Chief strode again into the room. For a moment they regarded each other.

"Well," the Chief said, "so Tarneverro's story was a lie. And you've based your whole investigation on it. It's not like you, Charlie, to be tricked like that."

Chan nodded. "If I had time to do so, I would droop my head in shame. However, I choose now to forget the past. From this point on, my investigation takes new turn——"

"What do you mean—from this point on?" his Chief demanded. "The case is ended—don't you know that?"

"You think so?"

"I'm sure of it. In the morning Shelah Fane tells Tarneverro she killed Denny Mayo. Mayo was his brother. In the evening, she's found murdered. What could be simpler than that? I'm going to arrest the fortune-teller at once."

Charlie raised his hand. "No, no—I advise against that. You forget his alibi, solid as stone wall, not to be shaken."

"We'll have to shake it. It's evidently false. It must be. Either those old people are lying to save him, or else he tricked them as he tricked you——"

"I do not think so," Chan said stubbornly.

"What's the matter with you, Charlie? Losing your grip? We never had a clearer case than this. The little matter of the alibi——"

"Something else, too," Chan reminded him. "Why did Tarneverro say he would call me down the beach to arrest a murderer? His words stick in my mind and will not be unlodged. I tell you firmly, this problem not yet solved."

"I can't understand you, Charlie."

"Only one thing made clear by Mr. Fyfe's interesting story. I know now why Mr. Tarneverro did not wish me to open letter written by Shelah Fane. He feared I would learn at once his tale of seance with the lady was false in details, and house of cards would tumble about his ears. Fortunate for him, letter when finally opened was so worded as to add strength to his lie. "Please forget what I told you this morning. I must have been mad—mad.' Then he knew that blow struck in the dark was not needed, after all. Must have wished to give himself a few resounding kicks." Chan paused. "Yes, Mr. Tarneverro has muddled me with his deceit from very start. Still, I do not believe him guilty of murder."

"Well, what do you propose to do?" the Chief demanded. "Just sit here and twiddle your thumbs, with me to help you?"

"I am no thumb-twiddler," replied Chan with spirit. "I propose to act."

"On what? We have no more clues."

Charlie took the diamond pin from his pocket. "We have this." He handed it over. "Will you kindly oblige by making study of same?"

The Chief examined it. "The pin itself is broken in the middle, isn't it? Half of it seems to be gone."

Chan nodded. "Undubitably gone. And when we find that missing end, our case is solved."

The Chief looked puzzled. "What do you mean?"

"How was pin broken? When watch was smashed, murderer wished to provide further evidence of struggle that might make smashing of watch more probable. So he tore off orchid flowers and trampled them beneath foot. When he ripped off flowers, pin unfastened and came with them.

No doubt it lay on floor, point uppermost. Perhaps that point drove deep into heel of murderer's shoe, and broke off there. Did this happen, and did it go unnoticed by killer? It might. If so, there may be tell-tale scratches on polished floors of house at Waikiki. I speed there at once to look for same."

The Chief pondered. "Well, there might be something in it, at that. I'll give you a chance to find out. Go along, and I'll wait here for news."

In the doorway, Charlie encountered Kashimo. The little Japanese was worn and dispirited. "Have combed town twenty, maybe fifty, times. Mr. Smith no longer exists."

"A fine detective you are," growled the Chief. "Smith is out there in a cell now. Charlie found him."

Disappointment and distress showed in the eyes of the Japanese. Charlie paused at the door and came back. He patted the little man's shoulder.

"Cheer yourself up," he said kindly. "Be good boy, attend all meetings of Y. M. B. A., and you will yet win success. Nobody is perfect. Take look at me. Twenty-seven years on force, and I am nowhere near so clever as I thought I was."

He walked slowly from the room.

Chapter XXIII

THE FATEFUL CHAIR

Charlie rode out to the beach for what he hoped would be his final call at Shelah Fane's house. The moon had not yet risen, the sky was purple velvet pierced by ineffectual stars, the flowering trees hid their beauty somewhere in the calm breathless dark. Twenty-four hours ago, in this same period of impenetrable night before the coming of the moon, the black camel had knelt at Shelah Fane's gate.

Though he knew now the secret in the woman's past, knew that she had done a grievous wrong, he still thought of her with the deepest sympathy. She had never stood in court to answer for her crime, but she had suffered none the less. What torture those three years must have been! "Perhaps in the end I may find a little happiness. I want it so much"—thus she had written in her last pitiful note. Instead she had found—what? The black camel waiting to carry her away into the unknown.

Whatever the motive behind her murder may have been, Chan reflected, the act itself was heartless and cruel. He was firmly resolved that the person who had killed her should be found and made to pay. Found—but how? Would the little pin resting in his pocket come nobly to his aid? He hoped desperately that it would, for it was his sole reliance now.

The banyan tree's shade was like ink on the front lawn of the huge rambling building that had been the famous star's last home. Chan parked his car, switched off its lights, and leaped nimbly to the ground.

Jessop, serene and dignified as ever, let him in. "Ah, Constable, I was rather expecting you. What a pleasant evening to be abroad. Mild and fragrant, I should call it, sir."

Chan smiled. "I am too busy man, Jessop, to have concern with perfumes of the night."

"Ah, yes, I presume your time is fairly well occupied, Constable. Is there—if I may make bold to inquire—any news regarding the homicide?"

Chan shook his head. "Not up to present moment."

"I regret to hear that, sir. The young people are on the beach—Miss Julie and Mr. Bradshaw, I mean. Whom did you wish to interrogate?"

"I wish to interrogate the floors of this house," Chan told him.

Jessop raised his white eyebrows. "Indeed, sir. My old father used to say that walls have ears——"

"Floors, also, may repeat a story," Charlie returned. "If you have no inclination for objecting, I will begin in living-room."

He pushed through the heavy curtains. Diana Dixon was sitting at the piano, softly playing. She got up.

"Oh, hello," she said. "You want somebody?"

"I want somebody very much," Chan nodded. "At end of trail I hope to find him—or her."

"Then you haven't yet discovered who killed poor Shelah?"

"I have not. But subject is unhappy one. Why are you not on beach? That is place for youth at this hour?"

Diana shrugged. "What's the beach without a man? And there aren't enough to go round, evidently."

"A situation rare in your neighborhood, I will wager," Charlie smiled.

"Oh, a change does us all good." She watched him as he stood there, looking impatiently about the room. "What are you going to do now? I'm so thrilled by all this——"

"Now, I am going to be unbearably rude," he replied. "I find myself in uncredible position of wanting to dispense with your company. Will you kindly wait on the lanai?"

She pouted. "I hoped you were going to ask me to help you."

"In such charming company as yours, I fear I could not keep mind on work." He held open the French window. "As a very great favor, please——"

With obvious reluctance she went out, and he closed the window after her. He did not wish to appear undignified in the presence of a witness, and it was his intention now to be undignified indeed. He turned on all the lights in the room and with some difficulty, got down on his knees. Taking a magnifying-glass from his pocket, he began a close scrutiny of the highly polished floor wherever it was uncovered by rugs.

For a long time he crept about, until his knees ached. But he did not mind that, for his efforts were richly rewarded. Here and there he encountered numerous little scratches which had been, without doubt, recently made. He breathed hard, and his black eyes shone with satisfaction.

Suddenly a brighter idea struck him. He scrambled to his feet and hurried to the dining-room. The table, he was happy to note, was the same size it had been on the previous evening. Jessop was putting away silver in the sideboard. He turned.

"I observe," Chan remarked, "that you have not yet reduced size of dining table."

"I couldn't, sir," replied the butler. "All the leaves are already out. The former occupants of this house, it would appear, were of a most hospitable temperament."

"Just as well," nodded Chan. He was pleased to see that the big table stood on the bare floor; the room was without rugs save for a small one that lay in the doorway. "Do me a great favor, if you will, Mr. Jessop. Kindly place ten chairs about this board, in identical positions they occupied last night."

Puzzled, Jessop obeyed. When he had finished, Charlie stood for a moment in deep speculation.

"They now stand just as they did when you served dinner guests with coffee, some twenty-two hours ago?"

"Precisely," the butler assured him.

Without a word, Charlie pulled back a chair and disappeared beneath the table. One by one, mute evidence of his activity there, the chairs were pushed away, while Jessop stared with an amazement rarely seen on his imperturbable face. With a flash-light added to his equipment, Chan made the long circuit. Finally he came up as though for air.

"Were place-cards used for last night's dinner?" he inquired.

"No, sir. It was a rather informal affair, and Miss Fane told me she would seat the guests herself."

"Then when they came in here for coffee, they sat in no prearranged order?"

"Oh, no, sir. They just sat anywhere their fancy dictated."

"Is there chance you happen to remember who sat in which place?"

Jessop shook his head. "I'm sorry, Constable. It was a somewhat disturbing evening. I was a bit—unnerved, I fear."

Charlie laid his hand on the chair at the right of the one the hostess would no doubt have occupied. "You can not, then, tell me who it was reclined here?"

"I'm afraid not, Mr. Chan. One of the gentlemen. I fancy. But—I—I really don't know."

Charlie studied a moment. "Thank you so much. The telephone is in the hall closet, I believe?"

"Yes, sir. I will show you——"

"No need to trouble," Chan told him. "I will find it."

He went out to the hall and shutting himself in the hot cubby-hole under the stairs, made numerous calls. Finally he rang up his Chief.

"Inspector Chan speaking," he said. "May I humbly suggest that you bring one other good man with you, and come immediately to house of Shelah Fane?"

"Something doing, Charlie?" asked the Chief.

Chan pulled the door shut as far as it would go. Little beads of perspiration began to pop out on his forehead.

"Pin is about to lead us to success," he replied in a low voice. "On floor of living-room repose plenty fresh scratches. What is more, during time of investigation last night, guests who expected to enjoy dinner sat down round dining table for abbreviated repast. Floor is bare beneath table, and in front of one chair—and only one—more scratches are in evidence."

"Who sat in that chair?" the Chief demanded.

"The murderer of Shelah Fane," Chan answered. "The name I do not yet know. But I have just now summoned to house six guests, who, with three already here, make up complete list. When all are assembled we lead them to dining-room and ask them, please; to sit where they did last night. Chair of dead hostess was at head of table, facing door to hall. Note who sits down in chair at right of hostess. Same will be person we so hotly seek."

The Chief laughed. "Going to make a big drama out of it, eh, Charlie? Well, that's all right with me, so long as it means success. I'll be with you pronto."

Chan returned to the hall, mopping his brow. He caught a glimpse of the coat-tails of Jessop, hastily disappearing through the curtains of the dining-room door. With an idle step he moved along, and came finally to the lanai, where he encountered Miss Dixon.

"Living-room is again at your disposal," he bowed.

She rose and came toward him. "Did you find what you were looking for?" she asked eagerly.

He shrugged. "Who in this world finds what he looks for? Success—what is it? A bubble that explodes when touched by human hand." And he strolled off toward the beach.

At his right, as he crossed the lawn, lay the pavilion, dark and empty to-night. Close by the sea, seated together in a beach chair intended for one person only, he came upon Julie and Jimmy Bradshaw. The boy rose.

"Why, it's good old Charlie," he cried. "Honolulu's noted sleuth. How are you, and what's the news?"

"News seems to be that spell of Waikiki Beach is still intact," Chan answered. "I am so sorry to interrupt this touching scene."

Bradshaw held out his hand. "Shake, Charlie. You're the first to hear about it. I'm going to be married. And oh, yes,—Julie is too."

"Plenty good news," returned Chan heartily. "May you have half the happiness I wish you—the full amount would be impossible."

"Oh, thank you, Mr. Chan," Julie said.

"You're a great old scout," Bradshaw remarked. "I'll miss you. I'll miss this beach, too——"

"What is that? You leave Honolulu?"

"Oh—sure."

"You depart from this lovely spot, about which you have written one million words——"

"I've got to, Charlie. Have you ever stopped to think about the effect of all this languid beauty on a young man's character? Devastating, that's what it is. On this crescent beach, fanned by the warm breath of the south, and so on—what happens to him? He droops, he stagnates, he crumbles. No more cocopalms for me. Redwoods, Charlie. Do you know about the redwoods? They brace you up. They're my trees hereafter. A big lumber and sap man from the West—that's going to me my rôle."

Chan grinned. "You have failed to win Miss Julie to your views on Hawaii?"

"It looks that way. Sold it to fifty thousand tourists, but not to the girl I love. That's life, I suppose."

"When you go from here, you will leave much beauty behind," Charlie said. "But you will also take much beauty with you, since Miss Julie goes along."

"Which remark, Mr. Bradshaw," Julie laughed, "should have come from you."

"It would have, presently," he answered.

Chan stood staring at the rising moon, the curve of lights along the whispering shore. The sad music of Hawaii came drifting up from the Moana courtyard. "To be young, in love, and on this beach," he said. "What greater happiness than that? Taste it to the full. It happens once, then time moves on. Moment comes when gold and pearls can not buy back the raven locks of youth."

"Why, Charlie,—you're getting sentimental," Bradshaw cried.

Chan nodded. "I think of my own courtship on this shore—so long ago. How long, you wonder? I am now father of eleven children—judge for yourself."

"You must be very proud of them," Julie ventured.

"As proud as they will permit," Chan answered. "At least, I have done my part to link past with future. When I move on, leaving eleven offspring, can any man say I have not been here? I think not."

"You're certainly right on that," Bradshaw assured him.

"May I speak with you in private for a moment?" Charlie said. He walked with the boy back toward the lights of the house.

"What's doing?" Bradshaw wanted to know.

"Plenty will be doing at any moment now. Within the hour I tell you who killed Shelah Fane."

"Good lord!" the boy gasped.

"First, I suggest a task for you. Miss Julie was Shelah Fane's dear friend. Go back and break news gently to her that it was Miss Fane who shot Denny Mayo. Same is now established beyond all doubt."

"You don't mean it?"

"I do. Impart news gently, as I request. Then blow will not hit her with such cruel force as in crowd of people. It will be unhappy shock for her, but she will soon forget. She has your love."

"All I've got, Charlie. Say—this is pretty considerate of you. But then—you think of everything."

"Within my limitations, I try to do so. When news is broken, both of you are to come at once to living-room."

"We'll do that, Charlie. Thanks."

As Chan entered the great room, Diana Dixon was greeting Martino, Van Horn and Jaynes, who had come down from the hotel together. The detective noted with satisfaction that all three were in dinner clothes—was it too much to hope they wore the same shoes as on the previous evening?

"Hello, Inspector," Martino said. "We came as soon as we could make it. What's in the air?"

"A little experiment," Chan answered. "Perhaps our case is *pau* to-night."

Jaynes was lighting a small cigar. "*Pau*—you mean finished? By jove, I hope so. They're holding a cabin for me on to-morrow's boat. I rely on you, Inspector."

"We all do," added the director. "I want to get off myself. Huntley—you and I might take that boat too."

Van Horn shrugged. "Oh—I don't care if I never leave. I was looking at that beach-comber last night. Shouldn't be surprised if he were the happiest man among us."

"Going primitive, eh?" Martino smiled. "I suppose it's the influence of that part you played down in Tahiti."

"It's the thought of Hollywood," responded Van Horn. "Of all the artificial places I've seen, that town wins the embossed medallion."

"Spoken like a true Californian," remarked Jimmy Bradshaw, entering with Julie. "Would you mind if I quoted you on that? Famous picture actor prefers Honolulu's simple ways to the fevered swank of the film colony."

"You do," returned Van Horn grimly, "and I'll deny I ever said it."

"Alas!" grinned Bradshaw. "All the movie actors' best lines have to be left out of their interviews."

Wilkie Ballou and his wife came in. The former wore a linen suit, with white shoes, and Charlie was troubled. If Ballou took the chair that was waiting for some one in the dining-room, then his case might be far from proof even now.

"What's it all about?" Ballou demanded. "I was going to bed early to-night."

"Poor old Wilkie can't stand excitement," Rita remarked. "As for me, I love it. Hello, Diana,—what have you been doing to-day?"

The curtain parted, and Tarneverro stepped noiselessly

into the room. He stood for a moment, staring about, a rather worried look in his dark eyes.

"Ah, yes," he said. "We're all here, aren't we?"

Jaynes got slowly to his feet, walked over and proffered a case. "Good evening," he remarked. "Will you have one of my cigars?"

"No, thank you," Tarneverro answered blandly "I don't use them."

"So sorry," replied the Britisher. "I rather thought you did."

Charlie stepped hastily between them. "Will you be seated, please? We are all here, yes—except my Chief. We wait few minutes for him."

They sat down. Rita, Diana and Julie chatted together in low tones. The men were silent, staring into space.

Presently there was a clatter in the hall, and the Chief strode in. After him came Spencer, big and competent-looking. Chan leaped up.

"Ah, Chief,—now we may go forward. I have explained that we desire to make small experiment. You know some of these people——"

Wilkie Ballou shook the Chief's hand. "I'm glad to see you here," he remarked, with a glance toward Charlie.

"Mr. Tarneverro is also known to you," Chan continued, oblivious. He introduced the others. "Now we will all proceed to dining-room," he finished.

"What! Another dinner party?" cried Rita Ballou.

"A peculiar dinner party," Chan told her, "at which no food will be served. Come this way, please."

They filed out, solemn and ill-at-ease now. The presence of the Chief and the burly policeman in uniform had served to impress them with the seriousness of the situation. Not unnaturally, they were asking themselves what all this meant? Was it a trap?

Jessop was on duty in the dining-room, grave and dignified. He waited, ready to seat them at the barren table with the same poise as though it had gleamed with silver, been snowy with linen.

"We are now about to make request," Chan said slowly. "I would remind you that this is important moment and you must think deep before acting. No mistake must be made. Will you kindly sit down at same places you occupied at this table last night?"

A little chorus of dismay greeted his words. "But I was so excited, I don't remember," cried Diana, and the others echoed her. For a moment they milled about, puzzled and uncertain. Then Jimmy Bradshaw dropped down at the foot of the table, opposite the empty chair of the hostess.

"I sat here," he announced. "I recall it perfectly. Julie, you were at my right. Mr. Van Horn, you sat at my left."

Julie and the picture actor, with Jessop officiating, took their places.

"Mr. Ballou, you were here beside me," Julie said, and Chan heaved a sigh of relief as the Honolulu man sank into his chair.

"So I was," Ballou remarked. "Thank you for remembering, my dear. Diana, you were at my right."

"True enough," Miss Dixon agreed, and Jessop held her chair. "And, Val, you were at my right."

"Of course," the director nodded, and sat down.

One side of the table was now completely filled—but it was not the side that interested Charlie.

"You were across from me, Rita," said Diana.

Mrs. Ballou took her place.

Two chairs, aside from the one at the head of the table, remained vacant, with Jaynes and Tarneverro left to occupy them.

"I believe, Mrs. Ballou, that I had the honor of sitting beside you," remarked Tarneverro, and took the chair at her right.

"So you did," Rita agreed. "And Mr. Jaynes was on the other side." She indicated the chair at her left—the portentous chair before which were tiny scratches such as might have been made by a broken pin protruding slightly from the heel of a shoe.

"I fancy we have it now," smiled Jaynes innocently and sat down.

There was a moment's silence. "You are seated just as you were last night?" Chan inquired slowly.

"We are not," said Huntley Van Horn suddenly.

"Something is wrong?" Charlie asked.

"It is. Mr. Tarneverro is at my left now, but last night Mr. Jaynes was in that position."

"Why, of course," Rita Ballou cried. She turned to Tarneverro. "You and Mr. Jaynes have exchanged places."

"Perhaps we have," the fortune-teller answered amiably. He rose. Jaynes also got up, and took the chair at Rita's right. After a moment's hesitation, Tarneverro dropped into the fateful chair. "I fancy we're all set now," he remarked calmly. "Jessop, you may serve the soup."

Charlie and the Chief exchanged a look, and moved away from the neighborhood of the table. They went into the hall.

"Tarneverro," said the Chief softly. "I knew it. Take a look at his shoes——"

But Chan stubbornly shook his head. "Something is very wrong here," he insisted.

"Wrong, nonsense! What's got into you, anyhow, Charlie?"

"Extremely wrong," Chan continued. "You can not convict a man with an alibi such as his. All broken pins in world would not avail."

"Then the whole thing's a flop, according to you?"

"So far—yes. But I do not despair. Permit me that I think a moment. There is some explanation of this. Ah, yes—come with me."

They returned to the dining-room. The group about that barren table looked at them expectantly.

"Kindly hold positions just as at present," Chan said. "I come back before I am missed."

He stepped through a swinging door into the kitchen, and they heard his voice in low converse with Wu Kno-ching, the cook. They waited in silence; even the obviously innocent appeared anxious and uneasy. Peresently Charlie returned, walking with unwonted briskness and with a grim look on his face.

"Jessop," he said.

The butler stepped forward with a rather startled air. "Yes, Constable?"

"Jessop, after these people departed last night, others sat at this table?"

The butler had a guilty look. "I'm extremely sorry, sir. It was not quite in order—I would not ordinarily countenance it in a well-run house, but things were rather at sixes and sevens—and we had had no dinner—so we just sat down for a bit of coffee; we needed it badly——"

"Who sat down?"

"Anna and I, sir."

"You and Anna sat down at this table, after the guests had gone? Where did you sit?"

"Over there—where Mr. Martino is now seated, sir."

"And Anna—where did Anna sit?"

"She sat here, sir." And Jessop laid his land on the back of Tarneverro's chair.

For a moment Chan was silent, staring at the butler with unseeing eyes. He sighed heavily, as one who after a long journey sights the end of the trail at last.

"Where is Anna now?" he asked.

"She is in her room, I fancy, sir. Up-stairs."

Charlie nodded at Spencer. "Bring this woman at once," he ordered, and the policeman disappeared. Chan turned to the table. "Our little experiment is ended. Please step back to living-room."

They got up and filed silently across the hall. Charlie and the Chief waited at the foot of the stairway. The Chief said nothing, and Charlie also seemed disinclined to speak. Presently Spencer appeared at the head of the stairs, accompanied by Anna. They descended slowly. His eyes like black buttons in the half-light, Chan faced the woman. With cool unconcern, she returned his stare.

"Come with me," he said. He led her into the living-room, and stood for a moment looking at her feet. She wore high, black shoes, in keeping with her sober uniform. The right one, Charlie noted, seemed somewhat thick about the ankle.

"Anna, I must make very odd request of you," he said. "Will you be good enough to remove right shoe?"

She sat down, and began slowly to unlace it. Tarneverro came forward and stood at Chan's side. The detective ignored him.

He took the heavy shoe from Anna's hand, turned it over, and with his penknife slit the rubber heel. A little half-inch length of gold pin lay exposed, and with a gesture of triumph he lifted it out and held it up.

"You are all witnesses," he reminded them. He turned to Anna. "As for you, I fear you have been grossly careless. When you stamped those orchids under foot, you failed to note this telltale evidence of your act. Ah, well—but for such brief moments of neglect, we would get nowhere in this business." He gave his attention to the shoe. "I note braces built along the sides," he continued. "Meant to protect weak ankle, I think. You have had an accident, madam?"

"My—my ankle was broken—long ago," she replied, in a voice barely audible.

"Broken?" cried Charlie quickly. "When? How? Was it

dancing on the stage you broke that ankle? Ah, yes—it was. Madam—I think you were once the wife of Denny Mayo."

The woman took a little step toward him. Her eyes were hard and defiant, but her usually dark face was white as Waikiki's sands.

Chapter XXIV

THE VEIL IS LIFTED

Charlie turned to Tarneverro. In the deep-set eyes of the fortune-teller he saw a reluctant admiration. He smiled.

"I have been plenty dense," he said. "This woman is on the scene by no coincidence. When you set up as lifter of the veil in Hollywood, you needed—what? Spies—spies to scatter about the place, and bring you morsels of gossip regarding film people. Your brother's wife had suffered accident, she was no longer able to work at profession, she was penniless and alone. You sent for her. What more natural than that action? You helped her to position, that she might help you."

Tarneverro shrugged. "You have a remarkable imagination, Mr. Chan."

"No, no—you flatter me," Charlie cried. "It has just been proved I have not imagination enough. Only one claim I make for myself—when light at last begins to stream in, I do not close the shutters. Light is streaming in now. Anna's task was not alone to bring you trivial information—she was also to assist you in solving matter of Denny Mayo's murder. Was that why you placed her with Shelah Fane? Had you already some suspicion of Miss Fane? I think so. Yesterday morning in your apartment, actress confessed her misdeed to you. At once you inform Anna that victory has come. You are in high spirits. Your own intention is honest one, you plan to hand Miss Fane to police. Otherwise you would not say to me what you did in Grand Hotel lounge last night. Then—what happened?"

"You tell me, Inspector."

"Such is my purpose. You learn that Shelah Fane is murdered. Without being told, you know who did the deed. The position is hard one for you, but mind works fast as usual. You invent false story about your seance with Shelah Fane, and boost me off on wrong trail at once. You talk about mythical letter Miss Fane was to write for you. Then, to your surprise and dismay, you find real letter was written. It may wreck plans at once, so you strike me down and obtain epistle. Needless act, as it turns out. You rage about, destroying photographs of Mayo to conceal relationship with him. You seek to befuddle me by involving innocent parties. Oh, you have been busy man, Mr. Tarneverro. I might forgive you, but I find it difficult to forgive myself. Why have I been so stupid?"

"Who says you've been stupid, Charlie?" the Chief asked.

"I do, and I remark same with bitter force," Chan answered. "My little duel with this fortune-teller should have been finished long hours ago. Matter was clear enough. I knew he employed spies. I gathered—though I paid not enough attention to fact—that some one had been spying on Miss Fane in Tahiti and on returning boat. I learned that Anna here bought bonds—matter which might indicate more income than simple wage as maid. I listen to Tarneverro's alibi and feel certain he did not do murder himself. What, then, explains his actions? Natural inference for good detective would have been that he protects some one else. Who? I read in newspaper that Denny Mayo had wife. I discover Mayo was Tarneverro's brother, and I hear that Mayo was slain by hand of Shelah Fane. Later—crowning touch—I am told Mayo's wife encountered accident and can no longer follow profession. Do I put two and two together? Do I add up simple sum and get result? No—I fumble around—I flounder like decrepit fish—finally I slide into happy harbor of success." He turned suddenly on Anna, standing pale and silent before him. "For I am in that harbor. It is true, is it not, madam? You killed Shelah Fane!"

"I did," the woman answered.

"Don't be a fool, Anna," Tarneverro cried. "Fight it out."

She gestured hopelessly. "What's the use? I don't care. I've nothing to live for—it doesn't matter what becomes of me. Yes, I killed her. Why not? She——"

"Just a moment," the Chief broke in. "Anything you say, you know, may be used against you."

"You're a little late with that, Chief," Tarneverro said. "She should have a lawyer——"

"I don't want one," Anna went on sullenly. "I don't want

any help. I killed her—she robbed me of my husband—she wasn't content to take his love—she ended by taking his life. I've had my revenge, and I'm willing to pay for it. I intend to plead guilty, and get it over with at once."

"Fine," approved the Chief. He saw the territory saved the expense of a long trial.

"You're mad, Anna," cried the fortune-teller.

She shrugged. "Don't mind me. I wrecked all your plans, I fancy. I spoiled everything for you. Forget me and go your way alone."

Her tone was bitter and cold, and Tarneverro, rebuffed, turned away from her. Charlie offered her a chair. "Sit down, madam. I desire to make brief interrogation. It is true that Tarneverro brought you to Hollywood?"

"Yes." She accepted the chair. "I'll take it from the beginning, if you like. While Denny was acting in the pictures, I continued to dance in London music-halls. I was doing well, when I had that accident—I broke my ankle—I couldn't dance any more. I wrote to Denny about it, and asked if I could come to him. I didn't receive any answer—and then I heard he had been killed.

"Arthur—Denny's brother here—was also playing in London at that time. He was kind to me—loaned me money—and then he told me he was going out to the States to learn who had killed poor Denny, if he could. After a time he wrote that he had set up in Hollywood as a fortune-teller, calling himself Tarneverro. He said he needed—help—that he could use me if I was willing to go into service. I had taken a position as wardrobe mistress with a manager for whom I used to dance. It was hard work—and the memories—I longed to get away from it all."

"So you went to Hollywood," prompted the Chief.

"I did, and I met Tarneverro secretly. He said he would place me with Miss Fane. He advised her to get rid of the maid she had, and sent me round the same day to apply for the position. He had discovered that Miss Fane and Denny were once—very close friends—and he thought I might be able to get on the trail of something in her house. He suggested that I change my appearance as much as possible—my way of doing my hair—he feared that Denny might have shown her pictures of me. I followed his instructions, but it was an unnecessary precaution. Denny—he must have lost my pictures—lost them or thrown them away. Miss Fane engaged me, and I was successful in the post. You see—I'd had maids myself. For a year and a half I was with her—helping Tarneverro. But I could discover nothing. Nothing about Denny, I mean.

"Yesterday afternoon Tarneverro and I met on the beach. He told me Shelah Fane had confessed to killing Denny—confessed it in his apartment that morning. He wanted to get a repetition of that confession with a witness to overhear—he planned it for last night in the pavilion. He would talk with her there alone, and I was to be hiding somewhere about. Then he proposed to send for an officer.

"I returned to this house, almost beside myself with hatred for the woman who had wrecked Denny's life—and mine. I got to thinking—sitting alone in my room. Tarneverro's plan began to look so very foolish to me. The police? I knew what one of your American juries would do with a woman like Shelah Fane—a beautiful, famous woman. They would never convict her—never. There were better ways than the police. I—I kept on thinking. I'm rather sorry I did."

Her eyes flashed. "No—I'm not. I'm glad. I planned it all out. Last night—during the party—that was the time. Plenty of people about—plenty of people who might have done it. I planned the alibi of the watch—I remembered it from a play in which Denny once acted. I was in the kitchen from twenty minutes before eight until ten after the hour. Jessop and the cook were there too. At eight-fifteen I located Shelah Fane in the pavilion—she was waiting there—waiting to make a good entrance on her party—as she always did. She was like that.

"I went to her room and got a knife—one she had bought in Tahiti. I wanted something to wrap it in—a handkerchief—a big one. The door of the blue room was open—I saw a man's clothes. I went in and took the handkerchief from the pocket of the coat—Mr. Bradshaw's coat, I think."

"Ah, yes," remarked Jimmy Bradshaw grimly. "Thanks for the ad."

"I went to the pavilion," Anna continued. "She didn't suspect. I came close to her——" The woman buried her face in her hands. "You won't make me tell that part. Afterward I broke the watch in the handkerchief, put it back on her wrist. But there was no other evidence of a struggle, so I tore off the orchids and trampled them under foot. I went out and buried the knife deep in the sand—I heard voices on the beach—I was frightened. I ran to the house, and went up to my room by way of the back stairs."

"And the handkerchief?" Charlie inquired. "You gave that to Mr. Tarneverro when he arrived?"

"Just a moment," said the fortune-teller. "Anna—when did you and I last talk together alone?"

"On the beach, yesterday afternoon."

"Have we communicated with each other since that moment?"

She shook her head. "No."

"Have I heard you say before that you killed Shelah Fane?"

"No, you have not."

The fortune-teller looked at the Chief. "A little matter," he remarked, "that I am rather keen to bring out."

"But the handkerchief——?" The Chief turned to Anna.

"I dropped it on the lawn. I—I wanted it to be found there." She glanced at Bradshaw. "It wasn't mine, you know."

"Very thoughtful of you," bowed the boy.

"On the lawn, precisely," said Tarneverro, "where I picked it up."

"And put it in my pocket," remarked Martino. "By the way, I haven't thanked you for that."

"Do not trouble," Chan advised him. "You were not the only one Mr. Tarneverro honored with his attentions."

The Chief went over to the woman's side. "Go upstairs," he said sternly. "And get ready. You'll have to go down-town with us. You can tell that story again—at the station." He nodded to Spencer to accompany her.

The woman rose, her manner sullen and defiant, and went from the room, with the policeman at her side.

"Well," said Ballou, "I guess we can all go now."

The Chief gave a sign of acquiescence. Wilkie and Rita left first, followed by Martino, Van Horn and Jaynes. The latter stopped to shake Charlie's hand.

"Thanks," he remarked in a low voice. "I shall make my boat. And on this boat—and all others in the future—I shall try to keep my head."

Diana went quietly up to her room. Chan turned to Julie.

"Go back to beach," he said gently. "Look up at stars, breathe clean fresh air and think of future happiness."

The girl gazed at him, wide-eyed. "Poor Shelah," she whispered.

"Shelah Fane's troubles over now," Chan reminded her.

"Do poor lady great kindness, and forget. Jimmy here will help you."

Bradshaw nodded. "I certainly will." He put his arm about the girl. "Come on, Julie. One more look at the coco-palms, and then we're off for the coast, where trees are trees." They moved toward the French window. Bradshaw smiled at Chan over his shoulder. "So long, Charlie. I've got to go now and tone down my adjectives so they'll fit California."

They went out, and Chan turned back into the room to find his Chief staring speculatively at Tarneverro. "Well, Charlie," he remarked. "What are we going to do with our friend here?"

Chan did not answer, but thoughtfully rubbed his cheek. Tarneverro, seeing the gesture, smiled.

"I'm so sorry," he said. "I've made you a lot of trouble, Inspector. But I was in a horrible position—you can realize that. Should I have handed Anna over to you at once? Perhaps; but as I told you last night, I saw immediately that I was responsible for the whole affair. Innocently so, of course, but none the less responsible. I ought never to have told her—but I wanted a witness. If only I had kept my discovery to myself."

"The man who looks back sees his mistakes piled up behind," Chan nodded.

"But I never dreamed Anna would lose her head like that. These women, Inspector."

"They are primitive creatures, these women."

"So it would seem. Anna has always been a strange, silent, unfriendly person. But there was one bond between us—we both loved Denny. When she proved last night how desperately she loved him—well, I couldn't betray her. Instead I fought my duel with you. Fought to the limit of my ability—and lost." He held out his hand.

Chan took it. "Only the churlish are mean-spirited in victory," he remarked.

The policeman in uniform looked through the curtains.

"Right with you, Spencer," said the Chief. "Mr. Tarneverro, you'd better come along. I'll talk to the Prosecutor about you. But you needn't be alarmed. We're not inclined to spend much money over here on chance visitors from the mainland."

Tarneverro bowed. "You're very encouraging."

"You got your car, Charlie?" the Chief asked.

"I have it," Chan told him.

The Chief and Tarneverro went into the hall, and presently Charlie heard the front door slam.

He stood for a moment looking about him at the bright room where his work was *pau* at last. Then, sighing ponderously, he stepped through the curtains and picked up his hat from a table in the hallway. Wu Kno-ching appeared suddenly from the dining-room.

Charlie gazed into the beady eyes, the withered yellow face of his compatriot.

"Tell me something, Wu," he said. "How was it I came upon this road? Why should one of our race concern himself with the hatreds and the misdeeds of the *haoles?*"

"Wha's mallah you?" Wu inquired.

"I am weary," sighed Chan. "I want peace now. A very trying case, good Wu Kno-ching. But"—he nodded, and a smile spread over his fat face—"as you know, my friend, a gem is not polished without rubbing nor a man perfected without trials."

The door closed gently behind him.